Tom Hood, Thomas Hood, Frances Freeling Broderip

Memorials of Thomas Hood

Tom Hood, Thomas Hood, Frances Freeling Broderip

Memorials of Thomas Hood

ISBN/EAN: 9783337374150

Printed in Europe, USA, Canada, Australia, Japan

Cover: Foto ©Raphael Reischuk / pixelio.de

More available books at **www.hansebooks.com**

MEMORIALS

OF

THOMAS HOOD.

COLLECTED, ARRANGED, AND EDITED BY HIS DAUGHTER.

WITH

A PREFACE AND NOTES BY HIS SON.

ILLUSTRATED WITH COPIES FROM HIS OWN SKETCHES.

IN TWO VOLUMES.

VOLUME I.

BOSTON:
TICKNOR AND FIELDS.
M DCCC LX.

COSSINGTON, BRIDGEWATER, ENG.,
June 5, 1860.

Messrs. TICKNOR AND FIELDS,
Boston, U. S.

Gentlemen: —

We grant you with pleasure all the right we can to reproduce the "Memorials" in the United States. In offering you the early sheets for republication, we wish you all success in the undertaking, and beg to sign ourselves,

Yours, truly,

THE CHILDREN OF THOMAS HOOD.

(FRANCES FREELING BRODERIP.)
(THOMAS HOOD.)

University Press, Cambridge:
Stereotyped and Printed by Welch, Bigelow, & Co.

Dedicated

TO

THE PEOPLE:

FOR WHOM THOMAS HOOD WROTE AND LABOURED.

HE SANG THE SONG OF THE SHIRT.

PREFACE.

In submitting the following memorials to the public, my sister and myself would wish, at the first outset, to warn those who think to find in them fine biographical writing, that the book is not for them. We have seen too many great men fail in that art, and we feel no desire to emulate them. Our own part in this work is small, being restricted to such explanations and amplifications as were necessary to connect the letters, to which we have added, here and there, characteristic anecdotes, to which reference is made in them.

Our language we have endeavoured to render as simple as possible. If therefore, at any time, it warms into a higher strain, it is solely at the promptings of the heart, and not by artistic design. Indeed, any such trick or premeditation could not have existed at the same time with the feelings called up by a task, how solemn, how sad, and how unutterably absorbing, none can tell, who have not experienced a like sensation of mingled pleasure and pain; for, although the latter predominate, there is some of the former in the performance of such a labour of love.

It is owing chiefly to this fact that the publication of these volumes has been so long delayed. To us, to turn over the MSS. for these pages — to consult the letters, written in that well-known, clear hand — was to recall to memory such a flood of recollections of dead joys, of long past sorrows, of gentle, loving deeds and words, that we may well claim to be excused if we were slow in our progress, and lingered somewhat over pages, that were often hidden from us by our tears.

Looking back now on my own emotion, while reading over these memorials, I can scarcely think how I should be so moved after the lapse of fifteen years, and I can fully realise how intensely painful must the compilation have been to my sister, who, as the elder, was more intimately connected with, and has a clearer memory of the events chronicled, than I.

We are well aware that there is considerable ground for the popular objection to Biographies, written by relatives; but we are of opinion, that, in this case, the advantages to be gained by the Editorship of some leading literary man of the day, are more than balanced by the intimate knowledge and understanding we have of all the incidents and acts of our father's life. Although, as will be seen, he numbered among his friends many distinguished writers, they can none of them know, nor could we impart to them our perceptions (if I may use the term) of that inner private life, which gave a stamp to the character his writings claimed for him — that of a benevolent, loving, Christian gentleman.

We are the better enabled to prepare these memorials, because we were never separated, for any length of time, from our parents, neither of us having been sent to a boarding-school, or in our earlier years confined to that edifying domestic Botany Bay — the Nursery — where children grow up by the pattern of unwatched, uneducated, hired servants.

How our father ever made of us companions, and was ready in return to be our playfellow, will be mentioned elsewhere.

Having then undertaken this "labour of love" ourselves, in preference, with all humility nevertheless, to entrusting it to others, comparative strangers, however distinguished; we repose, hopefully, on the generosity and consideration of the English people, with whom we have ever found our father's name a passport to the sympathies.

As regards the form and arrangement of these pages, a few words only are necessary. Each Chapter, with the exception of two, contains the events of a year; that having appeared to us the most simple and natural division. In the letters we have done our best to omit everything approaching to a repetition. If we have not, altogether, and at all times succeeded, we can only plead as an excuse the difficulties we have had to encounter; and the same must be said for any passage, which may give unintentional pain to those mentioned in it.

In the last volume we have ventured to reprint some of our father's less-known effusions, not included in the later editions of his works, and to offer to the public a few pieces hitherto unpublished, and, for the most part, more or less unfinished.

The illustrations consist, in the first place, of two facsimiles; the one of a sheet of the "Song of the Shirt," as first written out, and the other of the sketch for his own monument drawn by our father towards the close of his last illness. The remaining vignettes are from sketches rapidly dashed off by him for our amusement. Many of them are from sheets of similar oddities, which we used to find, to our huge delight, lying on our pillows occasionally of a morning. He had drawn them overnight, before going to rest, after the long hours of his literary labour were done. They may have perhaps too great a value in our eyes, but we have added them to complete the memorials, as indications, however slight, of the untiring humour, and self-forgetful thought for the pleasure of others, which could suggest and create them after the mental and physical labour of a weary night's composition.*

Having explained our plan in these volumes, I will add a few words on a subject which I feel it my duty to speak of rather plainly.

It has always been a popular misconception that men of letters, as a rule, are freethinkers. It is my own earnest belief, that the higher mental organization and refined sensibility of men of letters render them, almost to a fault, reserved in expressing a religious faith, for the very reason that they feel it so deeply and solemnly.

My father's religious faith was deep and sincere: but it was but little known to a world ever too apt to decide by hearing professions, rather than by scrutinising actions. Those to whom his domestic life was every day revealed, felt how he lived after the divine requirements: for he "did justice," sacrificing comfort, health, and fortune, in the endeavour; he "loved mercy" with a love that was whispering into his ear, even as he was dying, new labours for his unhappy fellows; and he "walked humbly with his God" in a faith too rare to be made a common spectacle; for, as he said —

"I consider faith and prayers
Among the privatest of men's affairs."

* Another reason for their insertion is, that they will give a fairer notion of his artistic skill, to which the cuts in the Comic Annuals did but inadequate justice.

* * * *

As regarded others' opinions, he was most indulgent.

"Intolerant to none
Whatever shape the pious rite may bear;
Ev'n the poor heathen's homage to the Sun
I would not rashly scorn — lest, even there
I spurn'd some element of Christian prayer;
An aim, tho' erring, at a 'world ayont,'
Acknowledgment of good, of man's futility,
A sense of need, and weakness, and indeed
The very thing so many Christians want —
Humility."

In a similar spirit, he bids us —

"Ne'er o'erlook, in bigotry of sect,
One truly *Catholic*, one common form,
At which, uncheck'd,
All Christian hearts may kindle, or keep warm.
Say — was it to my spirit's gain or loss,
One bright and balmy morning, as I went
From Liege's lovely environs to Ghent,
If hard by the wayside I found a Cross,
That made me breathe a prayer upon the spot —
Where Nature of herself, as if to trace
The emblem's use, had trail'd around its base
The blue significant Forget-Me-Not?
Methought the claims of Charity to urge
More forcibly, along with Faith and Hope,
The pious choice had pitched upon the verge
Of a delicious slope,
Giving the eye much variegated scope; —
'Look round,' it whisper'd, 'on that prospect rare,
Those vales so verdant, and those hills so blue;

Enjoy the sunny world, so fresh so fair,
But '— (how the simple legend pierced me thro'!)
'PRIEZ POUR LES MALHEUREUX!'"

I am impelled to quote one more passage from the "Ode to Rae Wilson," because the appealing advice contained in it has since been acted on. I wonder does any working-man, when he attends one of the special evening services held for the poor and the labouring classes in our metropolitan minsters and churches, ever think of his affectionate friend and advocate, who once wrote thus?

"Oh! simply open wide the Temple door,
And let the solemn, swelling organ greet,
With *Voluntaries* meet,
The *willing* advent of the rich and poor!
And, while to God the loud Hosannas soar,
With rich vibrations from the vocal throng —
From quiet shades that to the woods belong,
And brooks with music of their own,
Voices may come to swell the choral song
With notes of praise they learned in musings lone!"

Almost my father's last words were, "Lord — say 'Arise, take up thy cross, and follow me.'"

He had borne that cross during his whole life, but the quiet unobtrusive religious faith I have endeavoured to describe, supplied him with exemplary patience under severe sufferings, with cheerfulness under adverse circumstances, with a manly resolution to wrong no one, with an affectionate longing to alleviate the suffering of all classes, and with a charity and love that I will not do more than touch on, for fear I should be thought to be carried away by my feelings.

My mother was a fitting companion for such a husband: she shared his struggles, and soothed his sorrow, and was so much a part of his very existence, that latterly he could hardly bear her out of his sight, or write when she was not by him. We have been frequently obliged to omit large portions of his letters to her — it would have been sacrilege to alter them, and we did not feel it right to publish what was intended for her eyes alone — the tender epithets, and the love-talk; so fond, and yet so true. I quote here one passage, as a sample of those which occur so frequently in the letters.

"I never was anything, dearest, till I knew you — and I have been a better, happier, and more prosperous man ever since. Lay by that truth in lavender, sweetest, and remind me of it when I fail. I am writing warmly and fondly; but not without good cause. First, your own affectionate letter, lately received — next the remembrances of our dear children, pledges — what darling ones! — of our old familiar love, — then a delicious impulse to pour out the overflowings of my heart into yours; and last, not least, the knowledge that your dear eyes will read what my hand is now writing. Perhaps there is an after-thought that, whatever may befal me, the wife of my bosom will have this acknowledgment of her tenderness — worth — excellence — all that is wifely or womanly, from my pen."

Throughout his long illnesses she was his constant nurse and unwearying companion, nor did she long survive him. One trait in her character I record as an example for mothers. She never, even in the most unimportant matters, answered my childish inquiries as to the various things, which naturally attracted my young thoughts, with anything but the truth. I can truly say now that after-experience has never discovered anything, in which she deceived me, as some do, to put a stop to tedious questionings. The consequence is, that, in many matters of faith, hard to understand and grasp, the only reason I can give for holding them, but that is an all-sufficient one, is "that I learnt to believe it of my mother, and she never taught me what was untrue." That memory has been an anchor on which I have rested, when otherwise I might have lost myself in blind gropings after the intangible.

I must not close this preface (although it has already exceeded the limits I assigned it), without a grateful reference to Miss Eliza Cook, and the originators and promoters of the movement, which led to the erection of the noble monument to my father in Kensal Green; a monument which has not its peer in England, whether for the universal subscriptions which raised it, or for the chaste and unique novelty of its design.

From the managers and furtherers of the undertaking, or from the distinguished names on the subscription lists, it would be ungracious and invidious to select any for special notice; but a similar reason to that, which led me to connect my father's slight sketches with these memorials, induces me to select from the humbler names on the lists such donations as the following: "trifling sums from Manchester, Preston, Bideford, and Bristol — from a few poor needlewomen — from seven dressmakers — from twelve poor men."

I should be wanting indeed in appreciation of the people's love for my dead father, if I did not, (by incorporating them with this work,) endeavour to rescue from oblivion these tokens of the gentle remembrance, by the poor, of the Poet

"Who sang the Song of the Shirt."

T. H.

NOTE. The Vignette on page vi. is a sketch of the arms, which my father used to say he should adopt, if the Queen would give him a grant — "a heart, pierced with a needle threaded with silver tears," — the motto, "He Sang the Song of the Shirt."

The crest was one he selected in jest, quoting Shakespeare — "The ox hath his bow, sir; the horse his curb; and the falcon her bells;" so why should n't the Hood have his hawk?

It is worth noticing that the little silhouettes of Animals, &c., interspersed among the other vignettes, were drawn long before "Punch" appeared with his spirited little black cuts.

CONTENTS OF VOL. I.

CHAPTER I.

FROM 1799 TO 1835.

CHAPTER II.

1835.

CHAPTER III.

1836.

CHAPTER IV.

1837.

CHAPTER V.

1838.

MEMORIALS OF THOMAS HOOD.

CHAPTER I.

FROM 1799 TO 1835.

Birth and Parentage. — Apprenticed to an Engraver. — Goes to Scotland for his Health. — Assistant Sub-Editor of "The London." — Acquaintance with the Reynolds Family. — "Odes and Addresses." — He marries Miss Jane Reynolds. — Robert Street, Adelphi. — Birth and Death of first Child. — "Whims and Oddities." — "National Tales." — "Plea of the Midsummer Fairies." — Edits "The Gem." — "Eugene Aram." — Winchmore. — Birth of second Daughter. — Anecdotes, Fondness for the Sea, &c. — "The Comic Annual." — Acquaintance with the Duke of Devonshire. — The Chatsworth Library Door. — "Tylney Hall." — Connection with the Stage. — Is presented to his Majesty King William IV. — Lake House, Wanstead. — Anecdotes, &c.

THE public record of THOMAS HOOD has been long before the world — either in the quaint jests and witty conceits, that enlivened many a Christmas fireside; or in the poems, which were his last and best legacy to his country. All that remains is the history of his private life — that "long disease," as it was truly called, so long, and so severe, that it was only wonderful that the sensitive mind and frail body had not given way before. From his earliest years, with the exception of a few bright but transient gleams, it was a hand to hand struggle with straitened means and adverse circumstances. It was a practical illustration of Longfellow's noble lines —

"How sublime a thing it is
To suffer and be strong."

He possessed the most refined taste and appreciation for all the little luxuries and comforts that make up so much of the enjoyments of life; and the cares and annoyances that would be scarcely perceptible to a stronger and rougher organisation, fell with a double weight on the mind overtasked by such constant and harassing occupation. He literally fulfilled his own words, and was one of the "master minds at journey-work — moral magistrates greatly underpaid — immortals without a living — menders of the human heart, breaking their own — mighty intellects, without their mite." The income his works now produce to his children, might *then* have prolonged his life for many years; although, when we looked on the calm happy face after death, free at last from the painful expression that had almost become habitual to it, we dared not regret the rest so long prayed for, and hardly won.

His life, like that of most modern literary men, was very barren of incident; there is therefore little to relate, save the ebb and flow of health and strength —

"As in his breast the wave of life
Kept heaving to and fro."

The reader must bear this in mind, if wearied with the recurrence of the chronicle of sickness and suffering.

With the distinct and even minute foreknowledge of organic and mortal disease, liable at any moment to a fatal and sudden termination, it must indeed have been a brave spirit to bear so cheerfully and courageously, as he did, that life, which was one long sickness. He knew that those dearest to him were dependent on his exertions, and his mental powers were cramped and tied down by pecuniary necessity; while his bodily frame was enfeebled by nervousness and exhaustion.

Of my father's birth and parentage we can glean but few particulars; his own joking account was, that, as his grandmother was a Miss Armstrong, he was descended from two notorious thieves, *i. e.* Robin Hood and Johnnie Armstrong. I have found his father's name mentioned in "Illustrations of the Literary History of the Eighteenth Century," by J. B. Nicholls, F.S.A.: —

"*August 20th.* — At Islington, of a malignant fever, originating from the effects of the night air in travelling, Mr. Thomas Hood, bookseller, of the Poultry. Mr. Hood was a native of Scotland, and came to London to seek his fortune, where he was in a humble position for four or five years. * * * His partner, Mr. Vernor, died soon afterwards. Mr. Thomas Hood married a sister of Mr. Vernor, junior, by whom he had a large family. He was a truly domestic man, and a real man of business. Mr. Hood was one of the 'Associated Booksellers,' who selected valuable old books for reprinting, with great success. Messrs. Vernor and Hood afterwards moved into the Poultry, and took into partnership Mr. C. Sharpe. The firm of Messrs. Vernor and Hood published 'The Beauties of England and Wales,' 'The Mirror,' 'Bloomfield's

Poems,' and those of Henry Kirke White. Mr. Hood was the father of Thomas Hood the celebrated comic poet."

The above account is, I believe, tolerably correct, except that Mr. Hood married a Miss Sands, sister to the engraver of that name, to whom his son was afterwards articled. Mr. Hood's family consisted of two sons, James and Thomas, and four daughters, Elizabeth, Anne, Jessie, and Catherine. At his house in the Poultry, on the 23d of May, as far as we trace, in the year 1799, was born his second son Thomas, the subject of this memoir. The first son, James, was supposed to be the most promising, fond of literature, and a good linguist, a more rare accomplishment then than now. He drew exceedingly well in pen and ink, and water-colours, as also did one or two of the sisters. The elder Mr. Hood was a man of cultivated taste and literary inclinations, and was the author of two novels which attained some popularity in their day, although now their very names are forgotten. No doubt his favourite pursuits and his profession influenced in no small degree the amusements and inclinations of his children; and, for those days, they must have been a very fairly intellectual family.

James Hood, however, died at an early age, a victim to consumption, which ultimately carried off his mother and two sisters. After the sudden death of the father, the widow and her children were left rather slenderly provided for. My father, the only remaining son, preferred the drudgery of an engraver's desk to encroaching upon the small family store. He was articled to his uncle, Mr. Sands, and subsequently was transferred to one of the Le Keux. He was a most devoted and excellent son to his mother, and the last days of her widowhood and decline were soothed by his tender care and affection. Her death was, I have often heard him say, a terrible blow to him. I have now in my possession a little sketch of his, of his mother's face as she lay in her coffin. His sister Anne did not survive her very long,* but I cannot ascertain the date of either of their deaths.

An opening that offered more congenial employment presented itself at last, when he was about the age of twenty-one. By the death of Mr. John Scott, the editor of the "London Magazine," who was killed in a duel, that periodical passed into other hands, and became the property of my father's friends, Messrs. Taylor and Hessey. The new proprietors soon sent for him, and he became a sort of sub-editor to the magazine.

I am exceedingly indebted to the kindness and courtesy of Messrs. Taylor and Hessey (who have both survived almost all their contributors) for several particulars relating to my father's early life. From the latter gentleman's letter on the subject I have ventured to quote largely.

"I remember," he says, "often having seen the late

* The lines entitled "The Death-Bed," (in the "Englishman's Magazine,") and commencing,

"We watched her breathing through the night,"

were written at the time of her death. The poem has been frequently quoted, without the name of the author, and so, with several others of my father's writings, is not generally known to be his. Shortly after my father's death, when "The Serious Poems" were published, a Latin translation of "The Death-Bed" appeared in the "Times."—T. H.

Mr. Hood when he was a mere boy at the house of his father, whom I had the pleasure of knowing intimately for many years. He was, as far as I can recollect, a singular child, silent and retired, with much quiet humour, and apparently delicate in health. He was, I believe, educated at a school in the neighbourhood of London,* and at the age of fifteen or sixteen was articled to his uncle, Mr. Sands, as an engraver. His health, however, beginning to suffer from confinement, it was found necessary to put an end to that engagement, and he was sent to a relation in Scotland,† where he remained some years with great benefit. He returned to town about the beginning of the year 1821. In that year the

* This school was either at Clapham or Camberwell. I can remember my father's pointing it out to me, while we were living at the latter place. At that time it was converted into a naval school, I think. Of many schoolboy tricks and adventures, related by him, I regret that I can recal only very faint recollections, for they were very laughable, and might go among the *exempla minora* to prove the rule "the child is father to the man." Amongst other anecdotes, I remember one in which he was the instigator of a purely homœopathic revenge upon the footman, who was permitted to vend nuts, parliament, and marbles to the pupils. Monopoly of trade induced the man to raise the price above the "outside" standard, whereon characteristic retaliation was inflicted by raising the articles (that is the desk in which they were kept) by four cords to the schoolhouse ceiling. When the charges were lowered, the desk was permitted to follow their example. — T. H.

† According to his own 'Literary Reminiscences,' he was clerk in a merchant's office. But I doubt this, as most probably a "mischievous invention" for committing puns. He was two years in Scotland, and made his first appearance in print there — first in the Dundee paper in a letter, and afterwards in a local magazine. He did not, however, he says, adopt literature as a profession till long after. — T. H.

'London Magazine' came into the hands of Mr. Taylor and myself, after the death of the editor, Mr. John Scott; and Mr. Hood was engaged to assist the editor in correcting the press, and in looking over papers sent for insertion. This was his first introduction to the literary world; and here he first amused himself by concocting humorous notices and answers to correspondents in the 'Lion's Head.'* His first original paper appeared in the number for July, 1821, vol. iv. p. 85, in some verses 'To Hope.' I find nothing more of his until November of the same year, when his humorous 'Ode to Dr. Kitchener' appeared in the 'Lion's Head' of that month; a poem, 'The Departure of Summer,' in the body of the number, p. 493; and 'A Sentimental Journey from Islington to Waterloo Bridge,' in the same number, p. 508. From that time he became a regular contributor, and as many as twenty-four more papers of various kinds ap-

* "The Echo," in Hood's Magazine, was a continuation of this idea. Some of the replies to imaginary letters were very quaint. I append a few, extracted at random, because the magazine is not so well known or so often met with now, as to render me liable to the charge of quoting what every one knows.

"VERITY. It is better to have an enlarged heart than a contracted one, and even such a hœmorrhage as mine than a spitting of spite."

"'A Chapter on Bustles' is under consideration for one of our Back-numbers."

"N. N. The most characteristic 'Mysteries of London' are those which have lately prevailed on the land and the river, attended by collisions of vessels, robberies, assaults, accidents, and other features of Metropolitan interest. If N. N. be ambitious of competing with the writer, whom he names, let him try his hand at a genuine, solid, yellow November fog. It is dirty, dangerous, smoky, stinking, obscure, unwholesome, and favorable to vice and violence." — T. H.

peared, the last being 'Lines to a Cold Beauty,' in June, 1823, after which time I find no further production of his pen.

"Mr. Hood's connection with the 'London Magazine' led to his introduction to our friend Mr. Reynolds (and through him to his sister) and to the various contributors to the work,—Charles Lamb, Allan Cunningham, Hazlitt, Horace Smith, Judge Talfourd, Barry Cornwall, the Rev. H. F. Carey, Sir Charles A. Elton, Charles Phillips, Dr. Bowring, John Clare, Thomas De Quincey, George Darley, the Rev. Charles Strong, Wainwright, Hartley Coleridge, Bernard Barton, Richard Ayton, the Rev. Mr. Crowe, Rev. Julius Hare, Rev. Dr. Bliss, John Poole, Esq., &c. &c.

"At the end of the year 1824 the magazine passed into the hands of another person as proprietor and editor, and I have no means of ascertaining who were then its chief supporters; but I do not believe Mr. Hood contributed to it at all. Mr. Reynolds continued to write in that work till the end of the year 1824.

"It may perhaps be interesting to you to have a list of the articles contributed by Mr. Hood, and I have great pleasure in sending you the enclosed, which I believe is tolerably correct. Most of them, I suppose, have been reprinted.

"My acquaintance with Mr. Hood ceased about the year 1823, till which time I had enjoyed the pleasure of constant communication with him. Soon afterwards I went into the country, and, I regret to say, I never saw him again."

PAPERS CONTRIBUTED TO THE "LONDON MAGAZINE" BY THE LATE THOMAS HOOD.

Vol. IV. July to December, 1821.

Page 85. To Hope.
468. Ode to Dr. Kitchener.
493. Departure of Summer.
508. Sentimental Journey from Islington to Waterloo Bridge.

Vol. V. January to June, 1822.

Page 3. "Please to ring the Belle."
203. Faithless Sally Brown.
269. The Sea of Death.
311. To Celia.
375. To an Absentee.
404. Moral Reflections written on the top of St. Paul's.
422. The Stag-eyed Lady.
427. On Mr. Martin's Pictures and the Bonassus.

Vol. VI. July to December, 1822.

Page 141. Lycus the Centaur.
276. Hymn to the Sun.
304. The Two Peacocks of Bedfont.
388. "Now the loud cry." — Nimrod.
494. Midnight.
497. On a Sleeping Child.
517. Presentiment. A Fragment.
536. Sonnet, "Most delicate Ariel."

Vol. VII. January to June, 1823.

Page 96. Fair Ines.
187. Ode to Autumn.
215. Sonnet to Silence.
541. Sonnet written in Keats' "Endymion."
565. Sonnet to an Enthusiast.
636. Sonnet — Death.
660. To a Cold Beauty.

My father's first acquaintance with my mother's family must have commenced somewhere in 1821, through her brother, John Hamilton Reynolds. The father, Mr. Reynolds, was head writing-master at Christ's Hospital, and with his family then resided in that very Little Britain so quaintly and well described by Washington Irving in his "Sketch Book." Here, no doubt, many a cheerful evening was spent among such a pleasant circle of friends and acquaintances. John Keats, Edward Rice, and a Mr. Bailey were all familiar friends and constant correspondents of the young Reynoldses. I think however my father's intimacy dated rather later, for I do not think he was well acquainted with any of the above mentioned trio. But about this time must have originated his long-standing friendship with Mr. and Mrs. Dilke, who were known to all parties.

John Hamilton Reynolds was himself a writer for the "London Magazine," in which appeared several articles from his pen, under the signature of "Edward Herbert." He was also the author of a small volume of poems, "The Garden of Florence," which was favourably noticed at the time. To him, my father, in a very friendly manner, dedicated "Lycus the Centaur." A congeniality of pursuits and likings drew them together — a connection that was afterwards by my father's marriage with his sister to be still further strengthened. It was a pity it did not survive to the end, for on one side at least it was characteristically generous and sincere.*

* My uncle is often referred to in the letters as "John." A frequent correspondence was kept up between my father and him, which would have afforded materials of much value towards the compilation of these

It was "in the pleasant spring-time of their friendship," and "with the old partiality for the writings of each other, which prevailed in those days," that many pleasant versified encounters occurred. This may be instanced by the following verses which were inserted in the "Athenæum." When Miss Fanny Kemble took leave of the English stage, at her farewell performance she took off her wreath and threw it into the body of the house. The following verses were written by my father, as from a young farmer in the country.

MISS FANNY'S FAREWELL FLOWERS.

Not "the posie of a ring."
SHAKESPEARE (all but the *not*).

I came to town a happy man,
  I need not now dissemble
Why I return so sad at heart,
  It 's all through Fanny Kemble.
Oh, when she threw her flowers away,
  What urged the tragic slut on
To weave in such a wreath as that,
  Ah me, — a bachelor's button!

None fought so hard, none fought so well,
  As I to gain some token —
When all the pit rose up in arms,
  And heads and hearts were broken;

memorials. I regret to say they are unavailable, owing to Mrs. John Reynolds' refusal to allow us access to them. It is a great disappointment that the public should be thus deprived of what would become its property after publication — the records of one of its noted writers. — T. H.

Huzza! said I, I 'll have a flow'r
  As sure as my name 's Dutton.
I made a snatch — I got a catch —
  By Jove! a bachelor's button!

I 've lost my watch — my hat is smashed —
  My clothes declare the racket;
I went there in a full dress coat,
  And came home in a jacket.
My nose is swell'd, my eye is black,
  My lip I 've got a cut on —
Odds buds! — and what a bud to get —
  The deuce! a bachelor's button!

My chest 's in pain; I really fear
  I 've somewhat hurt my bellows,
By pokes and punches in the ribs
  From those *herb-strewing fellows.*
I miss two teeth in *my* front row;
  My corn has had a *fut* on;
And all this pain I 've had, to gain
  This cursed bachelor's button!

Had I but won a rose — a bud —
  A pansy — or a daisy —
A periwinkle — anything
  But this — it drives me crazy!
My very sherry tastes like squills,
  I can't enjoy my mutton;
And when I sleep I dream of it —
  Still — still — a bachelor's button!

My place is booked per coach to-night,
  But oh, my spirit trembles

To think how country friends will ask
  Of Knowleses and of Kembles.
If they should breathe about the wreath,
  When I go back to Sutton,
I shall not dare to show my share —
  That all! — a bachelor's button!

My luck in life was never good,
  But this my fate will harden:
I ne'er shall like my farming more, —
  I know I shan't the Garden.
The turnips all may have the fly,
  The wheat may have the smut on, —
I care not, — I've a blight at heart —
  Ah me! a bachelor's button!

To this Mr. Reynolds replied with the following —

LINES TO MISS F. KEMBLE,

ON THE FLOWER SCUFFLE AT COVENT GARDEN THEATRE.

BY CURL-PATED HUGH.

" Make a scramble, gentlemen, — make a scramble."
Boys at Greenwich.

Well, this flower strewing I must say is sweet,
And I long, Miss Kemble, to throw myself considerably at your feet;
For you've made me a happy man in the scuffle, when you jerk'd about the daisies;
And ever since the night you kiss'd your hand to me and the rest of the pit, I've been chuck full of your praises!

I 'm no hand at writing (though I can *say* several things that 's
handsome);
But that ignorance, thank my stars! got me off when I was
tried for forging upon Ransome.
I did n't try to get the flowers, which so many of your ardent
admirers were eager to snatch;
But I got a very good-going chronometer, and for your sake
I 'll never part with the watch!

I 've several relics from those who got *your* relics — a snuff-
box — a gold snap;
A silver guard and trimmings from a very eager young chap;
Two coat flaps with linings, from a youth, who defying blows
And oaths, and shovings, was snatching at, and I 'm sorry to
say missing, the front rose!

One aspiring young man from the country rushed at the
wreath like a glutton,
But he retired out of the conflict with only a bachelor's button!
Another in a frenzy fought for the flowers like anything crazy,
But I 've got his shirt-pin, and he only got two black eyes and
a daisy.

The thought of you makes me rich — Oh, you 're a real friend
to free trade;
You agitate 'em so and take their attention off — If you 'd
keep farewelling my fortune 'd be made.
Oh, how I shall hate to make *white soup* of the silver, or part
with anything for your sake!
I 'll wear the country gentleman's brooch, on your account,
it 's so very pretty a make!

I didn't get a bud — indeed, I was just at the moment busy
about other things;
I wish you 'd allow me to show you a choice assortment of
rings —

You understand the allusion; but I'm in earnest — that's
what I am;
And though I'm famous a little — domestic happiness is better
than all fame!

Well, you're going over the water — (it may be my turn one
of these days);
Never heed what them foreigners the Americans says!
But hoard your heart up till you come back, and if I luckily
can
Scrape up enough, you shall find me yours, and a very altered
young man!

Conjointly with my uncle Reynolds, my father wrote and published, although anonymously, "Odes and Addresses to Great People." This had a great sale, and occasioned no little wonder and speculation as to the author, as will be seen from the following letter from S. T. Coleridge to Charles Lamb. It appears to have been sent for perusal, as the copy I have is in my father's handwriting.

My dear Charles,

This afternoon, a little, thin, mean-looking sort of a foolscap sub-octavo of poems, printed on dingy outsides, lay on the table, which the cover informed me was circulating in our book-club, so very Grub-streetish in all its exteriors, internal as well as external, that I cannot explain by what accident of impulse (assuredly there was no *motive* in play) I came to look into it. Least of all, the title, "Odes and Addresses to Great Men," which connected itself in my head with "Rejected Addresses" and all the Smith and Theodore Hook squad. But my dear Charles, it was certainly written by you, or under you, or *una cum* you. I know none of your frequent visitors capacious and assimilative enough of your converse to have reproduced you so honestly, supposing you had left yourself in pledge in his lock-up house. Gillman, to whom I read the spirited parody on the introduction to Peter Bell, the "Ode to the Great Unknown," and to Mrs. Fry — he speaks doubtfully of Reynolds and Hood. But here come Irving and Basil Montagu.

Thursday night, 10 *o'clock.* — No! Charles, it is *you.* I have read them over again, and I understand why you have anon'd the book. The puns are nine in ten good, many excellent, the *Newgatory* transcendant! And then the *exemplum sine exemplo* of a volume of personalities, and contemporaneities, without a single line that could inflict the infinitesimal of an unpleasance on any man in his senses — saving and except perhaps in the envy-addled brain of the despiser of your *lays.* If not a triumph over him, it is at least an ovation. Then moreover and besides, to speak with becoming modesty, excepting my own self, who is there but you who could write the musical lines and stanzas that are intermixed?

Here's Gillman come up to my garret, and driven back by the guardian spirits of four huge flower-holders of omnigenous roses and honeysuckles (Lord have mercy on his hysterical olfactories!. What will he do in Paradise? I must have a pair or two of nostril plugs or nose-goggles laid in his coffin), stands at the door, reading that to Mc Adam, and the washerwoman's letter, and he admits *the facts.* You are found *in the manner*, as the lawyers say; so, Mr. Charles, hang yourself up, and send me a line by way of token and acknowledgment. My dear love to Mary. God bless you and your

Unshamabramizer,

S. T. Coleridge.

On the 5th of May, 1824, the marriage of my father and mother took place.* In spite of all the sickness and sorrow that formed the greatest portion of the after-part of their lives, the union was a happy one. My mother was a woman of cultivated mind and literary tastes, and well suited to him as a companion. He had such confidence in her judgment that he read, and re-read, and corrected with her all that he wrote. Many of his articles were first dictated to her, and her ready memory supplied him with his references and quotations. He frequently dictated the first draft of his articles, although they were always finally copied out in his peculiarly clear neat writing, which was so legible and good, that it was once or twice begged by printers, to teach their compositors a first and easy lesson in reading handwriting.

Of late years my mother's time and thoughts were entirely devoted to him, and he became restless and almost seemed unable to write unless she were near.

The first few years of his married life were the most

* I have reason to believe that the match was not entirely approved of by my mother's family — not perhaps unreasonably, for it could not have seemed very prudent: but the attachment was strong and genuine on both sides, and so the course of true love at length reached its goal, though not perhaps running very smoothly. The poems, "I love Thee," "Still flows the gentle streamlet on," and several others, were written at this time. — T. H.

unclouded my father ever knew, The young couple resided for some years in Robert Street, Adelphi. Here was born their first child, which to their great grief scarcely survived its birth. In looking over some old papers I found a few tiny curls of golden hair, as soft as the finest silk, wrapped in a yellow and time-worn paper inscribed in my father's handwriting: —

"Little eyes that scarce did see,
   Little lips that never smiled;
   Alas! my little dear dead child,
Death is thy father, and not me,
I but embraced thee, soon as he!"

On this occasion those exquisite lines of Charles Lamb's, "On an infant dying as soon as born," were written and sent to my father and mother.

I much regret that there is no record left of the pleasant days of this intimacy with Charles Lamb and his sister. It was a very lively and sincere friendship on both sides, and it lasted up to the time of Mr. Lamb's death. When my father lived at Winchmore, the Lambs were settled at Enfield, so that they were tolerably near neighbours. My father's "Literary Reminiscences," in "Hood's Own," are almost the sole memorials left of his acquaintance with all those, who form such a brilliant list in Mr. Hessey's letter.* But few now survive, nor are there

* One of them — Wainwright — in the 7th vol. of "The London" (1823) criticises my father's bent and style with such an accurate perception of them, as to forestal all later critics. My father wrote occasionally under the name of Theodore M——.

"Young Theodore! young in years, not in power! Our new Ovid! — only more imaginative! — Painter to the visible eye — and the in-any written memoranda upon which to found any chronicle of that period: living so near, and being on such intimate terms with many of them, was almost sufficient reason that but few letters remain to throw any light on the subject. Had they lived in the time of the penny post, there would probably have been a goodly collection of "notelets" or "chits," but in those days of heavy postage, a letter was a more serious undertaking.

In 1826 appeared the first series of "Whims and Oddities," which had a very good sale. It was dedicated to the "Reviewers" in a humorous sort of epigram as follows: —

DEDICATION.

TO THE REVIEWERS.

What is a modern Poet's fate?
To write his thoughts upon a slate:
The critic spits on what is done,
Gives it a wipe — and all is gone!

ward; — commixture of what the superficial deem incongruous elements! — Instructive living proof how close lie the founts of laughter and tears! Thou fermenting brain — oppressed, as yet, by its own riches. Though melancholy would seem to have touched thy heart with her painful (salutary) hand, yet is thy fancy mercurial — undepressed; — and sparkles and crackles more from the contact — as the northern lights when they near the frozen pole. How! is the fit not on? Still is 'Lycus' without mate! — Who can mate him but thyself? Let not the shallow induce thee to conceal this thy depth. * * * * As for thy word gambols, thy humour, thy fantastics, thy curiously-conceited perceptions of similarity in dissimilarity, of coherents in incoherents, they are brilliantly suave, innocuously exhilarating; — but not a step farther if thou lovest thy proper peace! Read the fine of the eleventh, and the whole of the twelfth chapter of 'Tristram Shandy;' and believe them, dear Theodore!"

This first series took so well with the public, that a second edition followed, — and some time afterwards, in 1827, a second series appeared, dedicated to Sir Walter Scott. This was followed by two volumes of "National Tales," a series of stories, or rather novelettes, somewhat in the manner of Boccaccio. These are now utterly out of print; they were published by Mr. W. H. Ainsworth, then living in Bond Street.

The "Plea of the Midsummer Fairies,"* a very favourite poem of his own, appeared in 1827, but it did not exactly suit the public taste, and many copies remained unsold on the publisher's shelf. My father after-

* This most artistic poem has latterly been more fairly appreciated in spite of its antiquated style. The art, truth, and pictorial skill, as in the "Haunted House," require patient and quiet criticism. I may mention in reference to this subject, that the first book (of course, by Lamb's rules, "Readings made Easy" and the like are not books) that I read was selected by my father, and was the "Midsummer Night's Dream." Of this I read all the fairy portion one summer's day, perched at an open window on a fitting couch composed of bales of "sheets" — probably the sheets of the very work which suggested this note. At that time I was about seven years old.

It is not out of place here to insert a sonnet by the late Mr. Moxon, of Dover Street. That gentleman was an old friend of my father's, whom I have frequently heard speak of him in the warmest terms, as one whose own talents enabled him to recognise genius in others, and whose integrity and liberality as a man of business were without parallel. My father, not often fortunate in his dealings, used to say, "Moxon is the only honest publisher I know," — a sentence which, though severe, was warranted by his experience, and the losses he had met with through dishonesty. It remains — a most grateful task — for my sister and myself to add our heartfelt tribute to our father's praise of Mr. Moxon. We shall never forget his generous arrangements for the publication of our father's poems after his death; and most deeply do we regret that Mr. Moxon has not lived to superintend

wards bought up the remainder of the edition, as he said himself, to save it from the butter shops.

The poem of "Eugene Aram's Dream" first appeared in an annual called the "Gem," of which in the year 1829 he was editor, but it was afterwards republished in a separate form with drawings by Harvey, an intimate friend of my father's.

In 1829 he left London for Winchmore Hill, where he took a very pretty little cottage situated in a pleasant garden. He was very much attached to it, and many years afterwards I have known him point out some fancied resemblance in other places, and say to my mother, "Jenny, that 's very like Winchmore." It is a pretty neighbourhood even now, when the great metropolis has

the publication of these Memorials of one, between whom and himself so cordial a friendship existed. — T. H.

SONNET.

TO T. HOOD, WRITTEN AFTER READING HIS "PLEA OF THE MIDSUMMER FAIRIES."

Delightful Bard! what praises meet are thine,
  More than my verse can sound to thee belong;
Well hast thou pleaded, with a tongue divine,
  In this thy sweet and newly-breathèd song,
  Where like the stream smooth numbers gliding throng:
Gathered, methinks, I see the Elfin Race,
  With the IMMORTAL standing them among,
Smiling benign with more than courtly grace; —
Rescued I see them — all their gambols trace,
  With their fair Queen Titania in her bower,
And all their avocations small embrace,
  Pictured by thee with a Shaksperian power —
Oh, when the time shall come thy soul must flee,
Then may some hidden spirit plead for thee. — EDWARD MOXON.

encroached far on the "Green Lanes," and in those days no doubt was considered quite in the country.

An amusing incident took place during their removal from town. A large hamper of glass and china had arrived from town by the carrier one morning, and the contents, being unpacked, were placed, *pro tempore*, on a dresser in the china closet. This wooden shelf had been only newly mortared into the wall, and when all this weight was put on it, of course it came suddenly down with an alarming crash. My father who was within hearing soon came to the scene of action, or rather fraction, and, after coolly surveying the damage, very quietly sent the maid to her mistress with the message "that the china which came *up* in the morning, had come *down* in the evening." This to his great amusement brought my mother, in a state of utter mystification, to the scene of the catastrophe. They were, however, both cheerful people, and the breakage was borne with tolerable philosophy on both sides.

He enjoyed playing off little harmless practical jokes on my mother, who on her part bore them with the sweetest temper, and joined in the laugh against herself afterwards with great good humour. She was a capital subject for his fun, for she believed implicitly in whatever he told her, however improbable, and though vowing seriously every time not to be taken in again, she was sure to be caught. Her innocent face of wonder and belief added greatly to the zest of the joke.

On one occasion soon after their marriage, my father was suddenly seized with rheumatic fever of a severe kind. On his partial recovery he was ordered to Brighton to recruit his strength. Sea air always produced a beneficial effect on his health; and for many years he was in the habit of visiting Brighton, or his favourite haunt, Hastings, for a few weeks.

At the time I mention he was so weak as to be obliged to be lifted into the coach at starting, but the next day, refreshed by the first breath of the bracing air, he was almost himself. At breakfast he offered to give my mother a few hints on buying fish, adducing his own superior experience of the sea, as a reason for informing her ignorance as a young housekeeper. "Above all things, Jane," said he, "as they will endeavour to impose upon your inexperience, let nothing induce you to buy a plaice that has any appearance of red or orange spots, as they are sure signs of an advanced stage of decomposition." My mother promised faithful compliance in the innocence of her heart, and accordingly when the fish-woman came to the door, she descended to show off her newly acquired information. As it happened, the woman had very little except plaice, and these she turned over and over, praising their size and freshness. But the obnoxious red spots on every one of them still greeted my mother's dissatisfied eyes. On her hinting a doubt of their freshness, she was met by the assertion that they were not long out of the water, having been caught that morning. This shook my mother's doubts for a moment, but remembering my father's portrayal of the Brighton fishwomen's iniquitous falsehoods, she gravely shook her head, and mildly observed, in all the pride of conscious knowledge, "My good woman, it may be as you say, but I could not think of buying any plaice with those very unpleasant red spots!" The woman's answer was a perfect shout. "Lord bless your eyes, Mum! who ever seed any without 'em?"

A suppressed giggle on the stairs revealed the perpetrator of the joke, and my father rushed off in a perfect ecstacy of laughter, leaving my poor discomfited mother to appease the angry sea-nymph as she could. This was a standing joke for many years, in common with the story of the pudding, which will appear hereafter.

My father's attachment to the sea, as I remarked before, was very great, and he seized every opportunity of

getting within reach of it.* He was much amused when one of his contemporaries, in a little sketch of his life, gravely asserted that he was destined for the sea, but would not carry out the intention, owing to his dislike of the great ocean. The only ground he could imagine there was for this assertion was, that in one of the Com-

* This cut was one of several sketches drawn by my father to teach his wife the names, &c., of the different craft at Hastings. — T. H.

ies he wrote a sort of burlesque account of first going to sea, with all its attendant horrors to a landsman of storm and sickness. But this I need hardly say was under a fictitious character, and quite the reverse of his own opinions. Although his life had twice been in danger owing to it, yet his love and relish for the sea and all belonging to it partook almost of yearning affection, which he has so beautifully expressed in a sonnet published in the last collection of poems, commencing —

"Shall I rebuke thee, Ocean, my old love?"

The allusion here is to the fearful storm he encountered in after years, when crossing to Rotterdam. But his first peril was of a different kind, as I remember hearing the story from his own lips. It occurred before his marriage, but in what year I cannot ascertain. He was in the habit of going frequently to Hastings, and there he enjoyed boating to his heart's content, accompanied by his favourite old boatman Tom Woodgate, whom he commemorated in a sea-side sketch. At this particular time my father had just recovered from a severe illness, and after a few days' stay at Hastings, he fancied a bathe in the open sea would do him good. He had often bathed so before; and being a good swimmer he used to go out in the boat some way from shore, and then undress and plunge in. This he accordingly did, being still weak, and when he came up from his first plunge he found himself under the boat. Knowing the full extent of his danger, he exerted all his remaining strength and dived again, when he succeeded in coming up at some distance from the boat. He said he should never forget his sensations when he saw the green water, "like a bubble" getting lighter above him; he could only compare it to the often described feelings of persons rescued from drowning, when the events of all their past life seem to flash before them in a moment. He was so utterly exhausted when he came up that he could scarcely support himself till the boat reached him. The boatman told him afterwards he was dreadfully frightened, for although the whole occurrence took place in perhaps less time than it takes to describe it, the interval was quite long enough for his experience to tell him that something was wrong. Great was his relief to see my father come up at a little distance, and lustily did he pull to his help. He owned that he was speculating how he was ever to go back to Hastings with the clothes and watch, as few would have believed his story. Fortunately this tragical end was averted, but it was a warning to my father ever after. He perfectly understood the management of a boat, and would often take the helm, but he never attempted bathing in the open sea again.

During one of his visits to Brighton my father made acquaintance with an old lieutenant in the Coast Guard, a great oddity, who used to drop in of an evening for a quiet rubber. From him my father learned his solitary song; the only one he was ever known to sing; and quaint and characteristic enough it was. It ran somehow in this fashion —

"Ŭp jumped the mackerel,
With his stripëd back, —
Says he, 'Reef in the mains'l, and haul on the tack,

For it 's windy weather,
It 's stormy weather,
And when the wind blows pipe all hands together —
For, upon my word, it is windy weather!'"

This is the only verse that remains as a family tradition of the song, but, if I remember rightly, it brought in the suggestions of the various fishes for sailing the vessel. Now my father, curiously enough, with the most delicate perception of the rhythm and melody of versifying, and the most acute instinct for any jarring syllable or word, and peculiarly happy in the musical cadence of his own poetry, had yet not the slightest ear for music. He *could* not sing a tune through correctly, and was rather amused by the defect than otherwise, especially when a phrenologist once told him his organs of time and tune were very deficient.* My father used to say on the very rare occasions on which he was ever known to sing, that he chose this particular song because if he *was* out of tune no one could detect him, especially as he made a point of refusing all *encores.*

At Winchmore Hill my father must have resided

* Several people observed this in him, and one, who was just safe-landed from a rhapsody on music, in which he had indulged before my father, who did n't sympathise, said — "Ah, you know, you 've no musical enthusiasm — you don't know what it is!" It was a dangerous thing to "snub" my father, for he generally gave as good as he took. In this instance he said — "Oh yes, I do know it — it 's like turtle soup — for every pint of real, you meet with gallons of mock, with calves' heads in proportion."

One discovery he did make in music, which was that you cannot play on the black keys of a piano without producing a Scotch tune, or what will very well pass for one. — T. H.

about three years; and here, in 1830, I was born. In the Christmas of the same year the first "Comic Annual" appeared. To Sir Francis Freeling, his friend and my godfather, was this volume dedicated by my father in the following words, — Sir Francis being at that time Secretary to the Postmaster-General: —

TO SIR FRANCIS FREELING, BART.,

The Great Patron of Letters, Foreign, General, and Twopenny; distinguished alike for his fostering care of the

BELL LETTERS;

And his antiquarian regard for the

DEAD LETTERS;

Whose increasing efforts to forward the spread of intelligence, as Corresponding Member of All Societies (and no man fills his Post better), have

SINGLY, DOUBLY, and TREBLY

Endeared him to every class; this first volume of "The Comic Annual," is with Frank permission, gratefully inscribed by

THOMAS HOOD.

A copy of this first volume was, I believe, sent to the late Duke of Devonshire, and this I imagine was my father's first introduction to him, as I find his Grace's letter of thanks for it, dated February 8th, 1831.

LONDON.

SIR,

Accept my best thanks for the beautiful copies of the "Comic Annual," which I have had the pleasure of receiving from you; you could not have selected a person who has enjoyed more the perusal of your works.

I am almost afraid of making the following request, but perhaps it may be as amusing as it *must* be easy to you to comply with it, in which case alone I beg you to do it.

It is necessary to construct a door of sham books, for the entrance of a library at Chatsworth: your assistance in giving me inscriptions for these unreal folios, quartos, and 12mos, is what I now ask.

One is tired of the "Plain Dealings," "Essays on Wood," and "Perpetual Motion" on such doors, — on one I have seen the names of "Don Quixote's Library," and on others impossibilities, such as "Virgilii Odaria," — "Herodoti Poemata" — "Byron's Sermons" — &c., &c.; but from you I venture to hope for more attractive titles — at your perfect leisure and convenience. I have the honour to be, Sir, with many excuses,

Your sincere humble servant,

DEVONSHIRE.

In accordance with this request my father, in April, sent the following letter to the Duke:

WINCHMORE HILL.

MY LORD DUKE,

On learning that Your Grace is at Chatsworth, I send off as many titles as have occurred to me; promising myself the honour and pleasure of waiting upon Your Grace with some others on the 14th, and am,

My Lord Duke,

Your Grace's most obliged and obedient servant,

THOS. HOOD.

The list of titles follows this. Some of them have lost

the point which the topics of the day gave to them, while others appear to be such *bonâ fide* works, that one does not always catch the hidden meaning. As an instance of this I will mention "The Life of Zimmermann (the author of 'Solitude'). *By himself.*"

TITLES FOR THE LIBRARY DOOR, CHATSWORTH.

On the Lung Arno in Consumption. By D. Cline.
Dante's Inferno; or Description of Van Demon's Land.
The Racing Calendar, with the Eclipses for 1831.
Ye Devill on Two Styx (Black letter). 2 Vols.
On cutting off Heirs with a Shilling. By Barber Beaumont.
Percy Vere. In 40 volumes.
Galerie des Grands Tableaux par les Petits Maîtres.
On the Affinity of the Death Watch and Sheep Tick.
Lamb's Recollections of Suett.
Lamb on the Death of Wolfe.
The *Hop*tician. By Lord Farnham.
Tadpoles; or Tales out of my own Head.
On the Connection of the River Oder and the River Wezel.
Malthus' Attack of Infantry.
McAdam's Views in Rhodes.
Spenser, with Chaucer's Tales.
Autographia; or Man's Nature, known by his Sig-nature.
Manfredi. Translated by Defoe.
Earl Grey on Early Rising.
Plurality of Livings, with regard to the Common Cat.
The Life of Zimmermann. By Himself.
On the Quadrature of the Circle; or Squaring in the Ring. By J. Mendoza.
Gall's Sculler's Fares.
Bish's Retreat of the Ten Thousand.
Dibdin's Cream of Tar—.
Cornaro on Longevity and the Construction of 74's
Pompeii; or Memoirs of a Black Footman. By Sir W. Gell.
Pygmalion. By Lord Bacon.
Macintosh, Macculloch, and Macaulay on Almacks.
On Trial by Jury, with remarkable Packing Cases.

On the Distinction between Lawgivers and Law-sellers. By Lord Brougham.

Memoirs of Mrs. Mountain. By Ben Lomond.

Feu mon père — feu ma mère. Par Swing.

On Dec. the 22nd, 1832, my father sent His Grace the following further instalment of titles, with the letter which is printed after them.

Boyle on Steam..

Rules for Punctuation. By a thorough-bred Pointer.

Blaine on Equestrian Burglary; or the Breaking-in of Horses.

Chronological Account of the Date Tree.

Hughes Ball on Duelling.

Book-keeping by Single Entry

John Knox on "Death's Door."

Designs for Friezes. By Captain Parry.

Remarks on the Terra Cotta or Mud Cottages of Ireland.

Considérations sur le Vrai Guy, et Le Faux.

Kosciusko on the Right of the Poles to stick up for themselves.

Prize poems, in *Blank* verse.

On the Site of Tully's Offices.

The Rape of the Lock, with Bramah's Notes.

Haughty-cultural Remarks on London Pride.

Annual Parliaments; a Plea for Short Commons.

Michau on Ball-Practice.

On Sore Throat and the Migration of the Swallow. By T. Abernethy.

Scott and Lot. By the Author of "Waverley."

Debrett on Chain Piers.

Voltaire, Volney, Volta. 3 Vols.

Peel on Bell's System.

Grose's Slang Dictionary; or Vocabulary of Grose Language.

Freeling on Enclosing Waste Lands.

Elegy on a Black-Cock, shot amongst the Moors. By W. Wilberforce.

Johnson's Contradictionary.

Sir T. Lawrence on the Complexion of Fairies and Brownies.

Life of Jack Ketch, with Cuts of his own Execution.

Barrow on the Common Weal.

Hoyle's Quadrupedia; or Rules of All-Fours.
Campaigns of the British Arm: By one of the German Leg.
Cursory Remarks on Swearing.
On the Collar of the Garter. By Miss Bailey of Halifax.
Shelley's Conchologist.
Recollections of Bannister. By Lord Stair.
The Hole Duty of Man. By I. P. Brunel.
Ude's Tables of Interest.
Chantrey on the Sculpture of the Chipaway Indians.
The Scottish Boccaccio. By D. Cameron.
Cook's Specimens of the Sandwich Tongue.
In-i-go on Secret Entrances.
Hoyle on the Game Laws.
Mémoires de La-porte.

LAKE HOUSE, *Dec.* 22, 1832.

MY LORD DUKE,

I am extremely obliged to Your Grace for the kind and early answer to my request concerning Lady Granville. With my best thanks I have the honour of presenting a copy of my "Annual," and sincerely hope to have the same pleasure for many years to come.

The enclosed titles were for a long time "titles extinct," —being lost with other papers in my removal hither: or, as Othello says, thro' "moving accidents by flood and field." Some memoranda subsequently turned up, but I feared too late for use; and besides I could not disentangle the new from the old.

This has been matter of regret to me, but I have made up my mind to send them to Your Grace on the chance of their becoming of use, and that some secret door may yet open to them, like those in the old romances.

I have the honour to be,

My Lord Duke,

Your Grace's obliged servant,

THOS. HOOD.

His Grace acknowledged the receipt of the titles in the following letter:

CHATSWORTH.

SIR,

I am more obliged to you than I can say for my titles. They are exactly what I wanted, and invented in that remarkable vein of humour, which has in your works caused me and many of my friends so much amusement and satisfaction.

I shall anxiously await the promised additions — but I hope that on my return to London you will allow me an opportunity of thanking you in person. There is hardly any day on which you would not find me at home at twelve o'clock, and after the 13th of this month I shall be settled in London.

I have the honour to be, Sir,

Most truly and sincerely yours,

DEVONSHIRE.

This letter, it will be remarked, was in acknowledgment of the first set of titles. After this many communications passed between His Grace and my father. Until the time of my father's death (I might add even after that time, when I think of his generous subscription to the Monumental Fund) the Duke's acts of considerate kindness never varied or failed. Among other little minor courtesies I find, among my father's papers, admissions to Chatsworth, and to the Private Apartments at Windsor. The "Comic Annual of 1831 was dedicated to His Grace, and that of 1832 to Lady Granville, by a permission hinted at in the letter of Dec. 22nd. But

His Grace's kindnesses were not always minor ones. Assistance of great service was rendered by him to my father in the shape of a volunteered friendly loan, the benefit of which will be seen in the ensuing letter:

LAKE HOUSE, *August*, 1833

MY LORD DUKE,

It will doubtless appear to Your Grace that one request brings on a second, as certainly as one Scotchman is said to introduce another, when I entreat for my new novel of "Tylney Hall" the same honour that was formerly conferred on the "Comic Annual."

If a reason be sought why I desire to address a second dedication to the same personage, I can only refer to the "*on revient toujours*" principle of the French song; and no one could have better cause so to try back than myself.

I hesitate to intrude with details, but I know the goodness which originated one obligation will be gratified to learn that the assistance referred to has been, and is, of the greatest service in a temporary struggle — though arduous enough to one of a profession never overburthened with wealth, from Homer downwards. Indeed the Nine Muses seem all to have lived in one house for cheapness. I await, hopefully anxious, Your Grace's pleasure as to the new honour I solicit, fully prepared, in case of acquiescence, to exclaim with the Tinker to the "Good Duke" of Burgundy, in the old ballad,

"Well, I thank your good Grace,
And your love I embrace,
I was never before in so happy a case!"

With my humble but fervent wishes for the health and happiness of Your Grace, and one not so favourable to the long life of the grouse, I have the honour to be,

My Lord Duke,

Your Grace's most obliged and devoted servant,

THOS. HOOD.

Between 1831–2 my father had some connection with the stage in the form of dramatic composition. It was probably at this time he made the acquaintance of T. P. Cooke, and, I think, Dibdin.

He wrote the libretto for a little English Opera, that was brought out, I believe, at the Surrey. Its name is lost now, although it had a good run at the time. Perhaps it may be recognised by some old play-goer by the fact that its *dramatis personæ* were all *bees*. My father also assisted my uncle Reynolds in the dramatising of Gil Blas, which, if my impression be right, was produced at Drury Lane. One scene was very cleverly managed, considering that stage machinery (which now-a-days is almost engineering) was then in its infancy. It was a scene divided into two, *horizontally*, displaying at once the robber's cave, and the country beneath which it was excavated.

It is much to be regretted that we have been unable to discover any traces of an entertainment which was written, somewhere about this time, by my father for the well-known inimitable Charles Mathews the Elder, who was heard by a friend most characteristically to remark, that he liked the entertainment very much, and Mr. Hood too,— but that all the time he was reading it, Mrs.

Hood would keep snuffing the candles. This little fidgetty observation very much shocked my mother, and of course delighted my father.

He also wrote a pantomime for Mr. Frederick Yates, of the old Adelphi Theatre, and on that occasion received the following quaint epistle, the writer being Mr. Yates's *factotum*, and moreover machinist of all those wonderful Adelphi pieces that made that tiny theatre famous, and delighted the play-going public of those days. Mr. William Godbee was also, I think, the contriver and inventor of Matthews' transformation dresses, for his entertainments, and especially famous for manufacturing queer wigs and head-dresses for him. He was a clever man, but a great oddity, as the following letter will show.

THEATRE ROYAL, ADELPHI, *July* 24, 1832.

Mr. Godbee's Respectfull Compliments to Mr. Hood, and he begs leave to state that he have Received a Letter this morning from Mr. Yates, who is in Glasgow, and he begs of him to go Immediately to Mr. Reynolds of Golden Square, to beg of him to Intreat of Mr. Hood to Favour him with a Coppy of his Pantomime of Harlequin and Mr. Jenkins, for Mr. Yates by some unfortunate circumstance have lost it, and the Dresses and Scenery are of no use to him unless he had the M.S. of The Pantomime. Therefore if Mr. Hood have it by him, and would Send it Enclosed in a Parcel to the Stage Door of the Adelphi Theatre, he would be conferring an Everlasting Favour on him. Honored Sir, if you should not be so fortunate as to have it by you, *Pray Oblidge* me with an answer by Post, as I dare not Send his Scenery and Dresses without the M.S. to Glasgow. I trust your Goodness of hert will Pardon me in thus troubling you. Permit me to Remain

Your Humble Servant,

WILLIAM GODBEE.

P. S. Dear Sir, I shal wait with all anxiety as I can't write nor send to Mr. Yates until I hear from you.

Whether poor Mr. Godbee's anxiety was set at rest, and the Pantomime found, is not now to be ascertained, but it is to be hoped it was.

Of all my father's attempts at dramatic writing I can find no trace, save one little song intended for a musical piece, which was written to the air "My mother bids me bind my hair":

My mother bids me spend my smiles
  On all who come and call me fair,
As crumbs are thrown upon the tiles,
  To all the sparrows of the air.

But I've a darling of my own,
  For whom I hoard my little stock —
What if I chirp him all alone,
  And leave mamma to feed the flock!

The "Comic Annual" of 1832 was dedicated by permission to King William the Fourth, who received the dedication and a copy of the work very graciously, and eventually expressed a desire to see my father. He accordingly called upon His Majesty by appointment at Brighton. My father was much taken with His Majesty's cordial and hearty manner, and I believe he was very well received. One thing I remember is the fact, that, on backing out of the royal presence, my father forgot the way he had entered, and retrograded to the wrong entry. The king good-humouredly laughed, and himself showed him the right direction, going with him to the door.

In 1832 * he left Winchmore Hill, owing to some disagreement with his landlord, who declined to make some necessary alterations; it was much to be regretted, and he always spoke of it afterwards in that light. He was induced to take a house in Essex,† — Lake House, Wanstead. He was overpersuaded to do so by some not very judicious friends, and he ever afterwards repented it. It was, however, a beautiful old place, although exceedingly inconvenient, for there was not a good bed-room in it. The fact was, it had formerly been a sort of banqueting-hall to Wanstead Park, and the rest of the house was sacrificed to the one great room, which extended all along the back. It had a beautiful chimney-piece carved in fruit and flowers by Gibbons, and the ceiling bore traces of painting. Several quaint Watteau-like pictures

* It will be seen by reference to the letters to the Duke of Devonshire, that this removal took place toward the end of the year — probably in October. — T. H.

† The house was the banqueting hall of the splendid mansion that used to stand in Wanstead Park. Between them spread a large lake, so that the festive parties came by water. This has now dwindled to a couple of ponds, connected by a ditch, but it was doubtless from it that the house took its name. — T. H.

of the Seasons were panelled in the walls, but it was all in a shocking state of repair, and in the twilight the rats used to come and peep out of the holes in the wainscot. There were two or three windows on each side, while a door in the middle opened on a flight of steps leading into a pleasant wilderness of a garden, infested by hundreds of rabbits from the warren close by. From the windows you could catch lovely glimpses of forest scenery, especially one little aspen avenue. In the midst of the garden lay the little lake from which the house took its name, surrounded by huge masses of rhododendrons.

In the early part of his residence at Wanstead, my father's boyish spirit of fun broke out as usual. On one occasion some boys were caught by him in the act of robbing an orchard; with the assistance of the gardener, they were dragged trembling into the house. My mother's father happened to be staying there, an imposing-looking old gentleman, who had not forgotten his scholastic dignity when looking on anything in the shape of a boy. A hint to him sufficed, and he assumed an arm-chair and the character of a J. P. for the county. The frightened offenders were drawn up before him, and formally charged by my father with the theft, which was further proved by the contents of their pockets. The judge, assuming a severe air, immediately sentenced them to instant execution by hanging on the cherry tree. I can recollect being prompted by my father to kneel down and intercede for the culprits, and my frightened crying and the solemn farce of the whole scene had its due effect on the offenders. Down on their knees they dropped in a row, sobbing and whining most piteously, and vowing never "to do so no more." My father, thinking them sufficiently punished, gave the hint, and they were as solemnly pardoned, my father and grandfather laughing heartily to see the celerity with which they made off.

On another occasion two or three friends came down for a day's shooting, and, as they often did, in the evening they rowed out into the middle of the little lake in an old punt. They were full of spirits, and had played off one or two practical jokes on their host, till on getting out of the boat, leaving him last, one of them gave it a push, and out went my father into the water. Fortunately it was the landing-place, and the water was not deep, but he was wet through. It was playing with edged tools to venture on such tricks with him, and he quietly determined to turn the tables. Accordingly he presently began to complain of cramps and stitches, and at last went in-doors. His friends getting rather ashamed of their rough fun, persuaded him to go to bed, which he immediately did. His groans and complaints increased so alarmingly, that they were almost at their wits' ends what to do. My mother had received a quiet hint, and was therefore not alarmed, though much amused at the terrified efforts and prescriptions of the repentant jokers. There was no doctor to be had for miles, and all sorts of queer remedies were suggested and administered, my father shaking with laughing, while they supposed he had got ague or fever. One rushed up with a tea-kettle of boiling water hanging on his arm, another tottered under a tin bath, and a third brought the mustard. My father at length, as well as he could speak, gave out in a sepulchral voice that he was sure he was dying, and detailed some most absurd directions for his will, which they were all too frightened to see the fun of. At last he could stand it no longer, and after hearing the penitent offenders beg him to forgive them for their unfortunate joke, and beseech him to believe in their remorse, he burst into a perfect shout of laughing, which they thought at first was delirious frenzy, but which ultimately betrayed the joke.

Nor was I,* though a mere child, more exempt than my mother from a few innocent pranks. I had a favourite but very ugly wooden doll, combining all the usual features of the race, a triangular nose, button mouth, and inverted eyes. This lovely creature I left by some chance in the dangerous precincts of my father's study. What was my horror and amazement next morning to find her comely visage thickly studded with bright pink spots! For some hours I dared not go near her, as she lay extended on the table, being firmly persuaded she had the measles, then very prevalent in the neighbourhood. My father was, of course, the author of the mischief, and perceived the success of his plan with infinite amusement. My fears, however, were not allayed till poor dolly underwent a thorough ablution, under which

* My sister was often the subject of such jokes. I myself was too young for any more advanced pleasantry than a "booby-trap" of light pamphlets, carefully disposed on the top of the study door, but I was often spectator of little plots laid for my sister, such as a pinch of damp gunpowder plastered round the wick of a candle, which she would light in order to fetch some book, or go on some pretended errand. — T. H.

purification her few remaining charms vanished for ever.

Though living at Wanstead, my father and mother still visited the sea-side at intervals; indeed, my father seemed always to yearn with a vague longing for the ocean, "his old love"—just as dwellers in towns long for green fields. In 1833 he wrote the following letter to Wright from Ramsgate.

Ramsgate, May 26, Wind E. N. E., Weather moderate. Remain in the harbour the Isis, Snow, Rose, Pink, Daisy, cutters; Boyle, steamer; John Ketch, powerful lugger.

In the Roads, the Mc Adam, with Purbeck stone. The Jane (Mrs. Hood) on putting out to sea, was quite upset, and obliged to discharge.

My dear Wright,

It was like your lubberly taste to prefer the Epsom Salts to the Ocean Brine, but I am glad to hear you do mean after all to trust your precious body, as you have sometimes committed your voice, to the "deep, deep sea." Should its power overwhelm you, it will only be a new illustration of the saying that "might overcomes (W) right."

(Jack enters to say the wind and tide serve, so am after a sail, which I hope, with respect to myself, will prove a "sail of effects.")

(3 P.M. Re-enter the Ann (a young lady friend of Hood's) with T. H., his face well washed, his coat dripping, collar like two wet dog's ears, and his old hat as

glossy as a new "'un." He eats a biscuit as soft as sopped granite, a dram of whiskey, and then resumes the pen.)

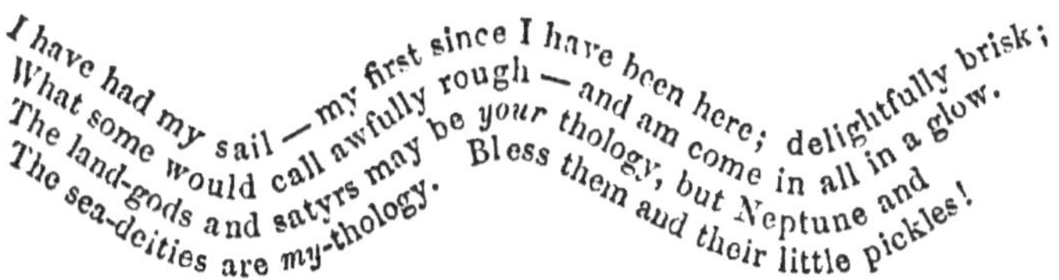
I have had my sail — my first since I have been here; delightfully brisk;
What some would call awfully rough — and am come in all in a glow.
The land-gods and satyrs may be *your* thology, but Neptune and
The sea-deities are my-thology. Bless them and their little pickles!

Although they are prose, I defy a poet to write better descriptive lines of the sea than the four last.

The Derby seems to have been highly creditable to Glaucus and the rest of the favourites. Outsiders (and sea-siders) for ever!

There come over here boats from France laden with boxes of white things, of an oval shape, the size of eggs; I rather think they are eggs, and I was much amused with an energetic question which one of our local marines put to one of the French ones, — "Where *do* you get all your eggs?" as if they had some way of making them by machinery. For certain the quantity is great, and the French hens must lay longer odds than mine. Please to copy the following verbatim, and send it to Dilke per post: —

Pencilled annotation on Prince Puckler Muskau, from Sackett's Library, Ramsgate, p. 212, vol. i.

"What a lie, you *frog-eating* rascal! What do you mean by telling such a twister?"

The weather is so fine, you will be a great Pump if you do not come here sooner than you propose.

When you talk of the *middle* of the week, you may as well embrace the *waist* of the week, and come down here at once by Tuesday's Margate steamer. Every hour will do you good, so don't stick Thursday obstinately on your back, like an ass ridden by *Day*. Seriously, I shall look for you, and my doctor says all disappointments will throw me back. Mind while you are on board, have a crust and Cheshire and bottled porter for a lunch. The last is capital! No entire can match that which hath been ripened and mellowed by voyaging. Even Ann Porter (the young lady referred to before) is improved by crossing the Channel. Don't forget the pig-tail, — that is the porter. And sit not with your back to the bulwark, on account of the *tremor* of the engine. The sound is as of a perpetual *gallopade* performed by sea horses. Just go to the chimney and listen. There was no illness whatever when I came down, — at least human sickness The only symptom I saw was the *heaving* of the lead.

* * * *

I remain, dear Wright, yours distantly,

THOS. HOOD, R. N.

P. S. Wind has veered half a point. Forgot to say we forgot my birthday on the 23rd, so are keeping it to-day *ex post facto*, but not completely as usual, for I had no artillery to discharge at one o'clock.

While residing at Lake House, my father wrote his only completed novel, "Tylney Hall," much of the scenery and description being taken from Wanstead and its neighbourhood. This was dedicated to the Duke of Devonshire. Here also was written a little volume containing a poem called the "Epping Hunt," with illustrations by Cruikshank. The frontispiece was an admirable likeness of an old gentleman who lived near us, a Mr. Rounding. He was one of the few surviving representatives of the genuine old fox-hunting squires of other days, living in hospitable style in a large old house, and keeping his pack of hounds. He was, I believe, the manager of those Cockney Olympian revels, the Epping Hunts, which, however, at that time were many shades better than they are now.

Brighton. March 23. 1828.

The Wreck.

CHAPTER II.

1835.

He is involved in Difficulties by the Failure of a Firm. — Birth of only Son. — Illness of Mrs. Hood. — Acquaintance with Dr. Elliot. — Goes to Germany. — Nearly lost in the "Lord Melville." — At Rotterdam. — Letters to his Wife. — Joined by her and the Children at Coblenz. — Letter from Mrs. Hood to Mrs. Elliot. — Acquaintance with Lieutenant De Franck. — Letters to Mr. and Mrs. Dilke, Mr. Wright, and Lieutenant De Franck.

AT the end of 1834, by the failure of a firm my father suffered, in common with many others, very heavy loss, and consequently became involved in pecuniary difficulties. "For some months he strove with his embarrassments, but the first heavy sea being followed up by other adversities, all hope of righting the vessel was abandoned. In this extremity had he listened to the majority of his advisers, he would at once have absolved himself of his obligations by one or other of those sharp but sure remedies, which the legislature has provided for all such evils. But a sense of honour forbade such a course, and emulating the illustrious example of Sir Walter Scott, he determined to try whether he could not score off his debts as effectually and more creditably, with his pen, than with the legal whitewash or a wet sponge. He had aforetime realised in one year a sum equal to the amount in arrear, and there was consequently fair reason to expect that by redoubled diligence, economising, and escaping costs at law, he would soon be able to retrieve his affairs. With these views, leaving every shilling behind him, derived from the sale of his effects, the means he carried with him being an advance upon his future labours, he voluntarily expatriated himself, and bade his native land good night."

This is extracted from a letter of his own in which he describes the whole course of his affairs.

To put the crowning stroke on all his sorrows and anxieties, my mother was taken most dangerously ill after the birth of their only son (Jan. 19, 1835), and for some time her life was despaired of. Then was first laid the foundation of that friendship with Dr. and Mrs. Elliot of Stratford, which only terminated with my father's life. Under God's permission, and thanks to the skill and care of their kind friend and physician, my mother was once more restored to comparative health. My father only waited to see her partially recovered, and then pursuing his plan he started for Rotterdam in the "Lord Melville," proposing to look out for some pleasant and suitable town on the Rhine where he could settle. My mother was to follow with her children as soon as she was able to bear the fatigue of travelling. At that time such a journey was no light undertaking; in fact, it required almost as much care and forethought as people think necessary in these days to exert on going to Egypt. My father's voyage was a disastrous one, for the fearful and memorable storm of the 4th and 5th of March, 1835, came on; when eleven vessels, including a Dutch Indiaman, were lost off the coast of Holland. To the mental and bodily exhaustion which attended this danger my father attributed much of his subsequent sufferings.

He finally fixed on Coblenz as the suitable place for a residence, and from thence he wrote the following letter to my mother. I have inserted it as a proof of his tender and watchful care of her, and the affection that considered even trifles worthy of attention when conducing to her comfort.

Somewhere about this time, perhaps a little while previous to his departure, the following sonnet was written to my mother.

SONNET.

Think, sweetest, if my lids are now not wet,
  The tenderest tears lie ready at the brim,
  To see thine own dear eyes — so pale and dim —
Touching my soul with full and fond regret,
For on thy ease my heart's whole care is set;
  Seeing I love thee in no passionate whim,
  Whose summer dates but with the rose's trim,
Which one hot June can perish and beget, —
Ah no, I chose thee for affection's pet,
  For unworn love, and constant cherishing —
To smile but to thy smile — or else to fret
  When thou art fretted — rather than to sing
Elsewhere, — alas! I ought to soothe and kiss
Thy dear pale cheek, while I assure thee this!

T. Hood.

Coblenz, *March 13th.*

At last, my own dearest and best, I sit down to write

to you, and I fear you have been looking anxiously for news from me.

In truth, I wrote a long letter at Nimeguen which I suppressed, having nothing certain to say. I will now tell you first that I am *safe* and *well* — which is the very *truth* — and then I may relate how I got on. I had a dreadful passage to Rotterdam: Wednesday night was an awful storm, and Thursday morning was worse. I was *sea-sick* and *frightened* at sea for the first time: so you will suppose it was no trifle: in fact, it was unusually severe. I went up at midnight and found *four* men at the helm, hint enough for me, so I went down again, and in the morning a terrific sea tore the whole four from the helm, threw the captain as far as the funnel (twenty paces), and the three men after him. Had it not come *direct aft*, it would have swept them into the sea, boat, skylights, and everything in short, and have left us a complete wreck. Eleven others miscarried that same night, near at hand, so you may thank the cherub I told you of: but such a storm has seldom been known. It was quite a squeak for the Comic for 1836. But when you come the weather will be settled, and such a sea comes but once in seven years. When you see four at the helm you may be frightened, but mind, not till then. Steam, I think, saved us; you ought to offer up a golden kettle somewhere. You were given over and I was given under — but we have both been saved, I trust, for each other, and Heaven does not mean to part us yet. But it made me very ill, for it was like being shaken up in a dice box, and I have had a sort of bilious fever, with something of the complaint Elliot cured me of, and could not eat, with pains in my side, &c., which I nursed myself for as well as I could.

I made two acquaintances on board — one gave me an introduction to a doctor at Coblenz, whom I have not seen; the other gave me an introduction to his father here, where I took tea to-night; their name is Vertue, so you see my morals are in good hands.

I got to Rotterdam only on Thursday night, and I supped there very merrily with the young Vertue and two of his friends.

On Friday night I stopped at Nimeguen, which is in a state of war, and could proceed no further till Saturday, which night I passed aboard, and on Sunday arrived and slept in Cologne.* Here I was detained on Monday by

* I have inserted here some lines from "Up the Rhine," which were written to my mother from this place. — T. H.

The old Catholic city was still,
  In the Minster the vespers were sung;
And, re-echoed in cadences shrill,
  The last call of the trumpet had rung;
While across the broad stream of the Rhine
  The full moon cast a silvery zone;
And methought, as I gazed on the shine —
  "Surely that is the Eau de Cologne!"

I inquired not the place of its source,
  If it ran to the east or the west;
But my heart took a note of its course —
  That it flowed toward Her I love best: —
That it flowed toward Her I love best,
  Like those wandering thoughts of my own;
And the fancy such sweetness possessed
  That the Rhine seemed all Eau de Cologne!

the steamer having broken a paddle, but made myself agreeable to an old general, Sir Parker Carrol, who took me with him to see the lions. I gave him a bulletin to carry to Dilke. Strange to say, the general once lived at their house. Also made acquaintance with a Rev. Mr. Clarke, a gentlemanly young man, and we started on Tuesday for Coblenz, where we slept; again on Wednesday to Mayence, slept there, and to-day he set off for Frankfort, and I returned here. At all these starts I have had to rise at five, and was too worn out and weak to undertake the walking plan I had concerted with Dilke, so I went up and down by the boat instead. Luckily, I got better on Tuesday, and that day and Wednesday and to-day being fine, I enjoyed it very much. From Cologne to Mayence is all beautiful or magnificent; I am sure you will enjoy it, especially if, as I will try, I meet you at Cologne.

I want you to see the cathedral. I am going to-morrow on foot to look among the villages; but my impression is, from what Mr. Vertue says, there will be some difficulty in finding anything there; but at all events there are lodgings to be had in Coblenz, which is a place I admire much. I therefore think you might start for Coblenz at once, without hearing further from me, when you feel able, letting me know, of course, your day of sailing, for in case of my getting anything at Bingen, &c., you would have to stop *here*, and unless I meet with something to my taste above, I shall make this our fixture.

Consult Dilke. For my part, if well enough, I think you may safely come on the chance, as it would take you five days: one to Rotterdam, one to Nimeguen, two to Cologne, and one to Coblenz. I am writing but a business letter, and you must give me credit, my own dearest, for everything else, as I wish to devote all the space I can to describing what will be for your comfort.* You must come to Rotterdam by "Der Batavier," which has female accommodations and a stewardess. You may tell the steward I was nearly swamped with him in the "Lord Melville," for he was with us, and will remember it. * * * * You must expect some nuisances and inconveniences, but they will do to laugh at when we meet, and "Der Batavier" is a splendid and powerful steamer. * * * * With my dear ones by my side, my pen will gambol through the Comic like the monkey who had seen the world. We are not transported even for seven years, and the Rhine is a deal better than Swan River. I have made a great many notes. My mind was never so free — and meaning what is right and just to all, I feel cheerful at our prospects, and in spite of illness have kept up. This will not reach you for four or five days, and then it would take you as much more to come, during which I should be sure to get a place, so do not wait to hear from me again. * * * You may reckon, I think, upon settling at Coblenz: it is a capital and clean town, and does justice to Dilke's recommendation. I have already begun some "Rhymes of the Rhine," of which the first is justly dedicated to your own self. But to-night is my first leisure. I have been like the Wandering Jew. How my thoughts and wishes fly

* At the foot of the letter he added a list of *fonetic* French words that my mother would require during the journey. — T. H.

over the vine-covered hills to meet yours; my love sets towards you like the mighty current of the great Rhine itself, and will brook no impediments.

I grudge the common-place I have been obliged to write; every sentence should claim you, as my own dear wife, the pride of my youth, the joy of my manhood, the hope of all my after days. Twice has the shadow of death come beween us, but our hearts are preserved to throb against each other. I am content for your sake to wait the good time when you may safely undertake the voyage, and do not let your heart run away with your head. Be strong before you attempt it. Bring out with you a copy of "Tylney Hall," which I shall want to refer to. I want no others, but the last Comic. If you are likely to be some time, treat me with one letter. Dilke will tell you how to send it. I long to be settled and at work; I owe *him* much, and wish to do C. Lamb while it is fresh. I hope Reynolds's spasms are gone. *They* could not do better than come up the Rhine this summer, it would not cost so much as Brighton — and such a change of scene. I have had some adventures I must tell you when we meet. I bought this paper all by telegraph of a girl at Cologne. We could not speak a word to each other, and the whole ended in a regular laugh throughout the shop, when she picked out of the money in my hand. Was not I in luck to meet the only *

* The increased facilities of travelling have made John Bull as much at home on the Rhine as by the Thames. Those who know Germany as it is, will hardly recognise it in my father's true and graphic delineation of it as it was. A great deal of what he says here was repeated in "Up the Rhine," but has still the charm of novelty to most, as that book is unhappily out of print. — T. H.

two or three English that were out, and make such friends with them. But I really am getting a traveller, and am getting *brass*, and pushing my way with them. I forgot to say at Coblenz the men frequent the Casinos, and the women make evening parties of their own, but I do not mean to give up my old domestic habits. We shall set an example of fireside felicity, if that can be said of a stove, for we have no grates here — the more's the pity. God bless you ever.

Your own,

T. H.

COBLENZ (at the Widow Seil's), 372, CASTOR HOF.

MY OWN DEAREST AND BEST LOVE,

The pen I write with — the ink it holds — the paper it scrawls upon — the wax that will seal it — were all bought by me *à la telegraph* — except that I had the assurance (impudence and ignorance go together) to look a pretty young German lady in the face and ask her for the use of her lips, not to kiss, but to translate for me, but she couldn't. The purport of this is to tell you what I think will give you ease and comfort — that I am fixed here in a snug, cheap, airy lodging — thanks to the kindness of the Vertues, who have taken great trouble for me. Lodgings *furnished* are scarcely to be had here at all, and when the Vertues came they had to stay at an inn seven weeks. They say, and I feel, I am fortunate. There are three little rooms, one backward, my study as is to be, with such a lovely view over the Moselle. My heart jumped when I saw it, and I thought, "There I shall write volumes!" My opposite neighbour is the

Commandant, so it 's a genteel neighbourhood. To-day I visited the Church of St. Castor, who is to be our patron Saint (vide address), and I saw a bit of his bone. Seriously it is quite a snuggery, where I should want but you and my dear boy and girl to be very happy and very loving. I went up a mountain opposite yesterday evening, commanding a magnificent expanse of view, but the thought would come that you were not in all that vast horizon. But it is splendid, and I 'm sure it is what you would enjoy. The Vertues have been very kind. I have just taken tea with them, and they will call to-morrow to see me set in. Widow Seil is a woman of property, and always aboard her own barges, travelling up and down the Rhine, and her daughter is here keeping house. She seemed wonder-struck this morning, and so was I, to reflect how we are to get on, for she knows nothing but German; but to-night I have delighted her by telling her in German (which I have poked out) to send to the hotel for my bag and cloak. She said over and over again "das is gude." I hope we shan't end in Eloisa and Abelard. In the fulness of her approbation the maid fairly gave me a slap on the back. You must know servants here are great familiars. The waiters at the inns are hail-fellows with the guests, and in truth but for them I must have foregone discourse, for they generally speak French. I find my French reviving very fast, and so I get on well enough.

I dine at a *table d'hôte*, and sleep here and breakfast, then coffee at the inn, and no supper. You can have your dinner sent in here, I mean for us all, very reasonable and without trouble; and on the first of May I can have Vertue's servant, for they are going to England. She understands English wants, and has a high character, so I think I have provided for you tolerably well.

Tell Dilke I am highly pleased with Coblenz, and quite confirm his choice — it is by far the best thing I have seen.

I do hope you will soon be able to come, and in the meantime I will do everything I can think of to facilitate your progress. * * * I should like a set of Comics for Vertue; and bring with you the bound up Athenæums, and your own bound books. Get the steward of the "Batavier" to see you ashore at Rotterdam, to the Hotel des Pays Bas, and in case of any difficulty about customs, which is very unlikely, send from the Hotel for Mr. Vertue, jun., there. The English ladies will explain for you, and he will lend his help, I feel sure. Let me know exactly when you sail from London, and I will meet you at Cologne somehow. Tell Fanny she may see soldiers here, if she likes, all day long. They are always exercising; it seems like — "A month he lived, and that was March!"

If she behaves well on the voyage, and minds what you say, I will show her wonders here. To-day has been beautiful — quite warm — and the weather looks well set in for fine. My little room has the reputation of being cool in summer.

I saw a vision of you, dearest, to-day, and felt you leaning on me, and looking over the Moselle at the blue mountains and vineyards. I long but to get to work with you and the pigeon pair by my side, and then I shall not sigh for the past. Only cast aside sea fears, and you will find your voyage a pleasant one. Your longest spell will be from Nimeguen to Cologne, when you must pass a night on board, but then I shall meet you to take care of the pair, and you will have a good night's rest. Get yourselves strong, there is still a happy future; fix your eyes forward on our meeting, my best and dearest. Our little home, though homely, will be happy for us, and we do not bid England a very long good night. Good night too, my dearest wife, my pride and comfort.

"And from these mountains where I now respire,
Fain would I waft such Blessing unto thee,
As with a sigh I deem thou now might'st be to me."

SUNDAY MORNING.

The hens do lay in Coblenz, they are cackling rarely under my window. I am located thus (here follows a sketch). Dilke will understand how good the look-out is, just at the junction of the Rhine and the Moselle; it is almost the corner house of Coblenz. I am charged a trifle extra because I eat two rolls at breakfast, so you see I improve in my habits: the Germans eat great suppers and little breakfasts. * * * For the sake of every one I keep myself in fighting condition, and have brought myself to look forward with a firm and cheerful composure of mind that I hope you will share in.

The less treasure I have elsewhere, the more I feel the value of those I have within my heart, and never could your dear presence be more delightful and blessed in its influence than it will be to me now. Our grapes, though sourish now, will ripen into sweetness by the end

3*

of the year, and I shall work like the industrious Germans, whom you will see labouring like ants on the face of their mountains. Tell the Reynoldses they could not do better than take a trip here in the summer, when it must be delightful. It cost me, illness included, but about £10 to get here, including Mayence, and I lost something by *change* in Holland. The Hotels, barring the first rates, professing to be English ones, are moderate and comfortable. My dear Fanny will enjoy herself here, there is so much bustle, barges, steamers, soldiering, and children like dwarf men and women.

Tell her I expect she will take great care of you and her brother on the voyage, and not give you trouble. The first thing I shall ask, when I see you, will be if she has been good, and if so I will take her with you to see the cathedral at Cologne, which with its painted glass, &c., will be to her like fairy land. * * * * You must bring blocks enough with you for the whole Comic, or more than that will be better, as I may do the Epsom or something else. Bring a good stock. * * * * Woodin would stare to see calves here, going to slaughter, seven days old, attended by dogs bigger than themselves.

I hear that the Ostend steamers got well knocked about in our storm, and had some men washed overboard; — my head still reels occasionally, and the stairs seem to rock, so you may judge what it was — the very worst for many years. The "Batavier" is an excellent boat; have *porter* on board her, as you will get none after Rotterdam; up the Rhine take Cognac and water, not the sour wine. Wrap yourself well up, and when the bustle of departure is over you may be very comfortable, but up to Cologne there is little worth seeing, except the towns, such as Düsseldorf. From Cologne to Coblenz is superb, and I shall enjoy it with you; but mind, be sure to come when you appoint, as I cannot stay long at Cologne.

Write to me "Poste Restante à Coblenz," as I go to the post-office every day to inquire, like Monsieur Mallet. You would be quite in the fashion here with a silk bonnet, and one of those cloaks with a deep cape to the elbows of plain or figured silk, or stuff, such as I saw about the streets of London before I left. It is very quiet here, except when Mrs. Commandant gives a party opposite, when there are carriages. You get a glimpse of the Rhine in front — you must not expect carpets here, and you will have stoves instead of grates, these are universal. By the bye Mrs. Dilke told me to have my linen well aired, I suspect it was only her ignorance, and that she had taken what is up in all the packets "*Dampschiffe*" for damp shirts. It signifies *steamboats*, — not an unnatural mistake. Bring me a set of Comics for my own use, your bound ones will do — Flanders brick of course — and my desk with all my papers in it. That box that was the tool chest, with handles, would be very useful for sending over all the Comic blocks in. * * * My young landlady has paid me a smiling visit this morning, and we have had a little conversation in German and English, which neither of us understood. St. Castor has just dismissed his congregation in various *grotesque gaieties;* the most distinguished feature was a violet and pink shot-silk umbrella. I have also had a visit this morning from a strange young gentleman, but for want of the gift of tongues he took nothing by his motion. I am in fact a sort of new Irving, with the girl here for a proselyte; she *will* hold forth, understood or not. Yesterday I gave two groschen to two little girls like Fanny, on the top of the mountain. They went apart, and after a consultation, one dispatched the other to present to me, I guess, an address of thanks, or to ask for more, I don't know which, but I think the former. I found on the same eminence a good honest fellow, very civil for nothing, and a good Christian no doubt, although like Satan he thence pointed out to me all the kingdoms of the earth.

Whenever my eyes leave the paper they see the Moselle still gliding on, and my own verses* occur to me with a powerful application of them to you, and my children all beyond the bluest of the blue hills. I shall give you good measure, and shall cross this letter, though I do not pretend yet to write letters worth reading, for my head is still confused, and I am but just settled down. Otherwise I have made many notes and memorandums, which I need not write either to you, who will I hope see the things referred to. The Vertues have called, and kept me beyond my time. They have begged me to make their house my home, and are very obliging. To-day being Sunday we dined in state, with a band playing, and I indulged in a glass of wine in which I drank your health. I have just bought with much trouble an instantaneous light to seal this letter with. I am become quite a citizen of the world, I talk to every one in English, broken French, and bad German, and have the vanity to think I make friends wherever I go.

* "Still glides the gentle streamlet on." — T. H.

Tell Dilke this, it will please him. Say to John I shall write him a long letter as soon as I hear from London, and also to Dilke. I have seen to-day the whole troops on the parade, governors, demi-governors, &c. Their bands do not equal ours, some of our drums would *beat them hollow*, and they have no good horses. * * * May God have all those I love, or who love me, in His Holy keeping, is the prayer of the subscribed,

THOMAS HOOD.

In accordance with the arrangements laid down by my father, my mother, accompanied by my brother and myself, went on board the "Batavier" on the 29th of March, 1835, and were joined by my father at Cologne. From thence we proceeded to Coblenz. I have inserted the following letter from my mother, as it describes better than I could do their first settling in their new home. Her descriptions also of what she saw are so evidently influenced and aided by my father's observations, that they are almost as interesting as his own.

372, CASTOR HOF, COBLENZ, 22*nd June*, 1835.

MY DEAR MRS. ELLIOT,

* * * * I was fortunate in my voyage here in having fair weather, and also in having the ladies' cabin of the "Batavier" to myself, with the exception of a young lady about fifteen, who was coming to a Moravian School at one of the villages on the Rhine. The stewardess too was a very respectable woman, and very attentive. We got to Rotterdam about six on Monday evening, and then some of my troubles began. We were

to set off by the Rhine steamer at six the next morning, and I desired them to call me at five; but the stupid chambermaid came and knocked at my door at twelve. I did not find out the mistake until I had with difficulty roused Fanny from her bed, and got her dressed. From being disturbed, when six came the poor child was so sick and ill, I was obliged to have her carried down to the steamboat. From Rotterdam to Cologne is very flat and uninteresting, and a very slow passage, as it is against the stream. We passed the night on board, which I should not have minded except for the children. I got some beds made up for them in the cabin, and thought they would be tolerably comfortable. But at nine we stopped and took on board a company of Prussian soldiers, with about twenty officers, who all came clattering into the cabin which was not very large, and the tables were spread for their suppers. After they had done eating, they played cards till three in the morning, when most of them were put ashore at Düsseldorf. We were to have arrived at Cologne at 12 o'clock, but to accommodate the Prussian officers, our steam was made to boil a gallop and we arrived at 10 A.M. So that I got to the Hôtel du Rhin before Hood, who was killing time on the parade. When he arrived I scarcely knew him, he looked so very ill. He made me stay a day here to refresh, which I very much needed; for my poor baby suffered much for want of his usual comforts, and I felt the fatigue with the children very much. Our stay allowed us to see the curiosities of Cologne which are well worth seeing; the Cathedral more especially: at the least so much as is finished of it, for it never will be completed unless the old days of Roman Catholic power and glory should return. The interior for *lightness* and elegance is perfectly exquisite. Hood says if the Loretto Angel had to carry away a Cathedral, he would choose that of Cologne. We saw all its wonders and relics, its golden shrine, inlaid with cameos and gems, and delicate mosaic; though some of the jewels by a dishonest miracle are converted into coloured glass. We saw the crowns of the Three Wise Kings, and also some admirable sculptures in ivory. I must not forget to mention the painted windows, which are splendid, and the tapestries in the choir from the designs of Rubens, which are quite in the style of the Cartoons. There is also a curious picture, very old indeed, of the Three Kings adoring the Virgin and Child — in parts recalling Raffaelle to my mind. In the old church of St. Peter, where Rubens was baptized, we saw one of his masterpieces — the martyrdom of the patron saint — they make you stoop and look at it, with your head downwards (like the figure of the martyr) to show the expression of the face, which is truly marvellous. From the church — what a next step! — we went to the masquerade room, which is of vast dimensions, supported by a range of pillars in the middle, in the shape of gigantic champagne glasses, out of which seem to issue a quantity of painted masquerade figures nearly covering the ceiling. The idea is better than the execution. German wit and humour, Hood says, are like yeast dumplings a day old.

Cologne itself is a rambling place full of crooked narrow streets, where you may lose yourself without much trouble. When Hood was there by himself he says he never went out but he was obliged to get a boy to show him home again. I wish I could praise its atmosphere — but as Head says in the "Bubbles," the Eau de Cologne seems to extract all pleasant perfume from its air. We started by steamer for Coblenz at seven on Saturday morning, and soon after, near Bonn, the fine scenery of the Rhine began to open with the towering Drachenfels and the seven mountains. The abrupt transition from flat uninteresting country to the mountainous and picturesque is striking and singular; for from this point nearly to Mayence, it is on both sides of the river high and varied in its features. The villages are very quaint and pretty, and almost as numerous as mile-stones. As it was the planting season, we saw the industrious peasantry working like ants among their vines on the face of the mountains; so small and yet so distinct as to remind one of the elfins and gnomes of German romance.

We arrived at Coblenz about six, and really the place justifies our friend's recommendation. The houses are good, the streets wide, airy, and clean, with here and there a bit of pavement in the English style, which I always found attracted my weary feet as if it had been a loadstone. The walking in Cologne was very rough, Hood calls it a stone storm, and says if a certain place is paved with good intentions, Cologne must have been paved with the bad ones. The very horses are compelled to wear high-heeled shoes to prevent slipping.

* * * *

As for Hood, he was in a wretched state of health, he had been sadly overdone before he left England, and the storm he was out in completed the mischief, otherwise he is fond of and used to the sea; but they were very nearly lost, eleven other vessels were wrecked the same night, in the same storm, in or near the mouth of the Maes.

Hood got worse day by day, but we could not prevail on him to have advice, though Mr. Vertue strongly recommended Dr. B—— who had attended his family while they were here. At last we were compelled to call him in, for Hood was seized with most frightful spasms in the chest. I cannot express how wretched, and terrified I was, for he said himself it was like being struck with death. His countenance was sunk and his eyes too. He was seized first at night, and Dr. B—— remained with him for two hours, and then left him somewhat easier, but the pain lasted, at intervals, all night, and left him next day as weak as a child. After this he had many similar attacks, but slighter ones. I wanted faith in our physician, but of course did not say so; their practice is so different to the English, they won't hear of calomel. However Dr. B—— certainly brought Hood round, and for the last fortnight he has got on rapidly, for which I cannot be too thankful. Dr. B—— recommends his going to Ems, for a little change, but he is too busy to spare time for it.

We are now very comfortably settled, we have a *little* kitchen, about three yards square, and Gradle our servant, with my superintendence, manages the cooking pretty well. I have actually been successful in a beef-steak pudding, and an Irish stew, and we have given up our "portions" and the table d'hôte. Lodging and washing are dear here, the latter as much so as in England, but food is cheap; mutton 3 groschen a pound, about three pence halfpenny. Beef and veal the same, but the latter is wretched, so young and so small; vegetables and fruit very cheap. The cherries are abundant, there is a walk out of one of the gates that is nearly a mile long, I should think, with cherry-trees all the way on each side, loaded with fruit; when in blossom it was a lovely sight. Grapes are of course very plentiful, and walnut-trees are planted everywhere: all the furniture is made of walnut wood, and very pretty it is. There is a walk here of rose-trees, the most beautiful you can imagine. They are standards, the stems nearly two yards high, of every kind and variety, all loaded with bloom. There is a triple row of about two hundred yards, it is the prettiest sight I ever saw. Mr. Maiden would be delighted with the cactus tribe here; they are splendid, four or five feet high, rich with bloom: the Cereus too are equally fine, they train them up spirally, and the effect is better than when they fall over the pot. The flowers of some of the cacti are of a rich peculiar crimson I have never seen before. The walks round Coblenz are so lovely that we have overdone ourselves, and have been obliged to stay at home for a day or two to recover. The moment you pass the gates of the town in any direction you are in a garden of Eden; orchards, cornfields, vineyards, villages, mountains crested with ruined castles, and through all flows the rapid, "arrowy Rhine," now almost of a sea-green colour — the blue Moselle runs into it just within view of the back of our house. Before I was well enough to walk much, Hood inveigled me up the twin height to Ehrenbreitstein.

"Ah, who can tell how hard it is to climb!"

He would not allow me to look behind, and I could see nothing before me but a fresh ascent at every turn, so I panted up to the top like the asthma personified. But the panoramic view well repaid me, I cannot describe it, for I never saw anything like it before. You see *across* the Rhine down into Coblenz, which lies under you like a map. Round the city is a fertile plain, as diversified in colour as a patchwork quilt, bounded by the distant mountains; you see snatches of the Moselle, and higher up the Rhine is divided by an island with what was a nunnery upon it. Only George Robins could describe all the other features, and for once he could not embellish. How I wish — to use a common expression — you could "enter into my *views*." To pass from nature to art, Hood took me into the Jesuit's church here, predicting that I should be half converted to Catholicism, and so, between you and me, was the case, for the altar-piece, screen, pulpit, &c., with all the apostles and angels, and the figures, appear to be of fine Dresden china, which you know all ladies have a great affection for. Fanny too has a bias to Popery, I think, there are so many processions, and children with flags, little girls in white with wreaths of white roses and valley lilies, and baskets of flowers. In short all she would enjoy at a London theatre with the advantage of freshness and the open air. Last Thursday was Corpus Christi day, and the host was carried in great state and pomp. They erected an altar over a public conduit at the end of our street, the said conduit having been prematurely erected by the French as a trophy of their *coming* triumph over the Russians. It is most laughingly inscribed.

"Mémorable par la Campagne contre les Russes, sous la Préfecture de Jules Douzan. Anno 1812.

"Vu et approuvé par nous, Commandant Russe de la ville de Coblenz le 1er Janvier, 1814."

So much for the foreign department, and now for the Home! You will be glad to hear the children have thriven recently to my heart's content. Fanny is very well and happy, my baby is a healthy little creature, and so "bronzy"* with brown and red, his Papa declares that at our first party he shall hold a wax-candle. He is as fat and hard as a German sausage, and so merry you would pick him out, as Dr. Kitchener recommends you to choose lobsters, namely, as "heavy and lively." N. B. Paternal vanity is answerable for the last sentence.

* * * *

The coffee here is really a sort of evening brown stout. It is roasted, or as they say here "burned" at home; and whatever be the cause, it is so different a beverage that Hood says he suspects with Accum that the English coffee is made from horse-beans. Tea is bad, and dear here. You may judge how good the coffee must be when I say that I do not regret it; besides the leaves are not in request here as there are no carpets. Hood says amongst the "Bridgewater

* This is an allusion to two handsome bronze figures of children reading, mounted as candlesticks, which used to stand on the drawing-room mantel-piece, and were heir-looms familiar to all his friends, so that the joke was a domestic one. — T. H.

Treatises," they might have instanced this as a manifestation of a Providence.

I have heard of German cousins, but I am sure we are not relations, or we should be more upon speaking terms.

"*We are only on talking terms with the Butcher, an Anglo-Prussian officer, and the Doctor (all in the killing line), but Hood manages to get on with a little bad French, which, as he lived at Wanstead, he very probably picked up at 'Stratford atte Bow,' notorious, as Chaucer declares, for such a jargon. All our dinners are ordered per dictionary, but we still get onions sometimes for turnips, and radishes for carrots. It sounds farcical, but it's true, that I sent for a fowl for my dear invaluable invalid (I mean Hood), and the servant brought back two bundles of goose-quills!*"

I need not make any remark on the foregoing sentence which has been written in my absence, but I must confirm the feathery fact.

* * * *

My baby has been vaccinated here according to law, as we should have been fined for omitting it; though where the original cow-pock comes from is a mystery, as well as the milk, for you never see a cow but once on a time in a cart: and good reason why, as peas, beans, corn, and clover run all into one, without hedges or fence of any kind.

It surprises me that we get sweet *milk, the Germans have such a* turn *for everything sour. The wine is sour, they* preserve *plums in vinegar, the very spring water at*

Ehrenbreitstein is acid, and called Sour Water! However, as a set-off, they pickle their walnuts with sugar and cloves. But the vinegar made of Hock or Moselle is superb, almost a wine of itself. I am pickling some cucumbers that I expect will be superlative.

That is Hood's again, for my letter is written by snatches as "my occupation isn't gone" like Othello's, but come. Fortunately my baby is fond of Gradle, and will go to her, which relieves my fatigue.

"*I should have said, carries off a good deal of my Fat Teague!*"

Hood *again!* I will not quit this letter again till I have finished it, he has "interpret himself so."

Our greatest present annoyance is, that if we poke out a short sentence of broken German, they give us such credit for our progress that they fancy we can return a whole volley of paragraphs. I regret very much that I cannot converse with one of our landlady's daughters, she has such a sweet voice, so pretty a face, that Hood is quite in love with her, but fortunately he can't declare himself. Female beauty, or even prettiness, is a rarity at Coblenz. A miller's daughter, a mile off is *the* paragon, Hood calls her the "Flour;" they say she is well educated too. I mean, if possible, to walk out and see her; strange to say, she is still single.

"*Joe Miller says, because there are two dams to ask instead of one!*"

We heard of her through a young English officer in the Prussian service here. He introduced himself to us, during our evening walk, being attracted by our King's English, and we were equally by his, as well as by his dog, which seemed *home made;* for you must know the Coblenz dogs are remarkably ugly and naturally like foxes, but after the first warm summer day, they were all converted by clipping the hinder parts into mock lions. He seemed determined to know us. First he told Fanny, who was not at all timid, to have no fear of his dog, who was not at all ferocious. As that failed to lead to an introduction, he walked back after us, and introduced himself. In truth we were equally glad to give him change for his English, which he declared he had by him till it had become burdensome. He has since called: he has been fourteen years in the Prussian service, but his heart seems to yearn after England and his family; his mother is an Englishwoman. He is a very nice, unassuming young man; as he is stationed at Ehrenbreitstein he has offered some day to help us to scale that impregnable fortress.

The English are beginning to come here now, last night's steamboat brought a number; the general opinion is that they will not swarm here, as they have done. Head's "Bubbles" sent a great number, but having once been they do not come again. It is said, that for the last two years their coming raised the price of everything fifty per cent. A war would break half the *banks* of the Rhine, — at least the magnificent hotels on them. Should you by any chance think of visiting the great river, we will send you all information — such as the professed guides do not condescend to give — for instance, if you wish for a clean face and hands, to carry a cake of soap, which you will not find in the best Inn's best bedrooms.

* * * *

While Hood was ill I felt very depressed and out of spirits, of course my own weak health rendered me but a poor nurse to him. I thought there was no end to my troubles, and felt as Rosalind says, "how full of briars is this work-a-day world." But I am now in much better spirits, and we get on better altogether. The comforts the English miss are not very portable, or they might bring them out, for instance, — a four-post bed, a Rumford stove, a kitchen range, and a carpet. But use reconciles, we almost feel native, and "to the manner born," so don't pity us, for we don't pity ourselves.

* * * *

Hood bids me describe a scene with Miss Seil, the landlady's daughter. I wanted some egg-cups, and in illustration I showed her the eggs, and she guessed so near that she snatched up a saucer and broke the egg into it, evidently wondering in her eg-otism that having eggs we did not know where to lay 'em. When I shook my head, she looked at me in despair, and seemed to say, 'What a pity that broken German and broken English should break good eggs!' Talking of eggs, you find them in the market of the gayest colours; and Hood says, 'Twigg would wonder what coloured hens they are that lay them.' I took the purple ones for egg-plums. They have apples now of last year's growth, and bring them to market, and put them in water to plump them out; and I can believe Head's story of the tailor eating a washhand-basin full of fresh Orleans plums, after seeing the countrymen eat the apples only half *un*-wizened out of the tub. The potatoes are small, and

Hood says he was nearly choked by some sliced up and fried, as he found afterwards, in the same pan which had cooked some bony Prussian carp the day before.

* * * *

The foregoing letter presents a fair specimen, here and there, of the dictations and suggestions, but more especially of the interpolations and additions, with which my father delighted to embellish my mother's letters. Whenever she left a half-finished letter anywhere in his reach, she was sure, on her return, to find "notes and queries" inserted, often much opposed to her original meaning, and frequently tending to the utter mystification of the recipient of the letter. Her handwriting was, although legible, rather peculiar, and he delighted in making it more so, — altering o's and a's, and changing t's into d's, to the utter confusion of her meaning. On one occasion this led to an absurd mistake. She had written to a friend to procure her some good Berlin patterns for slippers, &c.; but during her absence, my father got hold of her note, and, in his favourite fashion, altered and touched up the words. Some time after, she received a reply from her friend, asking what new English article it could be that was dignified by the name of "dippers!"

From the time of their arrival at Coblenz, my father's health continued very bad; and the necessity for constant work still continuing, there was little chance of amendment. Still his happy flow of spirits never failed him, as may be seen by his letters.

The first summer of my father's residence at Coblenz was pleasantly varied by his making acquaintance, as mentioned by my mother, with a young Prussian officer, M. de Franck. After their meeting during a walk by the Rhine, my father wrote him the following note:—

Sir,

I regret that I had not a card about me to offer to you in acknowledgment of a *rencontre* so agreeable. I beg leave to enclose one, lest you should suppose me infected with that national shyness, which makes foreigners so apt to consider us as a grand *corps de réserve*.

I have the honour to be, Sir,

Yours obediently,

Thomas Hood.

Lieutenant de Franck,
19th Polish Regiment, Ehrenbreitstein.

My father found in M. de Franck a very pleasant and agreeable friend, and a great help in all difficulties of German usage and language. He was his constant companion in all his fishing rambles and excursions, and used to drop in, in a quiet friendly way, of an evening, and play cribbage with my father and mother. They made the merriest and cosiest little party imaginable, generally finishing with some dainty treat of English cookery for supper. During my mother's enforced absences to superintend the cooking of these little edibles, the "two knaves" took the opportunity of changing her cards, moving her pegs, &c., secretly delighted at her puzzles and wonderings on her return. On these occasions my father generally kept them in a continual laugh by his flow of witty anecdotes and jokes.

The following is a letter to Mr. Dilke, the then editor

of the "Athenæum," and one of my father's earliest friends: —

COBLENZ, *May 6th*, 1835.

MY DEAR DILKE,

You ought to have heard from me before, but I was loth to inflict upon you bad news in return for your very kind letter, for every syllable of which I thank you, and instead of quarrelling with what you have said, I thank you for the meaning beyond. The truth is I have been unchanged from the hour I left you, my mind has not faltered for an instant, but though the spirit is willing, the body is weak. My health broke down under me at last, after a series of physical, as well as mental trials, and I am not a-Gog corporeally, witness my experiments in your night-gowns. "Tylney Hall," the "Comic," Jane's illness, and the extreme exhaustion consequent thereon, disappointment, storm and travel, came a pick-a-back, and I am not a Belzoni to carry a dozen on each calf, two on my head, &c. I broke down — not but that I fought the good fight, like a Widdrington, with a good heart, but I was shorn of my physical powers. The storm was a severe one. What pitched over, literally, stout mahogany tables, where eight or ten may dine, might derange any one; and the change of climate, which is really considerable (we had hotter suns in March than in England during May), had its effect. The safe arrival of Jane with my darlings, all better than I had hoped for, did me a world of good. * * * *

I assure you sincerely as to my personal feelings, with a decent state of health I could be very happy and contented; the presence of a very few friends would make my comfort complete. But I now suffer mentally, because my health will not keep pace with me. I have at last reluctantly called in medical aid; the whole system here seems based on Sangrado's practice, bleeding, blistering, and drastics. I had the prudence to mitigate his prescriptions, which in the proportion of two-thirds almost made me faint away. They do not recognise our practice here, or I could doctor myself. But according to Sir F. Head in "The Brunnens," Germans require horse medicines. I think I never in my life felt such a prostration of physical power, I can hardly get up a laugh, and am quite out of humour with myself. If I were Dick Curtis I could give myself a good licking, I mean my body, for not being more true to me. The "Athenæum" has been a great delight to me — it costs me here only two groschen, about two pence. Is it not singular that a fortnight ago, as the *only* exception to the rule, it cost me four or five groschen. I understand that throughout the Rhine, everything within the last two years has risen nearly fifty per cent. from the great influx of English. Notwithstanding this, many of the necessaries are very good and cheap, butter, bread, &c. I am going to make a calculation whether home cookery will not be the cheapest, though we have hitherto dined at the hôtel, *pour voir le monde.* I have bought some brandy here very good, though it is rather scarce, bottles included 2*s.* 6*d.* each, and some Oberwesel wine, something between Hock and Moselle, 1*s.* a bottle. I have got Jane some bottled Bavarian beer, which is very good. Butter is 8*d.* per pound, three rolls 1*d.*, and eggs about 2½*d.* a dozen.

I was going to resume this, but was prevented by what

soldiers call a night-attack. On going to bed I was seized with violent spasms in the chest, which after some time compelled me to send for the Dr. at midnight. I could only breathe when bolt upright, and rarely then at the expense of intense pain; I thought every breath would be the last. My Dr. certainly does me good, and, though a Jew, does not repeat his visits unnecessarily, but "waits till called for;" he talks a little English, and as Pope says I feel assured, "a little learning is a dangerous thing."

Jane said to him, "I wish you could give to Mr. Hood some *strengthening medicine;*" to which he replied, "Who is that physician you speak of?" But a more whimsical mistake arose out of my lay-up, which I must give you dramatically. Our servant knows a few words of English too, her name is *Gradle*, the short for Margaret. Jane wanted a fowl to boil for me. Now she has a theory that the more she makes her English un-English, the more it must be like German. Jane begins by showing Gradle a word in the dictionary.

Gradle. "Ja! yees — hühn — henne — ja! yees."

Jane (a little through her nose). "Hmn — hum — hem — yes — yaw, ken you geet a fowl — fool — foal, to boil — bile — bole for dinner?"

Gradle. "Hot wasser?"

Jane. "Yaw in pit — pat — pot — hmn — hum — eh!"

Gradle (a little off the scent again). "Ja, nein — wasser, pot — hot — nein."

Jane. "Yes — no — good to eeat — chicken — cheeken — checking — choking — bird — bard — beard — lays eggs — eeggs — hune, heine — hin — make cheekin broth — soup — poultry — peltry — paltry!"

Gradle (quite at fault). "Pfeltrighchtch! — nein."

Jane (in despair). "What shall I do! and Hood won't help me, he only laughs. This comes of leaving England!" (She casts her eyes across the street at the Governor's poultry-yard, and a bright thought strikes her.) "Here, Gradle — come here — comb hair — hmn — hum — look there — dare — you see things walking — hmn, hum, wacking about — things with feathers — fathers — feethers."

Gradle (hitting it off again). "Feethers — faders — ah hah! fedders — ja, ja, yees, sie bringen — fedders, ja, ja!"

Jane echoes "Fedders — yes — yaw, yaw!"

Exit Gradle, and after three-quarters of an hour, returns triumphantly with two bundles of stationer's quills!!! This is a fact, and will do for Twig.

* * * * I will now write as well as I can a description, which may serve to extract for the "Athenæum." The bound volumes were, though only a Dilke-send, like a God-send. You cannot think how well they read here, where there is nothing else to read. There's a compliment for you, worthy of our Irishman. On the first of May here, when I was wondering what would replace the *round*clays of the London sweeps, the deficiency was kindly supplied by a whirlwind, which made a great many sundries dance in its vortex. I was gazing from the window of the Belle Vue Hôtel opposite the bridge, when my attention was excited by a great cloud of German dust, waltzing after the German fash-

ion, to the great embarrassment of some untaught crows or rooks, who were flapping about quite bewildered in its mazes. It came from the direction where the Moselle mingles with the Rhine. The dust cleared off in about a minute, and the whirlwind itself became distinctly visible, travelling diagonally across the Rhine, at a leisurely pace, and showing to great advantage against the rock of Ehrenbreitstein, at that time bright with a gleam of sun, and strongly brought out by a mass of ink-black clouds; of a grey colour — slender, of equal width throughout — bellying before the wind, with a curve equal to that of the longest kite-string, and moreover towards the top, serpentining in three or four undulations, as if from various currents of air. The phenomenon presented the appearance of a narrow but long ribbon let down from the clouds. It apparently rose to a great height — I should guess a mile — and terminated above in a sort of ragged funnel of scarcely twice the diameter of the tube. I could not detect any circular motion; in fact, I repeat, it looked like a ribbon. On reaching the opposite side of the river it raised a surge on the bank, as well as a wash of linen which lay there, and which, after a few pirouettes, disappeared — of course it got a good wringing. I have since learned that it also made free with some skins from the leather manufactory situated near the Moselle, and carried them almost to Ems — I suppose to be *cured.* The whirlwind itself disappeared between Ehrenbreitstein and its neighbouring height, following apparently the road to the baths, as if to get rid of its dust.

But mark the truth of the proverb "one good turn

deserves another," the first had scarcely vanished, when looking upwards, I discerned overhead a second, but *parallel with* the earth, in the shape of a long black cloud, slowly revolving, and pointing in the direction which its predecessor had travelled over. It had the wind, as the sailors say, right fore and aft, and was somewhat shorter and lustier than the vertical one, ending obtusely towards the wind; but at the other, terminating in a long fine point! I could not help exclaiming as I saw it, "there's a *screw loose* in the sky!" for which even the Germans who knew English were little the wiser.

In expectation of seeing you this summer I have made a rough sketch of the thing, however incompetent, for a whirlwind especially demands a *Turner.*

My illness has been a sad hindrance to me in the "Comic," as to the executive, but I have collected some materials. I think I can hit off a few sketches like Head's as to the Germans. I have seen many funny things here.

Jane is evidently much better, and has walked up the hill to Ehrenbreitstein; and the children, thank God, thrive apace. The baby, Tom junior, has been vaccinated according to law here; he gets on well and is very good, giving as little trouble as a baby can. Fanny seldom walks out but with some little Germans walking parallel before and after, and wondering at her to her great amusement. She is quite a model here, for "strange yet true it is," *all* the children here are bandy-legged! You never saw such a set of legs as go to school daily down our street. But the people here are very stupid; mere animals; they take no interest in

Science, Literature, Politics, or anything I can find, but eating and drinking.

The "Athenæum," which I one day read at the table d'hôte before dinner, has I fear stamped me a *pedant.* Pray did you ever taste "*Mai Drank*" or May Drink; if not, you have a pleasure to come. I look forward to your advent with great joy, and hope some of you at least may come. For my own part, if God would but grant me a stomach, I have heart enough to stay here a couple of years. I only want health and strength. But those will come and the rest with them.

Thanks to Dr. B——, who acted as dragoman or interpreter, Jane has got her fowls at last! Only an old woman brought them alive and crowing! It so happened that to-day two hens have appeared for the first time, and the moment Jane saw them she thought we were still at fault, and that we were supposed to want to keep fowls. But the real ones have come home at last, dead and plucked, and we *have* hopes of one to-morrow, having been three days in getting it.

Oh! how I wish I wrote for A. K. Newman, and lived near Leadenhall Market! *Mon perruque!* how we are to get it boiled is a mystery yet unsolved. I guess Jane or I must just parboil ourselves by way of making signs. I only wonder, in my illness, when Jane sent for a doctor, Gradle did not bring me a bootmaker! But as Jane says, "there is a cherub up aloft for us."

I dined to-day on bread and Swiss cheese. I have no appetite, and German cookery is "rank — it smells to heaven!" Salt fish they wash till it is fresh, and what is fresh they just make sour enough for you to think it is *turned.* What ought to be sour — pickled walnuts — are *sweet,* tasting of cloves, — you never know where to have 'em!

* * * *

There are but few roofs in England under which my thoughts find a pleasant resting-place. So Coblenz would be a sort of Noah's Ark to me, but for the olive branch at 9, Lower Grosvenor Place. Jane sends her love to Mrs. Dilke and will write by the next post. News is scarce here both ways. A raft the other day carried away part of the bridge about half a mile; and though the Rhine is not so rapid now, they were about forty hours getting it back again! No great credit to their mechanical powers. God bless you all, if the benediction from an *Anti-Agnewite* be worth having. Kind regards to all friends. Rogers's Reminiscences to every one who cares to remember,

My dear Dilke,

Yours ever faithfully,

T. Hood.

19*th May*, 1835.

My dear Dilke,

I did not expect to write to you again so soon, but having to send the above, I do so.

* * * *

I have had a fresh attack of the spasms, — scarcely so severe as the first, but longer; they have left me so weak I can hardly walk. But the weather is favourable, and I try to get out, and take exercise and fight it off. The worst is over I think now, but it has been a sad hindrance to me. Next month we are going to alter our arrangements, and dine at home; with our own kitchen, &c., it will be much better and cheaper, and these one o'clock table d'hôte dinners cut up my mornings terribly. Thank God! Jane appears to get on in her health as well as her fatigues will let her, and Fanny is hearty and happy. But the babe is necessarily poorly from vaccination — he thrives otherwise famously. The air here seems very good and pure, and the country is beautiful now with the spring greens. We have heard the nightingale once, singing beautifully. Neither the Rhine nor Moselle, however, is very blue yet, — mud-colour rather, we have had so much wind and wet; but the "arrowy river" is fine anyway; what a rush it makes, as if there were something very good at the end of its course: here I could moralise, but I won't. I am washy and spiritless, and should degenerate into twaddle.

The "Athenæum," by special request, when I have done with it, goes to the Hotel, for the benefit of the English who come there. They are not numerous yet, but must be coming, when they do come, in shoals. I was diverted with one young fellow who came up to go to some clerkship at Mayence, a true Cockney. He thought his "dampschiffe" billet was a passport, so left the latter at Cologne, and came on here. He got me to explain the money to him, and after all was done, exclaimed in a real Bow-bell voice: "Well, arter all, there's no place like Lonnon!"

I also met at a shop here with a Parisian cockney — of whom I shall make a sketch à la Sterne — a cobbler's boy! He told me he came from Paris several times; asked me whence I came, — "from London." "Ah, Monsieur, est-il près de Paris?"

Pray tell Mrs. Dilke one of the last little table displays I have seen here. At the table d'hôte, the English are fond of copying foreign customs and manners. First pull out the crumb of your roll, about half of which roll up, and work between your fingers (if snuffy the better) into little balls as big as marbles. They will not look exactly like Wordsworth's "White Dough," but rather dirty putty. When you have used your quill toothpick, stick it up, bolt upright, in one of these dirty balls, a little flattened beneath, as you may have seen candles stuck in extempore clay candlesticks at an illumination. Should it (the toothpick) want cleaning, furbish it up with one of the other dirty bread balls; then it will be ready for further use! This I should think a very polite piece of manners, for I had it from a gentleman who wears a black velvet great coat and a ribbon at his button-hole, and who evidently does not think small beer of himself, or vin ordinaire, as I ought to say here. Mind, don't extract this in the "Athenæum" or 'twill be recognised. It is dangerous writing to the editor of a paper so in want of original extracts! Shall I write you weekly a foreign letter here, as your correspondent from Munich? There are no fine arts, or literature, or scientifics or politics here, but I can make them. Have you heard of our young sculptor, Hoche? his group of Goethe supported in the arms of Charlotte and Werther is just put up, but the pedestal is too low. Professor Swaltz's "Essay on the Architecture of the Catti" has made a great sensation here, and has quite filled all mouths, which a week ago were occupied with the project for having a new pump in the Rhein Strasse, and enclosing the parade with posts and rails. *Nous verrons.* In my next, I shall give you an account of the grand party at Prince Pfaffi's, &c., &c., &c. I could make you a *double number* of *very Foreign* intelligence. Or shall I send you some *free* translations from the German? They translate from me, and I ought to show my gratitude. If I may choose, I should like to make my first experiment on Kant's Transcendentalism. I have been to the Hotel of an evening, and got a good notion of German philosophy, — perhaps you are not aware that it is laid on with *pipes,* like the gas in London! I have tried to draw some of them, but a real smoker beats the pencil. It is a mistake, by the way, to say "he is smoking," he is not *active* but *passive,* — "being smoked!" How they suck their pipes, like great emblems of second childhood, so placid, so innocent, so unmeaning! "Mild as the Moonbeam!"

* * * *

My kindest regards to Mrs. Dilke and Wentworth, and believe me ever, my dear Dilke,

Yours very truly,

THOS. HOOD.

The following letter was addressed to John Wright, Esq., of the firm of Wright and Folkard, wood engravers of Fenchurch Street. This gentleman undertook the arrangement of the "Comic" during my father's absence, correcting the proofs, and superintending the more mechanical part of the work.

372, Castor Hof, Coblenz, *Sept. 12th*, 1835.

My dear Wright,

You will be glad to hear that I cannot write at great length to you, because I am busy, and able to be busy. You may imagine what a delight it was to us to see the Elliots, — they are so very kind and friendly. Besides, it was a comfort to have his opinion about me, though I am much better. I almost growl at feeding-time if the dinner is not ready. We dine at a very genteel hour — two o'clock — which is also the Governor's time. The universal people take it at one. But I find the difference more striking mentally than corporeally even; and ideas now come of themselves without being laboured for — and *in vain.* In fact, I know that I have a mind, or according to the famous form, "*Cogito, ergo sum.*" I believe that 's something like the Latin for it, but I forget, for *I had a Latin prize at school!* As I find a positive pleasure in the power, its exercise must be equally pleasant, and I think I shall get on rapidly; indeed, some evenings I have been quite delighted with my comparative fertility of thought. I have got some good stories, or hints for stories, from De Franck, whose loss I fear I shall shortly have to regret, for I really like him. How odd his knowing C—— and H. D——; there must have been some mysterious animal magnetism in his accosting me. A joke with him has led to my writing a poem of some 700 lines, which you will soon receive. My own impression is, if good enough for the "Comic," it had better be there to advance; but consult with Dilke, who will judge better than I can. I have been so unwell, I am down, and diffident as to what I do. I shall have some more Sketches on the Road, and some German stories, so I have not been quite idle even in bed. I did hope to be earlier this year, but, as all philosophers must say when it comes to be impossible, "it can't be helped." I am only too happy to exclaim, like the poor scullion in "Tristram Shandy," "I 'm alive." But some day I hope to make my account even with the storm; for there were some Eugene Aram-like verses rambled through my brain as I lay for the first night alone here — I believe a trifle delirious — but I remember something of their tenour, and I have a storm by me to work them up with. You see I am cutting out work for the winter. I went, the day the Elliots left, to Metternich, and in a wood at the top of a hill I found a large patch of wild purple crocuses in full bloom. I suppose they, too, had suffered a storm, and could not bud as they ought to have done in the spring. To-morrow I dine on game! — "Think of that, Master Brooke!" for it will make me think of you. I am sorry about Gilston Park. It would have turned all my hares white in one night, and then such a herd of *deers*. I have only three here, Jane, Fanny, and Tom; but they make a strong ring-fence about me. What a lot of Tremaines he must write to get it back again. *We* authors are an unlucky set — freehold, copyhold, or copyright!

Kind regards to all. God bless you, and send you

bright days, that we may meet in 1855 like two Rothschildren just come of age and into our fortunes.

Yours ever truly,

THOMAS HOOD.

P. S. — "Vallnuts* is in, and thrippins an underd, and will be lowerer!" Think of that!

In the latter part of September, or beginning of October, our friend left with his regiment for Posen, and the following letter was written by my father as if to himself from M. de Franck, as a quiz upon the bad memory of the latter. It is a curious jumble of wilful mistakes, and the changes are rung through every variety that can be thought of.

POSEN, *October 30th*, 1835.

MY DEAR MR. WOOD,

The departure of a friend for Coblenz affords me an opportunity of which I avail myself with much pleasure, and especially as it enables me to prove, in spite of your facetious hints of my inconstancy, that I am not unmindful of my absent friends. On the contrary, I assure you that on our march hither my thoughts often wandered back to Coblenz, and rested on you and your amiable wife and interesting family. Nay, although I am now quartered in a city of infinitely more bustle and gaiety,

* My father had a great fondness for nuts, which his doctors were very loth to allow him. On one occasion my mother kept a quantity of them in a chiffonnier, and used to lock the door that he might not get too many. He committed an amiable amateur larceny by taking out the drawer, and fishing the nuts out of the cupboard through the aperture. — T. H.

and have besides more multifarious military duties, still I can honestly declare, as this letter is a proof, that, in spite of such numerous avocations and distractions, my memory has never failed to recur to the many pleasant evenings I passed at your apartments in the Rhein Strasse. Indeed, I may almost say that I find Posen itself rather dull for want of such hours and companionship, and especially that of your lively little girl, whose remarks used to please me so very much. I never hear the name of Maria [Georgiana] but I think of her and her merry dark eyes, not forgetting her little brother Peter [William]. Sometimes I wonder whether Lina (you see I do not forget any one) gets more intelligible to her mistress, and I often wish my German could be again tasked to interpret between her and Mrs. Good. These are delightful reminiscences to me, and I shall cherish them to the last moment of my life. Let time rob me of what it may, it can never efface these traces of real friendship — even if I did not possess such a *souvenir* to remind me of you as the "Comic Manual" ["Chemical Annals"], which you were so kind as to present to me as a keepsake. I assure you, my dear Mr. Woodthorpe, I value it very much, and I did not forget it, and leave it behind me at a little wine-house on the right-hand side of the road between Pfaffendorf and Hocheim. The landlord's name, I think, was Steibel. Your story about "Was the other Dead Man a Beggar?" runs in my head as much as ever, and often sets me thinking of you; which always ends in the wish that I could say here to my servant, as I used when I was quartered at Ehrenbreitstein, "I am going to Mr. Blood's!" Even Juno seems to miss your indulgence; she looks melancholy, and, I dare say, longs in her heart to have another romp with your little boy, or a race with Miss Sarah round your garden. Poor Juno! I never take a walk with her of an evening without regrets at our separation. I assure you I have marked as a lucky day in my calendar the one on which I first met yourself, Mrs. Woodroffe, and little Margaret, on the banks of the Rhine. I can only comfort myself with the hope that I am allowed to live in your remembrances as you do in mine: in my mind's eye I see you all plainly at this moment, seated in that little room which looks on the Mosel bridge. As for little Caroline, I picture her, of course, surrounded with her dolls, or playing with her old favourite cart and horse. I suppose, by this time, through running about under a German sun, her little brother is as brown as she is; but there is no harm in that, for one is not very solicitous about having fair boys. If my memory serves me, the complexion of her other brother was very dark. It is very singular, but when I arrived at Posen, I did not find any old friends. You will say, of course, that I had *forgotten them;* but I will leave my defence to Mrs. Wedgwood, who used to stand my friend in such cases when you ran me so hard, and promised me a slice of bread and butter for a keepsake. The faithfulness and minuteness of my recollections in this letter ought also to speak for me. I can only say, if it should please Fortune, even twenty years hence, to throw us again together, you will find that neither your features nor the name of Woodley have escaped my memory, which was always reckoned a very good one. But we shall meet, I trust, in a much shorter interval than a score of years. I am tantalised here sometimes with rumours of our returning to Coblenz early in next spring. Should we do so, I suppose I shall hardly know Miss Flora again, for by that time her pretty black hair will be long enough to tie into tails, as the German little girls dress their heads. Pray give my love to her, and ask her if she remembers Lieut. von F—— and his dog Juno. There is a little girl here, thirteen or fourteen years old, just about her height of figure, and talking a little French also, who reminds me vividly of my little friend in Coblenz. She has the same black eyes and hair, and is equally fond of skipping-rope and swinging. If I remember rightly, those were little Katherine's favourite pastimes.

And now my dear Mr. Goodenough my time of duty warns me to conclude. It will give me sincere pleasure if you should think this letter worthy of a return in kind, in which case I beg you will be particular in giving me every information of yourselves and your family. Pray take care of your health, and do not neglect my advice about currents of air. I remember you had a discoloration under the eye as if from a severe blow through sitting in a thorough draught. You must not prosecute your medical [mathematical] studies too closely. By this time I trust Mrs. Woodbridge is quite well, and has no further occasion for the services of Dr. B——. I sincerely hope she will feel no more ill effects from the dreadful storm she encountered in coming from England. Have the kindness to present my respectful regards to her, with my best wishes for her health and welfare, and a happy and safe return in due time to Northamptonshire [Scotland]. I think you told me you came from Edinburgh, indeed I remember you had the Northern accent, which no doubt enabled you to pronounce the German so correctly. Pray give my love to Miss Anne, and tell her I hope she does not neglect her pianoforte. I remember all the airs she used to play to me. Her brothers, I fear, will have forgotten me, otherwise I should desire to be named to them with kindness. I shall eagerly expect every post to hear from you; and let me again beg of you to mention every one belonging to you, even your dog. You could not offer me a greater gratification; and if little Charlotte would add a P. S. in her own hand, for I remember she wrote very well, my pleasure would be complete.

Accept my kindest regards to you and yours, and pray believe me,

My dear Mr. Woodgate,
Your very sincere friend and well-wisher,
PHILIP DE FRANCK.

P. S. I shall watch the newspapers for announcements of your new works. I hope that some day you will publish another novel like your Tilbury House [Hall].

To JAMES WOOD, Esq., Coblenz.

372, CASTOR HOF, COBLENZ, *Nov. 3rd*, 1835.

MY DEAR WRIGHT,

I had yours with great delight, for I was *very* anxious about the fate of my box. I have made some inquiry and suspect the cause of the delay was that they were *things never sent before;* and that when examined at the frontiers between Prussia and Holland, they did not know what to do or to charge. I think such a delay not likely to happen again, but shall take every precaution. I had declared here what they were, and will in future get them sealed by the *Douane* here if I can. The MS. I will send post after post as I write it. I am glad what I sent made so much. Before this you will have found out what was to be done. * * * I am glad you liked Doppeldick. If I can only travel a bit in the spring here I will make "sich a Comic as never vos." I know nobody here now but R——, a teacher of languages, who drops in every Sunday. The last I had such a long palaver with him in French; and I really believe I must be to him as Horam the Son of Asmar, or one of the relaters of the Arabian Nights — though only in giving him an account of England — of which he asks me such questions as "have we any oaks?" almost if "we have any sun or moon!" I make him stare with truths sometimes. And though he is polite like all foreigners nearly, he almost constantly has an involuntary shake of the head.

* * * *

A shopkeeper, who also spoke French, one of the few I am on speaking terms with, died the other day of "nervous fever," being swelled like a man with dropsy! Verily I have no faith in the doctors here — we are sure to see a funeral every day — the population being only 20,000 including troops. I heard the other day of a man having *fifty-five* leeches on his thigh! My wig!

why they out-Sangrado Sangrado! One of their blisters would draw a waggon. If I should be ill again I will prescribe for myself.

I will conclude with a Coblenz picture. Jane in bed, smothered in pillows and blankets, suffering from a terribly inflamed eye. In rushes our maid, and without any warning suddenly envelopes her head in a baker's meal-sack hot out of the oven! prescribed as a sudorific, and the best thing in the world for an inflamed eye, by the baker's wife (there's nothing like leather!). What between the suddenness of the attack and her strong sense of the fun of the thing, Jane lay helplessly laughing for awhile and heard Gradle coax off the children with "Coom schön babie — coom schöne Fannische — mama kranke!" Encore! I sent a pair of light trousers which were spotted with ink to be dyed black; after six weeks they came back like a jackdaw, part black, part grey. I put my hands in the pockets like an Englishman, and they came out like an African's. I think seriously of giving them to a chimney-sweep who goes by here; full grown, long nosed, and so like the devil I wonder Fanny has never dreamed of him. There were two; but the other was stoved to death the other day at our neighbour the general's. They lit a fire under him when he was up. Our Dr. B—— who was sent for, told me gravely, that he could not revive him, for when he came, the man was *black in the face!*"

I forgot to tell you that when Gradle first proposed the hot flour prescription of the baker's wife, Jane had flattered herself that it was only a little paper bag of hot flour; and it was only when she was tucked in that she began to feel what a *cake* she was! I wonder what they do for rheumatism! God bless you!

Yours ever truly,

T. Hood.

P. S. Fanny sends her love, "not forgetting Jemmy and Freddy," and how they would like to come to Coblenz and see all the soldiers, and the generals. There is a man of the general's who rides upon a horse with a helmet on his head. I can almost talk German, I shall be glad to come back to England. Tommy has grown and is very fat. He has two sharp teeth, and he bites my fingers when I put them in his mouth. I am very happy here, because I can see the band go into the general's, I can say how many months make a year, and how many weeks make a month. I can write upon my slate A. B. C. and figures. And oh! I have a great house for my dolls, and three rooms in it! and I can't say any more for my head aches, and I have a great many teapots and mugs, and I have got a cold, and a kitchen! Good night, and love to you and Jemmy and Freddy.

"All of this stuff is Fanny's, every line,
For God's sake, reader, take them not for mine!"

Coblenz, 31*st Dec.*, 1835.

My dear Wright,

Your letter arrived yesterday evening to my great relief, for I began to get very anxious, supposing the book would be published on the 15th, and feel sure I shall be pleased with it, when I see it. All parties appear to have done their best, and for your own share I can only say that I feel you have done for me, as I would for you — your very best; so accept my best thanks accordingly. And now, what will you think of those abominable three months' old letters? up to this very hour they have never come to hand.

It has been a great nuisance to us, for we have not written to any one in the daily expectation of having something to answer, so that Dilke and I for example have not been on writing terms for three months, and I fear many things I had to tell him have escaped me.

To estimate our expectations and disappointments, you must remember we are here as in a sort of desert, with one friend, De Franck, and one acquaintance Ramponi, the language master, who jabbers French with me, and every now and then a fellow with an orange collar, *i. e.* a postman, comes to the very next door. And now you will laugh to be told that I am this evening going with De Franck to a grand ball at the Casino, where will be all the rank, beauty, and fashion of Coblenz, of course not to dance, but at De Franck's advice, who says that the German New Year ceremonies are worth seeing, and I mean to see all I can, and turn it to account. I expect to commit myself by laughing aloud, for when the clock strikes twelve I shall find myself all of a sudden the only unkissed, unembraced individual in the room; Franck dined with us on Christmas day, and by his help in the evening we had a pretty German celebration to the high delight of Fanny; but thereof no more, as we hope some day to introduce it in England. Our weather is variable, generally frosty — we have a little while had cold enough in all reason, the oil froze in the night light and the pound of butter in the middle, and as Katchen made a pudding in the kitchen the crust froze. The Rhine and the Moselle are full of ice, and the bridge being taken away, Franck for a month to come cannot stay with us later than nine in the evening, for he is quartered at Ehrenbreitstein on the other side, and must boat it across. He is really a treasure to us, thoroughly English, unpresuming, gentlemanly, and full of good sense, fond of a joke withal. Between him and the children it is quite a mutual flame; on their side, sometimes, so as to be laughable.

One night after his long absence I hung him up in effigy as a deserter, and he came in and found Fanny crying at it as if breaking her heart.

I have no local news to tell you, but that recently a priest at Cologne was convicted of poisoning a man from whom he had purchased an estate without paying for it. He is supposed to have given one or two their viaticum before now.

N. B. My thunder and lightning waistcoat is come! so I must go and dress for the ball. To you who know my *habits* all this must seem very funny as it does to myself. I expect to be highly amused.

Jane is going to curl my hair, and I am going to comb and brush it, more attention altogether than hair generally gets here. I drink, in a glass of holiday hock, to you and all friends, wishing many new years happier than the happiest you have ever known or unknown. 'T is pure rich juice of the grape, would you could taste it, the worst here, at 3*d.* a bottle, we should think something of in England.

With kind regards to all, yours ever sincerely,

THOMAS HOOD.

The following amusing letter to Mrs. Dilke is without date, although from many circumstances it was evidently written in the latter part of 1835.

372, CAST-HIM-OFF, GOD BLESS, 1835.

MY DEAR MRS. DILKE,

I write to you instead of *the D*—— because I am sick of him as a correspondent: as a countryman of Taylor's said, "who would go out with a fellow, that when you fire at him with a blunderbuss only returns it with a pocket-pistol?" even so have I sent Dilke huge letters full and crossed, enough to drive him blind and stupid, and give him a chronic headache; and what does he send in answer but a little letteret that cannot do anybody any harm? I suppose some day I shall come to, "T. H. is received" at the fag end of the Athenæum, amidst the mis-called Answers to Correspondents.

In short, I resent, as people resent who know the world, — that is, cut him when he is making advances. *You* shall have this, who will put it amongst the *haughty*-graphs you are most proud of, instead of telling me coolly that my "account of the whirlwind at Ehrenbreitstein, and the story of the tooth-pick you had mislaid, and had never been able to lay your hand on it since." It is long since he wrote so; but I can *harbour* malice quite as well as Margate pier. I scorn his paltry excuses for brevity without wit, and am astonished that he could have the face to plead "the disturbance of the gentleman overhead," whose noise he confessedly slept through. As for his cock and a bull about "Mr. Pap, who was burnt at Nottingham," I am of Jane's nursery opinion, that "*pap* oughtn't to be burnt," and that is a sufficient notice.

Regarding his whole 'pistle, in reality but a pocket 'pistle, candour compels me to say, I cannot conceive how any man alive could write a duller, "with Liston on one side of him, and Miss Kelly on the other." You see I do not spare him; but I have heard that in England it is a sort of genteel flirtation with the wife to abuse her husband to her face, so I mean to go my lengths. Poor dear wretched woman! I can well conceive your perplexity with him at those Kentish cliffs, for as you say "change of air *will* bring out any *complaint* that is hanging about." I can fancy him complaining that all the *chalk* was not *cheese*, and then the cheese not all *rhine*, in his megrims. Editors, as you say, are but bad travelling companions, and as Taylor would say, they are but bad visiting companions, or before this he would have left his card at least at our door; but he preferred Margate, and I can only say, *de disgustibus*, &c.

I don't wonder you "prefer *divines*," as I do, especially if they are not attached to any particular church or chapel; in token of which I last week gave a trifle to two Catholic priests towards building a new St. Castor's; being perfectly persuaded that the money would never be applied to its ostensible use. I hope all stiff and back-bone Protestants will be satisfied with this my apology.

They were very modest, and would take anything they could get, even copper, so I gave them a very small feather for the tail of the weather-cock.

If I recollect rightly your style of singing, you were also in favour of "tollol"eration; besides one of the priests allowed too that "*tous les hommes sont des hommes*," and I felt obliged to pay him for being converted so far into a Protestant. If Mr. Dilke exerted himself, he might get me a missionary stipend. The man's a brute, and I'll prove it by his own contrarieties; for if, as you state, his only wish on the coast was to "avoid the sea," why on the same principle of logic did he take you with him, but to get rid of you? Jane feels for you, and so do I, and indeed so do Fanny and Tom when you describe taking him by the fin, and hauling him up "all along the shore there" to the fish-market, only to hear him complain like a porpoise on land that he couldn't "get enough fish." As to lugging him up to the Fort, you ought to have recollected how little your own piano-*forte* used to interest him.

By your leave what you did with him was an error of judgment; you should have stuck him on a high stool at the parlour window, and made him pay every man in a blue jacket and trousers, one and threepence ha'penny. Besides, you forget his travels. Was it likely that a man who had crossed the Simplon, would care to cross a donkey? or that he who had seen St. Peter's at Rome, would give one of St. Peter's pence to see St. Peter's in Thanet?

You must have forgotten that he had been at Venice, when you took him to "Snobs' watering-place."

To get him into plain "yellow shoes and a pepper-and-salt dressing gown," must have been a mere Margate miracle after the outlandish nightcaps with no hole to 'em, but like tasselled rainbows, I used to find on the pillow of the spare bed at number nine. Even at Coblenz, here, — and he recommended Coblenz, — a plum-coloured coat, sky blue pantaloons, and a waistcoat of patchwork in silk is the costume. When he does make a holiday in future, pray make him look more like an Editor, that is to say, clothe him in all the "miscellaneous articles" you can muster. Judging by this costume, I suspect a good many of the Germans here are editors, and that accounts for Dilke wandering in this direction. But you will do well to egg him on in this fancy, for then, next year I may see you, and in the interim I will look out for German J. C——, S——, and Mrs. C—— to meet you, — not forgetting a Mrs. Pap, who (Dilke says in his confidential letter to me) is "a very sociable, good-tempered woman."

I am sure he means *her*, though he cunningly lays it on Mr. P. He says, "Mrs. Pap, whose husband was burnt at Nottingham — *the latter* is a very sociable," &c., &c. But don't be blinded so grossly.

Thank God you will have left ere this; a little longer and you would perhaps have been left, like Ariadne, on the shingles, looking at your husband gone off in a Pap-boat.

But "henuff hov 'im," as of course you used to say at Margate. * * Tom, Junior, who came to Cologne a little "shabby, flabby, dabby babby," has grown a young Kentuck, who can lick his father — as hard as nails, and as brown as rusty ones. — For his temper, only fancy mine "with sugar." So unlike Jane's "warm without." Then he is already so good on his legs. I wonder he ever required D. "to stand for him," and as to talking he can say papa when he likes. I have no doubt he only don't cut his teeth because he don't *choose.* In bulk, he is really a double number, but a good deal more amusing.

His love for Gradle is more beautiful than its object, for she is like a plain Chinese; but he will know better as he grows up.

Your Godchild is well and very good, but from seeing processions, &c., is half a Catholic, so if you please, you will come next year, and, according to your vows, teach her High Church.

I think we could make you very comfortable, — at least you would not need to lie in bed and eat split peas, as you did in Paris. Jane can cook a little. She had the honour of making the first pie ever seen in Coblenz, and the baker so admired it that he abstracted half the contents — greengages. Gradle can cook in the English style too, but she will not eat what she has so cooked, and yet I imagine it must be a good style, for a poor woman comes for "the broth the ham was boiled in," but Jane suspects that it is for a night-light, — being nothing but water and oil. You shall try it when you come. If you liked Tivoli, we have dozens of such tea-garden places. Mozelweis, Schönbornlust, the Salmiac hut, &c., &c. I took the Elliots to the first by moonlight, and gave them punch, but nothing to eat was to be had save some cold plum-tart. We are not too refined here to go to German White Conduits and Bagnigge Wellses. In the garden of Schönbornlust (which reminded me, by the way, of some of the shrubberies of Lake House), we saw the lady of our opposite neighbour, the general commander-in-chief of the Rhenish Provinces, or as Fanny calls her, Mrs. Generous (pro general).

His Excellency is much taken with our brats, and often, as he rides by, gives Fanny what she calls a "laughish smile." But the admiration of the Castor Hof is Tom, or as Fanny says, "all the boys that *traverse* the street call him *Timmus*," (she got the fine word out of the lesson-book). He quite takes after his godfather Dilke, in eating everything he can get, and plenty of it, and he is as stout accordingly — not fat but solid.

This has been a great blessing, and altogether we are as comfortable as need be. Our lodgings are very commodious and pleasant. A sketch I send Dilke will show our look out at the back: and we have a tiny kitchen — but it does — it does. We shall be able to give the Elliots a dinner on their way back.

I am writing in a little study with a bookcase and a sofa in it, so you see I am not without *my* luxuries; Fanny has a little bed-room next ours; Tom has regu larly outgrown his cradle.

Thank God, Jane and I have stopped growing, for as it is I cannot stretch at full length in the bed, except diagonally, because of the head and foot boards. The Prussians are universally shortish and the beds are in proportion, I ought to call them cribs. Ours is like "a coffin for two." So you may suppose we shall have no difficulty in finding *spare beds* for *you* when you come. Dilke must sleep upright in a cupboard. Mind you must not expect to be saluted when you arrive; it is not the fashion here, we have had many greater personages and they did not get a single gun. Queen of Naples, Princess of Beira, Prince Frederick of Prussia — not a pop — at last came the King of Würtemberg, and as nobody else did, he saluted himself with some tiny guns from his own steamer.

But you may get kissed a few; Lieutenant Franck told us that when the third battalion of his regiment came here, he had to be kissed by about thirty officers of it. It was a very droll effect to see these moustached veterans embracing each other, like boarding-school misses.

Franck, who is an Englishman, cannot bear it, and unluckily he is rather short. Allan Cunningham might escape it. I saw a young couple, lovers or newly married, kiss on separating in the steamboat, and, after going a few paces, the *lady* turned back and had another! The gent by this time had got amongst a party of English, for whom the scene was too funny to withstand, and as the lady's "second thought" took effect in the midst of us, we all burst into a general roar. The King of Prussia will not allow his officers to marry unless, independent of pay, the couple have between them about 180 per annum. I have some thoughts of writing a pretty little romance on the subject, — only fancy the distress of a pair of such turtle-doves £5 short!

Imagine them getting up to 79, and then the captain

obliged to sell out 10*s.* a year for a new uniform. Sitting in the *stocks* can be but a flea-bite to it. I should not like to be a father with money, for fear Wilhelmina or Charlotta should take it into her head to imitate Miss Blandy.

To be sure the king has some right to look after the officers' matches, for he pays their debts, (I wish I was in his service,) and altogether he seems to be very kind and considerate towards them. What I hear of his Majesty I like, and am therefore *pro tempore* his loyal subject, and drank his health on his birthday. Yesterday we toasted "the Snobs" in Hocheim wine, it only costs 4*d.* a bottle, and was quite good enough for such a pledge. I cannot help thinking your Margate trip has a little let you down, and you will want a jaunt up the Rhine to restore you to gentility. But pray cast off your Margatory manners and costume ere you come. One night there was *such* an English party at the gardens of the Weissen Ross, that Franck in horror told his brother officers they were French people.

"It warn't hus," we are among the respectables at present, and one comfort is, that when Jane has worn out her bonnet and all her caps, if we can't afford new ones, it's very fashionable for ladies to go bare-headed in the street.

Then for me a blue smock frock is a sort of sporting or pedestrian dress for gentlemen, (and though I can't walk much, or shoot, I can make believe,) when I have worn out my best brown and my old black.

I bought a cap to save my hat, and when I wear it, I am so thin withal, you would take me for a jockey who had been overtrained. But I hope to fill up again, for I am going to dinner with an appetite far sharper than our knives, which you may set your heart upon without hurting it. I feel quite a gourmand now, after going for months without dining, indeed it appears to have been a joke against me at the hotel, that I went to the table-d'hôte *not* to eat.

Now, I scold so, if the dinner is not ready at two! Jane likes nothing less than to hear me exclaim, "slow coach!" which means that our household affairs are not going on at the proper pace.

That will sometimes happen, for plain as she is, our Gradle has a lovyer (perhaps more), and goes out gallivanting. I wonder she has not lost him, for the departure of some five thousand troops to the reviews must have left many of the Coblenz servants at a loss what to do with their hearts. Comparatively we are as a city of the plague, and the streets appear deserted; the officers and men off duty were always lounging about them. Dinner and turn-out is as common here as tea and ditto in England.

We often see a party of a dozen officers in full twig go to dinner at two, and hop the twig at five or sooner, over the way. I cannot quite get out of my habit of sitting up to write at night, and when I am going to bed at eleven or twelve, and look out of the window, all Coblenzers are in bed; the only living thing is the sentinel at the general's. At noon the whole town literally smells of dinner; the shops are all locked up; and great is the consumption of grease and garlic. Dilke, who is anything but peaking and delicate, will laugh, and say he never met with anything *he* couldn't eat; but, upon my "davit," I saw a starved-looking dog in the steamboat refuse to touch a plate of scraps set before him by the steward. On looking over Jane's letter, for fear we should jostle on the same subject (you know we don't agree very well), I see she has given you a description of Gradle's dinner; so I refrain from mentioning it, and will only say that a knife, not without reason in Germany, is called a *messer*. As for Dilke (to recur to him), you know his infatuation about everything outlandish. Doesn't he send to (the further end of the Edgeware Road or where it is?) for German mustard—only because it looks dirtier than the English! I'll be bound, if it would give him time, he would give an elaborate panegyric on *Prussic* acid, because it is Prussian. Only try him! We would give a trifle here for a good Margate whiting for all his skits on that very delicate flavoured fish, at this distance almost *too delicate*.

I should like to have all the skate and flounders he refused; and if I possessed but a brill (that "workhouse turbot"), I almost think I should venture to ask his excellency to dinner; at a pinch we could enjoy sprats. I hear we *can* have oysters here in the season, rather stale-ish, that is to say they come like all other travellers, all "open-mouthed," as if they were looking at our lions. They eat them with vinegar and lemon, and Franck says you cannot eat them without; for though you have them in their *shells*, they taste a little *too* corpse-like; I think I could even eat the great big horse oysters *with their beards on*, that we used to leave to the coal porters and draymen about Lonnon. We have had those lobsters of Lilliput — small crayfish — we thought we must have bargained well when we got 25 a penny, but when Franck supped upon them with us in the evening, he said we ought to have got a hundred; perhaps we ought to have had a dozen for nothing. But the poor rich English are very much imposed upon! A *maître d'hôtel* (a very good authority), told me candidly on coming up, that there were three tariffs for the English, French, Dutch.

He stood in the middle predicament, and I have found his statement perfectly true. The good honest Germans are as great cheats as any, though I confess they look honest, they are so stupid-like, and perhaps honesty is stupidity. I had some shirts made here, and they not only changed the cloth I had bought of them, but sent me home some shirts so laughably short, I could only make shift with them; this was a respectable shop. Franck says he interfered once (he has a good national spirit about him), when he found some English deplorably fleeced at an Inn. The fact is, though we pay three times as much as the natives, it is still so cheap in com parison with England, "dear, dear" England, that one is blinded to imposition. In my last letter to Wright, I ventured to conjecture that there would be a revolution in England, if it were from so many English coming up the Rhine, and finding what a deal they can get for their money; not that they would wish to remove their *king*, but that they would wish their sovereign to go farther.*

* In these days, when we know more about the official — or shall

Only think how you may be charitable on next to nothing by giving a pfenning, the third part of a farthing; and in this blessed country there is something to be bought even for that low denomination. I wonder what you can get in England for a farthing, for the "little farthing rushlight" is only a fiction. Only fancy Fanny coming to me when Gradle is going to market, for a shilling to dine the whole household.

We have not tried, but I really believe you might have a snug little evening party for half a guinea! I suspect you never enjoy the sensation of fulness in the only place where repletion is a pleasure, in the pocket!

You might here go out of an evening with your bag *full* of money; and such is the nature of the coin, it would only suffice to pay for a lost game or two at shilling shorts. For example, fancy yourself the mother of a dozen strapping Wentworths (father or son they are both of a bigness), and even so does a little dumpy shirt-button-mould of a groschen (a penny), expand by changing into twelve goodly pfennings — each almost a ha'penny — whilst for a dollar (3 shillings), you get 6 pieces, each as big as the old eighteenpenny tokens. You might fell an ox with a long purse that had a pound translated into Prussian at the other end of it; I wonder Mrs. Fry never came here, one might do such a deal of good ostentatiously for a shilling a week. For my own part, I have not gone further in contemplation than a little feast to the poor

we call it, officious — interference of Continental Governments, is it not tolerably evident that the letters to Wright went Wrong, in consequence of such an awfully revolutionary desire as that of "change for a sovereign?" — T. H.

children in Coblenz, as I used to see the orphan school regaled in the avenue at the back of dear One-Tree Hill at Wanstead.

It would be a pretty sight in the Castor Hof; and fruits being cheap, only think that, buying wholesale, I could for three shillings give a hundred little ones nine greengages a-piece.

This would be as good as dining them: for you may read in the "Bubbles" of a tailor and his son who lived in the season on plums. If you would like to join in the entertainment, you might make all the parents drunk for about a fourpence a head, with music *ad libitum* for eighteenpence. I assure you I was in doubt at the hotel at a *table d'hôte* whether I could offer a penny farthing to a nice lady-like young woman, who had been so obliging as to sing, accompanied by her harp, all dinner-time. However, as the coin was neither silver nor copper, I managed not to be vulgar altogether, nor yet extravagant. You will be surprised to hear that *nothing* at all seemed to be very genteel, and some of the gentlemen gave it with a smirk and look as if they expected a salute in return. Never mind Dilke, *I* say Germans are not liberal (of course only speaking from the sample here), and yet we have an instance of liberality under our eyes enough to redeem a nation. How munificent are the poor to the poor, casting into shade the most splendid benefactions of princes!

Next door to us (a tavern) there lives a poor maniac; the house is her own property, and therefore the charitable lunatic asylums are closed against her. Her brother, and *heir*, ill-treats her, and is supposed almost to starve her, for the sake of the freehold; and the poor wretches at the back tenements, weavers and other famished human weazels (the woman who begs our ham-broth amongst the rest), thrust up to the poor mad creature, on the points of sticks, fragments of bread and food, of which, God knows, to look at them, they are scant enough themselves. This I call charity; and it makes me so pleased with the givers, that I wish I were but that King of Hams, the King of Westphalia, to allow them ham-broth to swim in if they so pleased.

And now, having given you this pretty episode to sweeten my asperities in my letter, I will leave you with an agreeable impression of human nature and myself. I have written a long letter, because I thought your kindness would be pleased with it, being a cheerful one, after some anxiety on my account. Besides, I write to you (I hope Dilke won't be jealous) *con amore*, seeing that we have been always very good friends, and have never disagreed but at secondhand. I mean when I could not put up with your pickled oysters, and you could not endure my preserved sprats. So I heartily reciprocate your "God bless" — which, I remember, when only females were in the case, used to be followed by a sort of smack that might have been heard from No. 9 to Pimlico palace. I do not know whether I ought — but the Germans do — and I 'd rather *you* than Dilke; and besides, I recollect how you sobbed and cried when Doctor S—— went away without offering ——. So here goes — consider it enclosed! On second thoughts I have judged it better to keep up appearances with your husband by writing to him. So that while I get you to remember me kindly to William and Wentworth and Taylor and Chorley and Holmes, and all other friends, I can get Dilke to forget me kindly to all the rest, which, I feel sure, he will punctually fulfil. He must have forgot *himself* when he went to Margate. I only wish when he goes to the coast again "may I be there to sea." Of course you did not dip him, for he is more than a mould already. Fanny asked, in her innocent way, "Did Mr. Dilke go about with a basket and pick up shells?" I told her "No; but he used to take a ride out on a donkey with you behind him on a pillion." I don't wonder at the child's wonder. In the name of Earl Goodwin (who rented the famous Sands), what did you do with his appetite? He is not a man to go about picking shrimps and teazing periwinkles out of their shells with crooked pins. As the sea air is sharpening, I wonder he did not eat you, who are as plump as a partridge, with Mrs. Pap by way of bread-sauce. Then the hot weather you both talk of must have made him open his coat wider than usual, that the wind might get down the arms. I think I see him courting the sea-breeze. "Upon my soul, Maria, this is a delightful place! So like Coblenz! So you call this Margate, do you, my beauty? Well —" (a grunt like a paviour's) "and I suppose you call that the fort — humph! Considering we might have stood before Ehrenbreitstein instead of it — hah!" (a sigh like an alligator's). "My God! — that we could be so insane! — how any Christian being could stay a month in it! — why I should hang myself in ten days, or drown myself in that stinking sea yonder! There is not one thing worth looking at — not one! I know what you are going to say, Beauty; but because the Crosbys and the Chatfields are such donkeys, and the Lord knows who besides, is it any reason because they don't act like common rational beings ——? But come along!" (no offer to stir though) "let 's go up to the market and look at the fish, for I suppose you know there is none to be had here, because it is so near the coast. To be sure, says you, there is whiting — and so there is at Billingsgate! If ever I go again to a watering-place — I believe that 's what you call it, Maria — it shall be Hungerford Market. My God! it is a madness — a perfect madness — to leave home and come down here to see — what? a parcel of yellow slippers and pepper-and-salt dressing-gowns." Here he draws down his mouth, and hoists up his shoulders, till his coat-collar hides his ears. "Well, it 's too late now to listen to common sense. It serves me right for being such an ass. By the time my holidays are over, I shall know how to spend them! But perhaps *you* like it better than I do, for there's no disputing of tastes.

"There may be something to recommend even Margate, though an angel from heaven couldn't find out what it is. I know *I* can't, unless it 's having a drunken noisy vagabond overhead to keep you awake all night long. But I forget, my darling, you don't sleep so light as I do — so much the better for you! Then there 's his sister that Mrs. —— what d' ye call her, Tops-and-Bottoms, with her infernal bobbings and curtseyings and over-civility. Damme if I know how to answer the woman! I suppose, according to Margate manners, we ought to ask her to Grosvenor Place. But mind, Maria, when she calls, I 'm at Somerset House! Come along" (not a stump stirred yet). "I suppose we must see what is n't to be seen in our salt-water Wapping. All *I* have seen is 'London butter,'—just think of that, Maria,—'London butter may be had here.' Why so it may in London without going sixty miles by sea for it; and you, my darling, as sick as a dog! Spasms! I don't wonder you 've had spasms; I 've almost had them myself. It 's the cursed negatives, and the place, rather than anything positive,—the utter bleakness and desolation of the country against the stinks of the sea-shore. Lord! that a man with a nose on his face should come here; and here too one has to remember that there are such places as Coblenz; and such a river as the Rhine. I 'll tell you what, Maria!" Here he tells you nothing; but stooping over his base, like the leaning tower at Bologna, he takes a very long pinch of snuff, and then anathematising, shakes the dust off his fingers against all Margate and all its inhabitants, present and future.

There! isn't that a portrait of him to the life — a cabinet picture — a gem! Pray take care of it, to be a comfort to you when you are a widow. Perhaps I shall send him a sketch of you as a companion picture, for I can fancy you quite as vividly. If I recollect rightly *you* were at Margate before, and liked it amazingly. Between your raptures and his disgusts I suppose you got up a quarrel, for I observed you say in your letter that "you are both getting a little more *reconciled*." He must have been awful — and I guess it was his splenetic attacks on the donkeys to vent his humane notions that originated the notice to visitors about "wanton cruelty." Take my advice *if ever you get him to Margate again* put him up to be raffled for. And now as the Germans say "ah chied!" or as you would say "a do."

Marry time Supremacy.

"If these pages should be the happy means of exciting one virtuous impression, or confirming one moral or religious principle, or lightening one moment of human suffering, or eradicating one speculative error, or removing one ill-founded prejudice, the writer will have his reward, and will not have written in vain."

I am,

My dear Mrs. Dilke,

Yours ever very truly,

THOS. HOOD.

P.S. I dined well to-day on such a haricot! that I'm persuaded Jane is the best cook in Coblenz. So I have done the handsome thing and *riz* her. She had nothing a-year before, and I have doubled it. We got a Westphalia ham against the Elliots' return, at five pence a pound. It is the finest I ever tasted; such a flavour, quite answerable to its odour, which is as unique in its kind as that of the best Eau de Cologne! They call it here the "rauch," answerable to the Scottish reek; but I will say no more here about edibles or you will compare me to Matthews, who began writing "The Diary of an Invalid," and ended a Gourmand. I should like to send you a real Westphalian, but then the *duty!* You ought to take one with you here, as Miss M—— did her sweetmeats from India; she brought a large box of them — preserved Lord knows what — but the customs demanded so much that instead of bringing them ashore she went and ate them all up on board herself. I had this from Dr. E——, who was called in to her after "the *Gorge*."

P. S. God bless.

CHAPTER III.

1836.

At Coblenz. — Letters from Mrs. Hood to Mrs. Elliot. — Letters to Mr. Wright and Mr. Dilke. — Accompanies the 19th Polish Infantry in their March to Berlin. — Letters to his Wife. — Returns to Coblenz. — Illness. — Letters to Lieut. de Franck, Mr. Wright, and Mr. Dilke. — Commences "Up the Rhine."

AT the beginning of this chapter, I have inserted the following letter from my mother to her friend Mrs. Elliot, not only as interesting in itself, but also as giving a correct history of the "trussing" of the Christmas pudding, to which such frequent allusion is made by my father in his subsequent letters to Mr. de Franck.

372, Castor Hof, Coblenz, 28*th Jan.*, 1836.

My dear Mrs. Elliot,

Your welcome letter arrived with many others in a parcel on New-Year's eve.

You may not have seen Mr. Wright to hear that his parcel was packed up to send here, when finding that it was not safe to enclose the letters he had to take them out, and a friend of the Dilkes coming to Düsseldorf undertook to convey them to us; she was detained a fortnight at Rotterdam, as the persons who undertook to put the luggage on board neglected to do so. From the time you left us, with the exception of one from my sister C——, two days after your departure, and a few from Mr. Wright, who saw the "Comic" through the press, we did not have a letter from a soul; post after post went by in vain expectation; first we were impatient, then we were angry, then astonished, and asked each other "Stands England where it did?" The man used to turn the corner of the Nagel Strasse, and come with his hateful lemon collar to the very next door, nay, even to our own, but not to us. Hood was dressing to go to the civil Casino ball with Herr Franck when the delightful parcel arrived. He was sorry he had to go, and kept his friend waiting, while he read some of the long looked-for letters.

I must now earnestly and gratefully thank you and my kind friend the Doctor for going to C——. My mother's letter expressed how much comfort you had afforded her by that visit; she seemed cheered by your good account of us, and I feel quite happy to think she will look on our absence with less regret now she knows we are going on so well. We are all well now except Hood, who every now and then has a slight return of illness and weakness, which I trust when the spring comes he will get over. * * * I have recovered the use of my eye in spite of all mis-management, but I suffered great pain. I had three spots on the white, or rather the red of the eye like seed-pearl. You will recollect that the people here are most of them troubled with weak eyes. Hood says they are generally brown but *border* on red. I forgot to tell you in its proper place, that is to say round my eye, that I was ordered leeches which were applied by a sort of barber-surgeon, an official not now known in England.

Hood desires me to make known the best part of his practice, namely, put the leeches for five minutes into a basin of tepid water, which makes them lively, and eager to bite; obviating the tediousness and trouble of the English method. And fortunately Hood in his candour ventured to approve of the plan, and drew upon himself the retort of "*Now*, Sir, you may write to England, and tell them how to put on leeches." But the Germans do not know *where* to put them, for he put one in the corner of my eye. We have since had the following bill: "To his Lady to put blood-suckers at your eye, six shillings," which charge, translated into English, according to the relative value of money, would be twelve shillings for merely putting them on, exclusive of the "blood-suckers;" but Hood thinks the method is worth attention, and I only mention the charge as a warning to any friends you may have coming up the Rhine, as a sample of what we find too surely obtains throughout as regards the English; this man never receiving more than a third from the natives.

We are getting wiser every day, and have paid for it, but could not have arrived at the truth without the help of our friend Lieut. de Franck, who is an Englishman by birth and at heart, but will pass for a German. It is too certain there is a separate table of charges for the English; and the superlativest thing a countryman can do going up the Rhine, is to insist upon the German price, always a half, sometimes a third. De Franck tells us a major's pay is a very handsome income, and it is exactly £280 a year. As they have a certain style to keep up, you may imagine how cheap living is *to the natives.*

Hood is so disgusted with their illiberality in this respect, that he likes to publish it as much as he can, especially as the English are the greatest benefactors to the Rhenish towns. I am not sure whether I shall be able to restrain him from going to the steam-packets, when they arrive with the English, to say, "Take care of your pockets."

I will now give you a pleasanter subject — Hood's description of the ball at Casino on New Year's eve. I made him sit by me and dictate it. "My ticket to meet all the rank, beauty, and fashion of Coblenz cost me only twenty groschen, and it was well worth every shilling of the money. His Excellency General De Borstell, commander of all the Rhenish provinces, was there, and so was my tailor, and the man of whom I bought my black stock. To be sure, although in one room, there was a West End. The rank particularly occupied the top corner; so the right-hand and the left corner next the door seemed to be the favourite with the snips and snobs. To do the latter justice, they behaved with much more decency and decorum than would have prevailed in such a motley assemblage in London. How would you stare, too, in London, to see at a ball a score or two in the uniform of common soldiers offering their partnership to the ladies! But the fact is, as everybody must be a soldier in Prussia, there is no purchasing commissions: some of the common soldiers are the sons of barons. The dances were waltzes, gallopades, and contre-danses, the last like our quadrilles. They mostly danced well, especially the waltz, which is such a favourite, that I saw girls stand up for it — steady-looking, decidedly serious as a Sunday-school teacher, whom I should as soon have expected to see whirl off with a young man round the room after sixty other couples. They made my head spin at last with looking at them. But the music was beautiful — excellently played. I think *I* could at least have *flounced* about *in time* to it myself. The instruments were many and various. They seemed never to tire of the whirligig; and De Franck says, they often waltz upon those *polished* floors, similar to the Duke of Orange's you saw, where we can hardly walk without breaking a leg, as the Duke of York did. I was amused to see De Franck and a young lady each pull out a card or little book, and register something in the Tattersall style of betting; it was an engagement to each other to dance together at a certain ball, perhaps a month to come. From time to time, the company refreshed themselves in a suite of rooms laid out with tables, each company paying for its own. For my own part, I got on pleasantly enough amongst a party of Franck's brother officers, one of whom instantly tendered to me a glass of Cardinal, *i. e.* Bishop (only cold), with wine, sugar, and the rind of a small green orange they grow here, of the size of a cotton ball, and which has the peculiar property, that a little too much of the rind in the mixture will infallibly give you the headache! I wish I could say much for the beauty of Coblenz; but there were only, to my taste, three or four with any pretensions. The great favourite was a Miss N——.

The officers hardly reckon it a ball without her. Yet she is not handsome; her nose is decidedly plain — snubby even; but she seems clever, which is rare enough here, I guess. I had also a young wife of sixteen pointed out to me as interesting, but she looked too like a school-girl. As to dress, I always get scolded because I could never describe if Miss A. or Miss B. was in blonde or bombazeen. So you must excuse the millinery, especially as, being all grades, they wore all sorts of fashions.

"At last came the dance I had come to see! Exactly at twelve, bang went a minor cannon in an adjoining room, and the waltz instantly broke up, and the whole room was in motion, everybody walking or running about to exchange salutations, and kisses and embraces with all friends and acquaintances male and female. Such *hearty smacks* and hugs, and hand-shakings to the chorus of 'Prosit neu jahr! Prosit neu jahr!' Some of the maidens methought kissed each other most tantalisingly, and languished into each other's arms, I am afraid because so many nice young men and gay officers were present to see it; but then the fathers and mothers were as busy kissing and be-kissed. With some of the older folks it was quite a ceremony; and I should think the demand on the sentimentals was very great. And there all the while stood your humble servant — the poor English creature — the disconsolate — the forsaken — the dummy — and looker-on — and what you will — with my lips made up and my arms empty — a lay figure — while the very fiddlers were hugging! Of course I could not kiss my tailor, or embrace the man

I bought the black stock of. But luckily I recognised two young ladies I have met at the Vertue's. (You see I stuck to the *Virtuous* though Jane *was not* present.) We had never been on speaking terms, as they did not like to own to French far from the best quality. However, I convinced them mine was no better, and we complimented each other with a good deal of 'bad language.' So I went and looked a salute at them, which made them smile, and then the officer who had presented me the glass of Cardinal, came and shook hands with me; and even this, which was my *all*, comforted me. It was really a funny scene, and if you will give a large party on New Year's eve, and have plenty of beauty and fashion, I will introduce the custom on my return. I mean to try and draw it." *

So much for Hood's New Year's eve. I must now tell you my story about the Christmas pudding. The Lieutenant was with us on Christmas day, and enjoyed my plum-pudding so much, that I promised to make one for him. Hood threatened to play some tricks with it — either to pop in bullets or tenpenny nails; and I watched over my work with great vigilance, so that it was put in to boil without any misfortune.

I went to bed early, telling Gradle to put it, when done, into the drawing-room till the morning. Hood was writing, and says, it was put down smoking under his very nose, and the spirit of mischief was irresistible. I had bought a groschen's worth of new white wooden skewers that very morning. He cut them a little shorter than the pudding's diameter, and poked them in across and

* This forms one of the illustrations of "Up the Rhine." — T. H.

across in all directions, so neatly, that I never perceived any sign of them when I packed and sealed it up the next day for De Franck's man to carry over to Ehrenbreitstein. He came to thank me and praised it highly. I find that while I was out of the room Hood asked him if it was not well trussed, and he answered "Yes" so gravely that Hood thought he meditated some joke in retaliation, and was on his guard. At the ball the truth came out — he actually thought it was some new method of making plum-puddings, and gave me credit for the woodwork. He had invited two of his brother officers to lunch upon it, and Hood wanted * to persuade me that the "Cardinal" officer had swallowed one of the skewers! Now was not this an abominable trick?

We have had very severe weather, and at first suffered much from the cold, for the stoves are dreadful and unsatisfactory substitutes for a good English fire. The Rhine bridge was taken up, and the people crossed the river to and fro in boats. This has been inconvenient to the officers who live at Ehrenbreitstein, as the private and public balls are numerous at this season, and crossing the Rhine through broken ice in an open boat at twelve, one, and two in the morning, after dancing, is not very agreeable. They attempted putting up the bridge again two days ago, after a week's complete thaw, and got it a quarter over on each side, but yesterday there came

* And nearly succeeded in doing so, innocently assisted by the officer in question, with whom the pudding had not altogether agreed. As he did not know English, and my mother was not yet up in German, a pantomime ensued on his part expressive of indigestion, but construed by my father as descriptive of the agonies of an internal skewer. — T. H.

with a storm of wind large masses of ice from other rivers that flow into the Rhine, and tore up the fastenings, crushing the boats, and breaking them into pieces. They have, however, got it up to-day again partly, and if fresh ice does not come, it will all be up by eleven or twelve to-morrow. The week before last we read an account in a Coblenz paper that the ice had stopped at the Lurlei (I dare say you recollect that singular and picturesque rock above St. Goar), and that it was "mountains high," not having been so before in the memory of man. We found from De Franck everybody was going to see it, and we nobodies wished to join them. It was a bright day, clear and frosty, and I who had not before been above Coblenz, enjoyed the scenery greatly. We left here at half-past nine, and arrived at St. Goar to dinner at half-past one. We set off after dinner to see the ice, which, we were told, extended far beyond what we could reach that evening, having to return here. The Germans, who are apt to exaggerate, had talked of icebergs not to be found, but still the sight was well worth seeing. Supposing you have not forgotten the Lurlei, imagine that narrow passage blocked up with a storm of ice; for the immense pressure had heaved it up in huge waves and furrows, eight or ten feet high, each ridge composed of massive slabs of ice tossed about in all directions. At every bend of the river there had been a dreadful scuffle, and the fragments were thrust upwards end-ways. But the mighty river would not be dammed up — you saw it now and then in a narrow slip rushing like a mill stream — then it plunged under the ice and boiled up again a hundred yards farther. At one bend of the river a green orchard was covered with great blocks hurled over the bank, one could not suppose how. There were some ridges, or rather ruts, so straight and evenly shaved down, that one fancied some giant of the mountain had driven his car through the middle of the ice, and that his wheels had left these traces and deep furrows. But on considering it, Hood discovered that the middle ice had moved, while that on the sides was stationary, and the friction had worn it as smooth as if cut with a knife. We went to Oberwesel, part of which was under water. We had not time to proceed farther, though we both agreed that we could have gone on, and on, and on, to see more. We hear that higher up a church was surrounded with masses of ice so that only the steeple was perceptible. The Moselle ice carried away a youth of sixteen, who was playing on it, and a similar and somewhat romantic incident occurred on the Rhine. On the island just above the bridge resides the Countess of P——, who walking out by herself to see the ice floating down, managed to fall in; perhaps she was pushing the loose bits of ice as the children do. Heaven knows what foolish process brought her to do it — but in she plumped! As Hood says, "some German cherub that sits up aloft" brought a willow bough to her assistance, and there she hung, well preserved in ice, a good long spell — till a young man, the son of one who had been at law with the Count, her father, about some hundreds of thalers, came in a boat and rescued her. There has been much speculation whether the law-suit would be dropped by the old gentleman, out of gratitude to the preserver of his daughter. However, I have not heard the result. Unfortunately the young lady is not a beauty, or even interesting; being very short and stout, with a coarse red complexion, and tow-coloured hair. Our friend says she attends the balls, and although always elegantly dressed with a jewelled order of crown and cross on her bosom, all agree she looks like some peasant-girl from the *mountains* — and one of the *plain*est too! Hood foretells she will give her preserver a lock of her tow-coloured hair, and advise her father to proceed with the law-suit. This is his splenetic idea of German gratitude.

I am going to intrude a double letter upon you, and I fear a very confused and blundering one. I am always very busy, and now especially so from Gradle not behaving well. Indeed she has so the upper hand of me, and goes her own course of late so obstinately, that we decide upon parting with her! The love affair (if one may so degrade the term) with Joseph, the carpenter, soon after you left became annoying; every evening he was at our door for two or three hours, and so she left us to attend to ourselves. When it got cold weather, and she had a pain in her face, she brought him into the kitchen; at last he was here at all times in the day. I could not go into my own kitchen, but there he stood or sat smoking his pipe, and she *would not understand* that we did not like it; so we got Herr Ramponi, an Italian master, who calls here sometimes to gossip with Hood, to say our mind, and she promised everything in the way of amendment, but her temper, as the Vertues told us, is very ungovernable. She has carried on the connection, and our children, when she is sent to take them out, are we find always kept standing on the banks of the Rhine or Moselle, while she talks to Joseph, who is at work there. As we cannot now depend on her, and I find her very insolent to myself, without the power to answer or check it, Hood insists upon her going.

Tom was seized with the measles, poor dear, and was *very ill* one day. It is not, they say, thought anything of here, but we moved his bed for warmth into Hood's study, kept fires night and day, and Hood and I never left him till quite well, which he is now, though a little weaker. He is an everlasting amusement to us with his little tricks — says "ja" and "ah chied," pronounced "a chee," and takes off his little black cap bowing as ceremoniously as a young German. We hear that there is going to be a very grand review of all the Prussian troops by the King next September; and they half think, and all wish it may be in the neighbourhood of Coblenz; it will be a grand sight — the pioneers will throw temporary bridges over the Rhine — the tents would be pitched on the plain on the other side of the Moselle facing our back windows — there will be 80,000 men, and it would be only a pleasant ride from here to see their evolutions and sham fights, De Franck being good information for us where best to go. The King would reside (if here) in the suite of rooms that run along the front of the General's opposite to us; and the place would be very gay and amusing. Of course it would even tempt travellers to abide here, as such a sight does not offer every day. The Dilkes wrote by the parcel your letters came in — he was very much dissatisfied with their trip to Margate, and kept saying continually "and we might have been on the banks of the Rhine."

Passing down Chancery Lane a month after their return, he heard the mistress of a greengrocer's shop say "that gentleman was at Margate when I was there!"

Our friend Franck has just been here on his way to the military ball at the Casino. He tells us that General Von Borstell has written to the King to beg he will have the review here, if possible, but they are afraid that the Minister of Finance will object, on account of the expense, as the farmers ask so much here for their crops, and the King always pays for the damage which is done by the troops during their sham fights; they trample over everything.

On the 11th February, the Carnival commences, but they seem to think it will not be a good one this year, it was so expensive on the last occasion, though I think to the sober English, the best is but mere trumpery and folly; it is well, however, to see all these novelties before settling again at our dear English fireside, which I look forward to with all hope and comfort. Hood promises himself the pleasure of writing to Dr. Elliot, to whom he feels much indebted for even his flying advice, as it has done him much permanent good. The steel wine appeared to be of such benefit that he really missed it when he chanced not to take it, and he has had no return worth mentioning of his complaint. He says he has entirely to thank the Doctor, that in medicine he is not an *Infidel*, and that here, for once, he has no double meaningless meaning, the double practice upon himself and his better half: he hopes the Doctor will not accuse him of presumption that he intends to practise here himself, — but only upon himself, and he prays God earnestly that he may not have need of such bad advice.

Hood means to go to Mayence, Frankfort, the Baths, &c., and also up the Moselle, to Trèves (I remaining here with my babes), if he can, next spring and summer — meditating a work for which he has already some matter and drawings, something like the "Brunnens," and yet not like it; he hopes you got the Comic he desired to be sent, and that it did you no harm. Through some mismanagement of not hearing how the book printed, he had too much, and so some of the writing stands over for the next. I was very angry at this, who saw how very hard he worked up to the last. We have not received it yet, which seems odd, but I suppose the difficulty of sending a parcel when the Rhine steamers do not go, prevented Mr. Wright forwarding that, and also the books you so kindly sent Fanny, for which she sends her love and best thanks, — they *will* be a treat as her little stock is quite exhausted now.

How we missed you! Though it could scarcely be called a glance: as the packet went smoking down the Rhine, we felt as if left upon a desert island, and walked back to look at our untouched luncheon, sad and silent. We then said to each other, "What shall we do?" and both agreed we must "go out a-pleasuring," — so off we set to take coffee at a roadside wine-house at Metternich; we walked up a steep hill through a pretty wood, and took by surprise a beautiful plot of large purple wild crocuses, which covered an open space at the top; they seemed out of place and season, and so did we. We brought home all our handkerchiefs full, and they lasted in water very long, as if for a souvenir of the day,—that was our last excursion from home, till we went to the Lurlei; for Hood, getting better, set to work—it was then "all work and no play," but I do not recollect seeing him get through it better—he finished with good spirits, and boiled over afterwards with some droll sketches for the work I told you of. Talking of boiling, I must, in self-conceit, say that I am improving decidedly in my cooking, having started several things lately "in the fancy line." Yesterday morning I set to work very seriously to make some potted beef, and succeeded, little thinking what ungrateful jests I should draw upon my poor head from Hood.

Being proud of my own fabrication, I produced it at tea, when De Franck came, and then commenced the jokes of the good-for-nothing. He asked with apparent interest, how it was made, and I said, "I pounded it in a pestle and mortar." "But, then, dear, we have not got one, you know."

In short, he insisted that, like the Otaheitan cooks, I had *chewed* it small; and as I happened, having the face-ache, to put my hand to my jaw at the time, it seemed a corroboration, of which he made full use. Upon this hint, he huddled joke upon joke, till we were convulsed with laughter, and to-day Franck declares he laughed in the middle of the night. Hood called it "Bullock jam," and when I asked him what he would eat, he replied "what you *chews*." To be sure, an ox here, after he has been in his time a plough-horse, a dray-horse, and a horse of all-work, might give an Ogress the face-ache.

I have also attempted a mince-pie on a large scale, which was so relished that the baker abstracted half the contents before it was baked. Talking of mince-meat, the Lieutenant tells us a very active poison has been discovered in German black-puddings, of course from the blood being in a bad state. There have been several martyrs. This bit of information is aimed at the Doctor, — Hood hopes it would hit him in the stomach.

* * * *

Hood desires me to say he will write to you without expecting you to be a correspondent, but there is at present no news worth postage. He is busy collecting materials, which Head has let slip out of his head. * * * Did you ever hear of bathing in malt? It is a German remedy. You see written up here, "Beer Brewery, and Bath House," — Hood will have it they bathe in the beer. As you recommend porter sometimes, he sends you this hint, and of course, as Head insists, the patient will take care "to put the head under," with the mouth open; pray prescribe it, perhaps an object that went in white and meagre, would come out "brown stout;" he thinks little children may be done in the small beer.

Dr. B. is going to London in the summer, he said to *me* when my eye was bad, "In Germance we do cure everything, all but Death, that is the divine law." We asked him how they cured the typhus fever, and he said, "Oh! to be sure with cold water!" De Franck says, some time back, they prescribed the same remedy for everything, and every pump in the place was an apothecary.

Pray accept our best thanks, and kindest regards, and believe me,

My dear Mrs. Elliot,

Yours very sincerely,

JANE HOOD.

The steam-packets commenced coming up the Rhine to-day, and the bridge is up again. One seems more comfortable at these signs of better weather, though it may be long ere the Dampschiffe bring any friends to us, and seldom that we cross the bridge. Hood and De Franck are talking of wonders they are to do in the fishing line (not meant for a pun). The perch are very fine and at St. Goar we saw the salmon jump, and they say they are to be caught with a line. I think Hood is laying out for more than he will have time for: he must, if he has health, travel for his new book; and then the other Comic will have to come out earlier if possible.

I have been amused during my needle-hours by Hood reading some French books, which we get at a library here, but they have no more, so that the stock is almost run through. When I read the Athenæum I long to see the new books spoken of. I could relish the sweepings even of Mr. Dilke's study; there are several libraries here, but no English books. I have quite a thirst for new books, we often speculate on how we shall behave on our return to England.

Hood's is rather a greedy style — he says he will stop at some coffee-house directly he lands and have some *bread and cheese and porter*, and, then he will call at Williams' noted shop at the Old Bailey for boiled beef.

This is shockingly John Bullish, is it not? My dear little boy splutters out with much anger Gradle's washing of bones, with fried onions and potatoes, which she calls soup. The other day she took him to the butcher's with her — on their return while talking with her, I saw him looking distressed, and quite heaving with something odious to him, and upon inquiry, I found he had got some brown bread given him by the butcher's frau, with fat-skimmings of the water they boil their sausages in, spread like butter upon it. I felt very angry. However he shows such signs of a good spirit of his own, that I think he will not submit to such feedings as that again.

I hope that your dear little baby goes on well, and that your fine boys are flourishing around you. Willie must have enjoyed all the novelties you had to tell him.

Children of intellect are delightful listeners, I think — only sometimes their questions are puzzling and difficult to answer.

Have you seen anything of the new residents at Lake House? If you have, speak of them when you write next. Heaven send they have the taste to leave that lovely garden untouched, of which I cannot help thinking with regret, and also the drawing-room: the house has been repaired, we have heard. Pray write soon, remembering that your last bears date October 14th.

Tell us all about yourselves, and the children. You cannot tell what a treat letters are to us, especially after the long famine we have endured.

Think of this and of the poor exiles, and write, write, write to far Germany. I mean to be so gay as to go to the play here, which is three times a week. They play an opera called the "Zampfer," which is very fine music, they say; and they finish early, which is very pleasant for me, who cannot depend upon Gradle's care of the children.

I must conclude, as the post-time nears. Please give our compliments to Mr. Maiden. God bless you all. The best wishes of the season to you.

Believe me ever, my dearest Mrs. Elliot,

Your affectionate friend,

JANE HOOD.

372, CASTOR HOF, 31*st January*, 1836.

MY DEAR WRIGHT,

We have been anxiously waiting to see our promised parcel, and as it has not come at this present writing, I have made up my mind to let you know, fearing it may have stuck at some of the custom houses on its way through. Should it have been despatched, pray let us have all the particulars, that I may try to recover it. You may, however, have heard of the ice; if so, and it has deterred you from sending, I am now able to tell you that the ice is all gone, our bridge will be up again, if it is not already, and the papers announce that the *Rhine* steamboats will start for the season to-morrow.

I have been very anxious — for except your last before Christmas, we have only had the *back* letters, and those by Mrs. L——, which came to us on New Year's Eve. I long to know what luck my book has had. It seems odd to me not to have seen the Comic yet; but judging from the fragments sent, which I had not time to look at before I last wrote, it is excellently got up on all hands, myself included. The cuts come very well indeed, and the text seems very correct: quite as much so as *I* could have made it. As this is only a business letter, I must refer to the Dilkes for particularities as to our domestic concerns, they have each had long epistles.

I think I told you De Franck is come back for good. He fishes, and means to fish more, in the Rhine and Moselle, as there are really good fish; both sport and profit may be looked for here (where we are very badly off for sea-fish, even *salted*). Perch, Barbel, Roach, Jack, and higher up, even Salmon, and a peculiar fish, not English: rod and line fishing is free. De Franck wants a few things, and I want an outfit for bait fishing, I do not pretend to troll, or throw a fly; do as you judge best for me. Pray do not forget to send me plenty of blocks, as I shall have much use for them — I have, however, a present supply. I do much wish, and almost hope you may come this spring. You may pay in London, per the "Batavier," the whole fare here, which is the cheapest way; with liberty of staying at any place on the road a few days, as at Rotterdam, Nimeguen, or Cologne, and then on again. Should you come, I project some pedestrian rambles, inland — to see the people and country. — I know enough German now to get along like *ile.*

I keep my health tolerably well, and hope to be better. The winter has tried us all with colds, coughs, face-aches, &c., and Tom has had the measles, but mildly. As Ollapod recommends, I am taking my "spring physic" — (N. B. I am my own M. D.) — and mean to go into mental and bodily training for a good campaign. It is a great thing for us, De Franck's return, in every sense, for he will save us from a great deal of imposition, of which the honest Germans hereabout are too fond. And he is a very good fellow as a companion, without thinking that he is our only one. I must cut this short, for Franck is come, and we have to get him to scold Gradle, and give her warning. She gave us a message from her priest, and when we sent her out with the chicks this morning, she took them to church. So we mean to protest as good Protestants, and Jane is quite a Luther at it. My kind regards to Mrs. Wright, and all of your name, and all friends of other names. Kiss my Godson, and "Prosit neu jahr!" from

Dear Wright, yours ever truly,
THOS. HOOD.

P. S. Postage is not dear. Pray let us know how matters go on. We have not the thousand and one occupations and acquaintances, and so on, to divert our anxieties like those of your great city: and molehills seem mountains. Franck swears that potted beef story kept him laughing all night. "Ah Chied!"

AT HERR DEUBEL'S,
752, ALTEN GRABEN, COBLENZ, *June 20th*, 1836.

MY DEAR DILKE,

Many, many thanks for your letter, and the kind interest and trouble it evidences on my behalf. They are such as I might have expected from the best and last friend I saw in England, and the first I hope to meet again. * * * *

We are in much better lodgings, at the same cost,

though our address, literally translated, is at "Mr. Devil's, in the Old Grave." We are now near the Moselle bridge, in a busy, amusing street, but out of the town in three minutes' walk.

We did not part with Miss Seil without some serio-comic originality in her struggles between extortion and civility. One moment she kissed Jane like a sister, and the next began a skirmish. First came Suspicion that, as we left a little before the time agreed on, we would not pay up to it. Satisfied on that point, Content fell to kissing. Then Memory suggested we had broken two or three old chairs and a glass, but finding we had replaced or sent them to be mended ourselves, she fired a fresh salute. Away we went, and then, Avarice prompting, she sent a volley of chairs, &c., we had *not* broken, to be repaired, and requested the use of the rooms. That promised so soon as we should have cleared out and cleaned up, she fell to compliments again; but sniffing that she meant to whitewash, repair, and brush up at our cost, we were obliged, in self-defence, to hold the keys. Thereupon she had the *locks picked*, and set to work, and hinted she would favour me with the bills. So I entered into the correspondence, and as she had sent Jane a quantity of notes in German, I thought it only fair to give her one in English, which I knew she must carry half over the town to get translated, and then, I fear, it will not be very flattering. I pointed out to her that she had no right to both rooms and rent, and as picking locks *is* a grave offence in Prussia, she must have, and had, presumed on a foreigner's ignorance of its laws. This has shut her mouth, and stopped the bills, and also the *billing.* Gradle marched on the 1st of March (military again), and, I am sorry to say, made a bad end. First, as Tom didn't at all want physic, she showed, or let him find his way (whilst his mother was out) to the cupboard "wot holds the honey-pot." Secondly, having "vained de Bibi," she did her best to unvain him again, and set him roaring all at once after his "Mutter." Thirdly, as Fanny had the face-ache, she opened all the windows directly our backs were turned, and, having taken a fit of cleanliness, she was busy one day brushing down the dust from the ceiling and walls over Missis's gowns. She had warning for the 1st of March, but, as Jane is as unlucky as "Joe,"* this of all years was leap year. It is too certain the dear departed made a per-centage on everything she bought for us. I declined to sign a certificate of honesty Vertue had given her, so she cast her eyes on Joseph, the carpenter, whom she got to marry her, induced by the fortune of a "bibi" two years old, and 150 dollars saved out of the 60 she had received from Vertue and us. Joseph's mother, whom he partly supported, dying opportunely the day before she left us, the wedding was fixed for the fortnight after the funeral; but, owing to some mysterious interdict of the priest, did not take place till a fortnight later.

We have now a servant with a seven years' character, and the consequence is everything is much cheaper, albeit she is not a good bargainer. Of course, though we do not quarrel, we have plenty of *misunderstandings.*

* "Unlucky Joe," is the best character in my father's novel, "Tylney Hall." — T. H.

We have changed our butcher, and gained a penny per pound; ditto laundress, and saved nearly a dollar a week. In short, Jane, whatever be her political principles, is a practical reformer; and I look on with a Conservative eye, lest the spirit of change should go on madly too far, and I be *Skeltoned* like the rest.

By the bye, I do not wonder at the separation of that worthy couple, the ——s. I should rather think they never met — or, at least, only like the Rhine and Moselle, which show a very decided inclination to keep themselves to themselves from the first moment of union. Jane and I, however, take the warning, and shall be particularly careful of quarrelling, as she has not "*a piano*" to be the harmonious means of bringing us together again.

As for "chimney ornaments" (except a very tall, long-nosed gentleman in black, remarkably like our English "devil," who sweeps for all Coblenz), we have not even a chimney-piece. The climbing boy here is really one of the finest men in the place. He sweeps the chimney, — the long iron pipes of the stoves are cleared by a live Friesland hen, a sort of fowl which has its feathers turned back the wrong way. When she is in the pipe a fire is made, and the heat forces her to make her way into the chimney with the soot among her ruffled feathers. She then cries "grauchschlacht!" which is the German for "all up!" and this is at least as true as some bits of Von Raumer.

I am writing this gossip partly to amuse Mrs. Dilke. The barber-surgeon I settled with thus: He wrote that in consideration that I might not be able to afford it, he consented to take one dollar instead of two. To which I replied, that I merely resisted an imposition, and should hand over the difference to the poor. This I did to the poor of Arzheim, near Ehrenbreitstein, where 280 have suffered from scarlet fever; and a subscription was opened by public appeal from the over-burgomaster of Coblenz, and is now closed, after two months' collection, having raised twelve pounds! — a smallish amount for a city containing a governor-general, two commandants, over and under-presidents, ditto burgomasters, and about twenty-five to thirty carriage families, and many rich tradesmen: but these are anything but the honest, conscientious, liberal, orderly, warm-hearted, intellectual Germans we give the country just credit for. The Coblenzers have other attributes. To return to my *leech-gatherer*. I do not intend to want again either physician or apothecary. I am no believer in astrological conjunctions, but I must insist on a sinister aspect in that case. A Jew doctor playing into the hands of his brother-in-law, the apothecary, who has been described beforehand by "Gil Blas," viz.: "He goes strictly to mass, but at the bottom of his heart he is a Jew, like Pilate, for he has become Catholic through interest."

As Jews must not be apothecaries here, and Hebrews do not forgive apostacy in their own brothers even, I fear their good understanding must be allowed to be ominous. Now for a bit of farce in one of the same tribe. He came to me to draw up an advertisement for him in English, on the strength of which, I suppose, he has set up here as Professor of Philosophy and *English*. Franck knows an officer who has *learned*, and he cannot understand his English at all. The officer will have his revenge when he has to drill the Professor! We are now more *au fait* here, but we have to fight every inch. I am now in health and spirits and do not mind it; but I wish, for the sake of the lovely country I am now able to enjoy, I could come to other conclusions. I am not writing from spleen or prejudice, or resentment at the loss of money, but to give you my cool and deliberate impressions for your guidance; and a resident has peculiar opportunities for observation. Prejudice be hanged! and I will help to pull its legs. But I want fair play for my countrymen, against whom there is much illiberal feeling, which is the more annoying, because Germans from other parts, who think well of us, are surprised to find opinion against us on the Rhine where it would be presumed we are so well known. As a sample of what I mean, there is Schreiber's sketch of "Die Engländer in Baden" referred to in your No. 431 of the "Athenæum," which I wish had fallen to my lot to review. I would have answered him with facts. The charge that the rectitude of many of the English is not to be uniformly depended upon is a grave one, on which I might retort fairly from my own experience as equivalent to his; and choose for my motto, in a new sense, "Beware — for there are counterfeits *abroad*." With few exceptions judging from those I have had to do with, I should put them in two great classes — Jew Germans, and German Jews. It may seem a harsh verdict, but it is *forced* upon me. As for the English quarrelling about coachmen's fares, &c., it is hardly worthy a traveller to squabble about petty over-charges, but extortions may become too gross and palpable to put up with. There is all along shore here, now-a-days at least, a sharking, grasping appetite, which growing by what it feeds on, has become ogre-like; and knowing the English to be rich, they have not known where, prudently, or with good policy, to stop. There was a colonel here, the other day only, crying out, naturally, at being charged in this *cheap* country five shillings for a bed; the landlord of the hotel in question chose at the Carnival to burlesque an English family travelling: he has told me, the English are by far his best customers, but the ridicule was congenial to the spirit of the inhabitants. The truth is, we are marked for plunder; and laughed at, for the facility with which we are plucked, as if it were a matter of difficulty to cheat those, who in some degree confide in you — for we do generally set forth with a strong prepossession in favour of German honesty. I believe in it myself, but not here, where the very peasantry (whom I like) seem to lose it. The other day a woman, who used to sell us a sort of curd cheese, taking advantage of Fanny, who carried the money, took six instead of three groschen, and has never since put in an appearance. Again, a man, who left a flower for Jane's approval, who declined it, called for it over night quite drunk, took it away, brought it back next morning, and made her pay for it because a bud was broken! these two are within ten days. Schreiber taunts residents like ourselves with "a petty and ridiculous economy," but it is mere resistance to extortion directed pointedly against the English. I never will concede that the rule, that we are to be robbed, only because we are, or are supposed to be, rich, is anything but a brigand feeling. Yet so it is. There is a separate tariff, well-understood, and tacitly acted upon, so that you shall see an English and German gentleman sitting at the same table d'hôte, eating the same dinner, and drinking the same wine, but at very different cost! It is quite a freemasonry, and the very figures in the *carte* stand for several amounts. One night we sent for a bill of fare for supper, and De Franck pointed out to me roast beef, (in English) four groschen, and directly under it, the same dish, (in German) three groschen. These things are somewhat repulsive to those who happen to be their guests, should they chance to find besides that their character is attacked as unfairly as their purse. I *know* that they retail stories about us, which have falsehood on the face of them, such as the Bible story in Schreiber, which is altogether out of keeping. As to our getting into rows and trespassing, I used to watch the steamer's arrival, and never saw a disturbance, but with a *German* lady, accused by the steward of secreting a spoon. But that Englishmen *might* get into rows I think very possible, and natural; I expect it myself. The lower class, not mere thieves and vagabonds like Londoners, but apprentices, workmen, and boys almost well-dressed, are blackguardly disposed.

Fishing has brought me in contact with them. I have *never* been without annoyance, and it is positively *unsafe* to stand within pelt of the Mosel bridge. Those officers, who have taken to it after our example at Ehrenbreitstein, have positively had to post men to defend them from *large* sticks and stones. I hope, as the clown says, here be *facts*. Good or bad politically, the making all men soldiers serves to lick these cubs into human shape; it makes them cut their hair, wash themselves, and behave decently, in fact as Puckler Muskau says, the men, who have served, and those who have not, are different animals indeed. I wish I could with honesty write more in the tone of Mrs. Trollope, whose book, by the way, I have just read; but although so treacley, it does not please the natives. Heaven knows why, for she does not object to one thing in Prussia, but the smoking. She is however, wrong there in one point, as may be gathered from the pretty strong sentiments she puts into the mouths of the German girls against pipes. A likely matter when they have been used to sniff "*backy*" from the father, who took them first on his knees, to the brother they played with.

On the contrary, and quite the reverse, they embroider tobacco bags for presents to the young gentlemen as English girls knit purses. But so Anti-English a writer as Mrs. T., who never omits an opportunity of letting down her countrymen, might be expected to be blind to the Anti-English feeling abundant in these parts. There is no doubt of its existence, I manage to read their papers, and the tone is the same.

Extracts for example headed, "Distress in *Rich* England." Like "the haughty Isle of shopkeepers," a phrase made use of by Schreiber. 'T is the mark of the beast; they covet our riches, they resent our political influence, and perhaps are jealous of the distinction shown to the English in *some* of the highest quarters. In spite of Raumer (a *jewel* by the way) I think the spirit enters into our commerce.

The merchant here, I had your wine of, said he did not hope for any reduction of our duties on their wines, because the Prussian Tariff is so very unfavourable to us. Our goods are in request, so that even they simulate English labels, &c., &c., but I think their introduction is not coveted by the powers. My little package was detained some time at the frontier, on the frivolous pretext, that the weight of every article, a fish-hook for instance, was not specified. I believe the tariff is also adverse to French and Italians; all I know is, many of their products are bad and dear: say, oranges from two pence halfpenny to 3*d.* a piece; salad oil dear and execrable, &c., &c. And now to Schreiber again; I take his for my text-book, because he represents the mass. Their usual ridicule of our habits, &c., might fairly and with interest be retaliated. For instance an Englishman with coat-pockets "big enough *to hold a couple of folios*," is no more ridiculous a figure than a German with ditto capacious enough for a pipe and a bag of tobacco; but this far from unusual sneer at our literary and reading propensity is somewhat misplaced in Intellectual Germany *the country of Goethe.* A book here seems a bugbear. I think I told you of the remark of the Jew Doctor on seeing a "Times" paper; in the same style my new Doctor took up the "Athenæum," supposing it to be a monthly.

When I said, "weekly," he threw up his hands and eyes, and wondered how we found time for it. Time, however, is the thing least wanted here, for they do not live at *our rate*, and consequently have more leisure; but it is not "learned leisure," from simple want of will.

They prefer the Virginian to other leaves, — and volumes of smoke.

The "Rhein und Mosel Zeitung" supplies them with abundant reading, and its standing articles, probably therefore favorite ones, are on beet-root, sugar, and railroads.

Their talk is of thalers, thalers, thalers, except when they smoke in the hotels of a night, or at the Casino, and then the Quakers could not hold a more silent Conversazione.

Galignani *is* prohibited, and the only English papers allowed are the "Globe," "Courier," and the "Albion," or some such name. So much for the Intellectuals. Personally I cannot complain, for a Colonel has translated my Eugene Aram for his wife, having heard of it through Bulwer's novel: Bulwer (who is a demi-god here) and the Pfennig Magazine, and native works on medicine and mechanical arts, are the main bulk advertised here, but I guess not much sold. Another fact, and I quit the subject. The extorting spirit is known and admitted by some of the better class — Jane, at request from the other side, has formed a very agreeable intimacy with a Miss von B——, who was educated at Nieuwiëd, and speaks tolerable English. She *volunteered* to accompany Jane to buy anything, saying she knew the English were imposed on, and informed her that her late father, a lieutenant-general, paid Dr. —— at the rate of ten silber groschen or a shilling a visit. He charged me forty-five, or four shillings and sixpence a visit, for being an Englishman. What follows is, I think, conclusive as to what I have said of a sort of free-masonry, &c. I happened to doubt whether the majors and captains here could afford to keep up such equipages on their pay, when F—— referred me to another officer (of ancient Polish family), I have met, and he frankly told me that they could. But supposing a major with family, &c., to make a certain appearance, and live in a certain style on his pay 2000 dollars, I must at once *for the same things* set down 1000 more for being an Englishman.

It follows that tradesmen, inn-keepers, all who have to do with the English, exact a *profit* of 33 per cent. *extra*, and yet cannot be pleased with their customers. Suppose some English Schreiber, in inditing a sketch of the German watering-places, were to adopt the portentous text of "take care of your pockets." * Suppose he were to end his book with a sarcastic hint of Sir Peter Teazle's, "I must go, but I leave my character behind me!" I give you the facts, because in the Athenæum you are sometimes called upon as a judge, between the natives of both countries, as in Schreiber's case. I do not want, like Jonathan in England, "a war, and all on my own account," nor, Irish-like, to whiten the English by blackening the Germans. Above all, I speak only of what I have seen and know, or have heard from good witnesses, and my locale is Coblenz; though the same thing may prevail on the other routes

* My father enlarged on this text in "Up the Rhine," where he gives a song, one verse of which I extract. — T. H.

"Ye Tourists and Travellers bound to the Rhine,
Provided with passport, that requisite docket,
First listen to one little whisper of mine,
Take care of your pocket! Take care of your pocket!"

of the English, *pro ex:* Baden. It is for you that I have set it down, and I beg you to believe, in no spite, or resentment, or prejudice; but to put you on your guard, and prepare you for perhaps a very altered state of things on the Rhine, not belonging more to the natives than to human nature, except in degree. But I wished justice for my countrymen, and disclaim personal vengeance, though I confess to have felt irritation. The tone of my book will be quite otherwise, I know it is unwelcome to read as to write such passages, and especially to introduce such actors on such a stage, with the Rhine and its mountains for the scenery. And moreover there is good and beautiful and whimsical to discourse of pleasantly, so pray read the foregoing in the same spirit that its author writ, and then hand over the substance of my remarks to the censor to be used "as occasion may require." Fair play is a jewel, and I like to see it set in the "Athenæum. Besides I do not know your Editor personally, but I suspect him of a little over-leaning towards the Germans. I picture him with "an awful fell of hair," and a serio-comico-metaphysico-romantico visage, moulded in brown bread made rather heavy, a big body made dropsically corpulent by fattening on thin wine, and a pair of stout legs of no particular shape, on which he partly walks, partly marches, having been drilled when a student. Like Pope and Cowper, and others of the learned, he wears a cap; but with a conceited cock on one side, and hangs a tassel from its apex. On his forefinger, a huge ring with an engraved stone or glass, that might serve Mrs. von D—— at a pinch for a jellymould; and he has chains enough on his bosom to hang him in. His waistcoat seems cut out of the train of Iris's court-dress, set off by a snuff-brown coat, and sad-green breeches — a sort of hybrid between a peacock and Minerva's fowl — grave and gaudy. When he eats, he prefers after soup the meat that was boiled in it — a mere residuum — like the patent ginless bread of Pimlico. He seasons it with mud-coloured mustard. He drinks a wine so sharp, that like the "Accipe Hock" of the Templar, it pierces your very vitals. When he is awake he dreams, when he is asleep he snores music, that, as Zelter says, by its very noise, "reminds you of the universal silence!" If he look pensive it is because he cannot fathom the immeasurable, grasp the infinite, or comprehend the incomprehensible. Should he be a little cracked he writes — when he gets purblind he paints, and you have the portrait of his mistress the Muse, as a little old woman with red toads dropping out of her mouth. Poet or Painter, he tries to be sublime, and makes a monster a "most ridiculous monster," or rather a herd of monsters, and makes them act monstrously, like the fantastic shadows in Carpenter's microscope, supposing you had mixed their drop of water with a ditto of brandy. If he smiles, it is with the idea of "reading much, learning much, and dying young!" by a horse-pistol with a leaf out of Bettine for wadding. Whilst he smokes he pastoralises; drunk, he moralises; sober, he romanticises; mad, he philosophises. There, Wolfgang von Dilke, there's a rally *à la* Randall, in return for your fighting me up into a German corner. By the bye your notices made me long to read Von

Raumer's England. It must be a capital book, but methinks he is apt to make azure of Prussian blue. Yet when I spoke of him here to our doctor, he seemed not to like him, and said he was considered a Jacobin. For example, too much credit is taken as to their contented and tolerant clergy. For instance, *here*, this is a Catholic province; the magistrates and a few more Lutherans must tolerate perforce a whole population nearly of unreformed. Prussia is formed of many provinces, some oughts, and some crosses, like the old game on the slate, and to be intolerant would be only to set one province against another, "hey dog — hey bull!" so that it would be dangerous for one party to tyrannise over the other.

A thing occurred here the other day that made a great sensation: the priest or curé refused to bury a drawing-master, who professed, but had not attended, his church, for many years. He said he was forbidden by the rules of the Council of Trent. The Lutheran minister was applied to, who buried him at once, and as it is usual to preach a funeral sermon for each defunct, the following Sunday his church was crowded with Catholics, Jews, and all denominations, who were eager and curious to hear how he would treat the subject. He preached a good temperate sermon on the text "Judge not, that ye be not judged," which made a great impression. The plan here, which is good, is that of both religions the ministers are paid by the King or State, an arrangement I should like for England and Ireland, — or let every one pay their own, as in America. As to Education, I think our Government does wisely not to interfere too rashly. Something may be left to the sense of the people. The infamous boarding-schools of former times are dying or dead, and replaced by proprietary ones without Government interference. If they meddle, let it be to reform Oxford, and the like; and, least of all, let us have the School a dependant on the Church, — with a Parson-Usher in each, preaching and teaching German philosophical "spiritualism," and "illumination and sanctification," which "reaches far beyond steam-engines and hydraulic presses."

But even Von Raumer is not reliable. Come lay your Frankfort hand, just above your Heidelberg or Darmstadt stomach, on your Dresden heart, and tell us with your München mouth, do you really believe the story of the factory boy's lament for pigs and poetry? Did you ever with your Ingelheimer eyes, on the Royal Birthday in London, see the innumerable children with flowers and flags, or hear with your Langen Schwalbach ears their chorus of "God save the King"? Again did you never hear with your Berlin auriculars, that row of street blackguard boys notorious *throughout* Germany, and characteristic of the Prussian capital, which Von R. with his national taste for music calls "the prattle of little children"?

As for his quizzes on our cookery (Mrs. Dilke, I am appealing to you and your old cook, who went away and is come back again), *is* English soup so sloppy that it must hide its weakness by a covering of pepper and spice? Lord help the man! he has been souping with the Sick Poor! I never saw any soup or broth in England but when cold was a perfect jelly, "as you might chuck over the house." As for his pepperless rice soup, *chacun à son goût*, but was not Bedreddin Hassan capitally sentenced for not putting pepper in a cream-tart? What does he mean by the "monotony of our roast beef, roast mutton, roast veal"? Why should not roast beef be roast beef, and always roast beef, like "the bill, the whole bill, and nothing but the bill?" I like that decided style. Is it any better for being, as here, roast horse, or with rank oil, or turned butter, sometimes like roast "sea horse"? Is Williams's boiled beef any the worse for being *only* boiled beef, is it better for being here like land stock-fish? Is our roast veal worse than theirs? — how they roast it is a culinary miracle, unless on a lark spit. Their seven-day calves, and seven-year porkers ought, according to Lamb's celebrated wish about his sister, to "throw their joint existences into one common heap!" I defy you to eat their roast mutton here, without scriptural reminiscences of rams, and burnt offerings. And then for *his* sauce about *our one* sauce for fish, don't they make pickled salmon of everything with scales, fresh or salt, with vinegar, vinegar, vinegar? As for his twaddle about Phidias and Praxiteles being French cooks, and his comparison of our joints to "an Egyptian divinity in simple dignified repose, *with arms and legs* closely pinioned in the same position!" (he has mistaken a trussed turkey for a round of beef or a fillet of veal) I will only say a village jobbing carpenter would be ashamed of such a *style!* Egyptian indeed! don't they poison everything with garlic, and consume Egyptian wages (onions) enough to build a new set of pyramids? Now for his Linnæus and Jussieu, if our vegetables *do* "appear in puris naturalibus," is it not better than if they were in "*im*puris naturalibus," full of "snips and snails," and the huge red slugs that crawl about here, in size and shape looking like live German sausages! How do *they* dress vegetables! Why make salads of them first, and then boil them, or *vice versâ.* I do believe the "Devil sends cooks," and they are German ones. The French are *artists,* the Germans are *daubers* in cookery. They are (in all that is grub-berly) lubberly, blubberly, and in regard to cleanliness, not over scrubberly! Was n't I nearly choked once by fishbones amongst a dish of fried potatoes? 'T is fact, and did n't I see a starved dog refuse to take the place and portion of a German gentleman unexpectedly absent from his accustomed place at the table d'hôte? Von Dilke be hanged! Catch him having a German cook at the Clarence! Have n't their own doctors discovered that their sausages contain an active poison, and is not every one of their messes a slow one? I *will* stand up for our English kitchen, especially now Jane is a cook in it. Vive Dr. Kitchener! if he is n't dead: and an echo responds from Düsseldorf, very like Mrs. L——'s voice, "Vive Dr. Kitchener!" When she last wrote to Jane she was watching a hash with one eye, according to his "oracle." Ask Head about German cookery, he says their sauces are always either sour or greasy, but I have gone a step beyond his experience, they can be sour and greasy too. And now for a triumphant clincher as to the respective merits of German and English cookery. There is a sort of *mésalliance* that occurs in England sometimes; nay I know personally of an instance, for W.

C. married the woman that dressed his dinner, but I have now before me "Der Preussiche Staat, in allen seinen Veziehungun," an authentic work, and I cannot find one instance of a German, who married his cook. This is not prejudice but statistics! But don't let this frighten you, Mrs. Dilke, from coming here, lest you should have to feast on *pommes de terre frites*. Jane can stew, and boil, and roast, and bake. You should hear her battering her beef-steaks, as if they were the children, or see Tom walk in with his little wig powdered or floured, from his mother-sick fit having interfered with her fit of pigeon-piety. You should hear De Franck congratulating her on her high health, or Miss von B. on her rosy English complexion, when the real secret is fried chops. So I speak not complainingly, but critically only, of the national cuisine.

You *must* come to the grand manœuvres (end of August), which will be well worth seeing. Better to see than be *born to*, say you. De Franck amused us much with his description of drilling the Dominies. Every man here must be a soldier, and two years is the rule; but the school-masters have the *indulgence* of only six weeks of it. But then in those six weeks they are expected to become as proficient as the "two year olds," and accordingly they are hard at it, soldiering "from morn till dewy eve"—the poor sedentaries! Franck described them drawn up with round shoulders, bent thighs, and other pedigogical attributes, so weak, and so bewildered! Sometimes an unlucky Dominic mounting guard, has even to put up with the gibes, nay missiles, of his quondam scholars, whom he cannot, for once, punish.

Is it not laughable to picture to oneself? What a subject for me! I must make a new revolution at Stoke Pogis, and let the mayor, having been up the Rhine, attempt to form a Landwehr. You know the place Dilke, just fancy Dominie Sampson, with a musket on his shoulder, standing *at ease* on Ehrenbreitstein.

Pray tell Mr. Reynolds* what he has escaped by being born, as Dr. Watts says, in a Christian land. He is an excellent *Blue*, but would not turn up well with *Red.* What a "six weeks' vacation!" What a march of mind for the schoolmasters abroad! It must seem to them like a nightmare dream, till assured of the reality, by feeling instead of the long flowing locks, affected here by the student, the bald *regulation* nape. The situation must seem as bewildering as Dr. Pangloss' with a tulip-eared bull puppy between his knees. Fancy Westminsterian Braine learning the "brain-spattering art." Imagine Dr. G—— mounting guard at the Mint, or Principal O—— standing sentinel by the Regent's bomb, whistling "Lawk a' mercy on us, sure this be not I," with a pantomime change, in the distance, of the London University into Sandhurst College. Our doctor's son is doing duty as a private in De Franck's regiment, so is the son of another M. D., and they are under no slight apprehension of having to carry a knapsack at the review. How should you like a taste of that same? Imagine yourself wanting to march in *three divisions*, in request by Lord Hill, Holmes, and Mr. Jack Junk, at the same time. Fancy Wentworth dancing at one of his mother's genteelest parties in the uniform of a private of the Tower Hamlets. And what

* My grandfather, head writing-master at Christ's Hospital. — T. H.

a review you would make; mind, not a criticism. Yourself, with your eye-glass, in the Rifles; A. Cunningham in the Grenadiers; Chorley in the band; H—— in the Artillery; T—— a Lancer; the stout C—— in the "Light Bobs;" and John F—— a "worthy Pioneer." Alas! for the "Athenæum!" Mrs. Dilke would have to be a suttler! By the bye we got our present lodgings in spite of the captain of the —th, who would have given five dollars a year more; but his wife, a termagant, was well known as the "suttler," (her nickname amongst the military,) and our landlord would not have her at no price. I hope Jane won't lower his rent still further. * * * *

There are some here, in appearance to the eye, anything but gentlemen, in the best sense of the word. You cannot mistake them.

Perhaps they have got the worst attributes of the French Revolution, a *nominal equality*, which puts the low, base, vulgar, and rich on a *false level* with "God Almighty's gentleman," which rank I do seek with all my heart; and endeavour that the English character shall not suffer at my hands, and though I resent, on public grounds, what I meet with, I am content to be a dweller here, whose character is to be judged by its own merits. But I feel the question gravely, and recommend it to your consideration. *I* may be prejudiced, but *F*—— is a good witness. Give me credit for honesty, when he tells you he as readily fights, what you may call, my prejudices, as those of the Germans. After all, *cui bono*, what I write? Why, after all, I appeal to the "Athenæum," because it is as free from party and prejudice as myself, *and no more.* There 's a hit for you, Big Ben, in answer to your " write-hander."

Besides, it has, and must have, an influence from its honesty, impartiality, and ability, and therefore, with all my humble three dittos, I endeavour to give it the benefit of my views.

W——, the other officer, says the same thing of the Rhenishers.

He calls them " méchant," and says they are a much better sort of people elsewhere. He says, moreover, that some Germans, lately returned from Switzerland, have made the observation, that the people there are corrupted and deteriorated, in the same way as I judge them to be partly here. There are two subjects which form handles against us, and are rather favourite topics here,— Ireland,— and the Duke of Wellington's remarks on the discipline of the Prussian army,— which have provoked much angry discussion.

As for Ireland, I am glad to see there is a chance of righting her at last, but what a sorry figure do some of the Peers cut !

I have just got the Athenæum containing Raumer. He is very flattering to us in some things, but his true picture of Ireland gives one pain, abroad,— to think what foreigners *must* conceive of our wisdom or government. I doubt, however, of the wisdom of returning for a remedy to the good old times when " *mendicant* monks imparted *their* goods to the poor." He learnt to *bull* in Ireland, seemingly. Again, I do not clearly understand whether the " unhappy nation that has been for four-and-forty years seeking for liberty in all directions," refers to

France or England. But, in either case, I do not agree with his prescription of "moderation, contentedness, and humility," by which I understand a sort of waiters on Providence, gaping for "a thrice happy Prussian's" condition, a "free, proprietary peasantry, — a contented and tolerant clergy, and well educated youth," at the hands of the Tories or their equivalents. But I, perhaps, misunderstand him, — the issue, being to be Murrayan, gave me the impression. The two countries are widely different; what a *good, absolute* King can do here, cannot be done with us. If our peasantry were free and proprietary, I think they would work as hard, and be as contented as the Germans. But the English labourer, labour as he may, can but be a pauper; and it seems a little unreasonable to require him to sit at Hope's or Content's table, eating *nothing*, with the same cheerfulness and gaiety as the barber's brother at the Barmecide's.

They have just carried by, in procession, with boys, two and two, a *dead schoolmaster!* Poor fellow; have they drilled him to death, or is he a deserter by anticipation? What a new translation they have of "*cedant arma togæ!*" How would Othello's pathetic farewell to arms read to a Prussian Pedagogue? Methinks he would have the black boy well horsed for it. Well! poor * * * * is gone, and, parodying Coleridge's apostrophe on the death of the Dominie, "May he be wafted to heaven by disembodied spirits that are no *Corporals!*"

* * * *

I was very much amused the other day with R——'s account of his taking an emetic.

He says he sat for an hour expecting naturally something would come of it, but nothing stirred.

It agreed with him just as well as if he had taken any other wine than antimonial. It was rather comfortable than otherwise. So he had recourse to warm water, of which he drank about a dozen large cups consecutively, but they made themselves quite at home with the wine. Then he tried tea, — in hopes of "tea and turn out," but it staid with the wine and water. So he had recourse to the warm water again, which staid still, and so did some soup which he took on the top of all: and then, despairing of the case, he went to bed with his corporation unreformed! Now, was not this a tenacious, retentive stomach, so determined never to give up anything it had acquired, good or bad; a lively type of a Tory! It would make a nice little fable done into verse like Peter Pindar's.*

We have had several little excursions. One to the Laacher Zee, amongst the volcanic mountains. We went on Whit-Monday, but it ought to have been *Ash*-Wednesday, considering the soil of the road we went through. Their proper scavengers would have been Cinderellas. The walls and houses thereabouts are built with lava, and the lake itself is supposed to occupy an extinct crater. What a lovely, little, secluded lake it is, embosomed in trees, and perched on the crest of a mountain, not like an eagle's nest, but a water "Roc's." It is said to be, in the middle, 200 yards deep, and the water is

* It is not improbable that the emetic was rendered innocuous by R——'s having been long used to German cookery, which had made a modern Mithridates of him in this respect. — T. H.

supernaturally clear. We fished, but of course could catch nothing, though there be huge Jack and Perch; in truth, as I could see my line from the top, of course they could see it at the bottom. There is a decayed church and cloisters, and the monkery and gardens afford delightful residence. There is also a referendarius here who does not care for it; what a taste! He is seldom there. It is a delicious spot. I honour the olden monks for the taste with which they pitched their tents. Methought as I walked in their cloisters I could have been willingly a Benedictine myself, especially when I saw a pair of huge antlers over one of the doors, — like a sign of "good venison within." We have booked this place for you to visit, when you come. Indeed, we thought of you, at our "champêtre," and drank your healths in our wine, for as the "hospitallers" have quitted, we had to carry our cold baked meats with us. The return was through a country reminding me of some of the romantic parts of Scotland, but on a larger scale, and more diversely wooded. Through mountain-passes, and by rapid, winding, trout-streams, we suddenly came upon Tönnenstein; a little Brunnen in a lovely glen. I asked the priestess (a buxom young damsel in a Cologne cap, which you know is somewhat like a muslin soup-plate) very gravely whether the water was good for a man "with a wife and children," and she replied as gravely in the affirmative, handing me a glass of *bubble* without *squeak*. With wine and sugar, it drinks like champagne, but it is good neat. But, Lord! what an effervescing, gunpowder plot of ground do we Germans live upon! I scarcely seem safer than your brother at Chichester.

Every spring beneath us seems boiling hot, or boiling cold. And if I was a freeholder, I should feel some quakings in reckoning all between the sky and the *earth's centre* as my own. I should certainly content myself with tilling the upper crust of the soil instead of being too curious in mining. Bless us all! should our Teutonic Terra be seized with active inflammation in her stomachic regions, instead of the evident chronic one she suffers under! If we have any living Saurians below, as the Rev. Kerby opines, they must be salamanders. How little do the infant Germans,* with an eruption on all their heads, dream of another that may happen under their feet. We have been once or twice to Lahnstein, a favourite resort here, on the river Lahn, where we have obtained the credit of fishing with "a spell," on account of our success; when the old native anglers had failed, simply because we fished at the top and they at the bottom. They have no notion of fly-fishing. The only attempt we ever saw was a Captain of Engineers gravely fishing in the Moselle with a hackle-*fly* and a *worm*, at once; but the *infancy* of his art may excuse the *tops* and *bottoms*. For the sake of Mrs. Dilke, I must relate two adventures at Lahnstein, the first almost as laughable as Mr. L——'s. Whilst we were fishing, all of a sudden I missed De Franck,—but spied him at last up to his neck in the middle of two rocks between which he had slipped in jumping from one to another. He made a strange figure when he came out,

* My father elsewhere remarked this prevalent peculiarity of the German children's heads. It would seem to denote their Scandinavian origin, as descendants of the Scalds. — T. H.

— the best lay figure for a River-god imaginable, — for German sporting jackets have an infinity of pockets, and there was a separate jet of water from every one, as well as from his sleeves, trousers, and each spout of his drowned moustachios (N. B. they 're very long). He did not seem much improved, when, having gone to the Inn, he returned in a suit of the landlord's, who, though twice as tall, was not half so stout. However, we did not care for appearances, for we thought nobody would notice him, as it was not a holiday, and there was no company. But we were mistaken. The landlord's dog sniffed a robbery, and knowing his master's clothes again, insisted on stripping the counterfeit, and was obliged to be pulled off *vi et armis*. The landlord was very much distressed, and made a thousand apologies; and, to do him justice, was a very obliging, honest, reasonable fellow, and certainly deserved to be paid better than *with his own money, out of his own waistcoat pocket*, by De Franck, as we discovered afterwards. This was the comic part, now for the tragic. In the meanwhile, Jane, whose legs are not so elephantine as they were, you will readily suppose, made shift to scramble, with Miss Von B——, up to the ruined castle of Lahn-eck.

Having seen everything on its old ground-floor, female curiosity, prevailing even over female fear, tempted them up a dilapidated staircase to one of the mouldering attics; and then, how unfortunately fortunate! some half-dozen of the topmost stairs caught the contagion of curiosity, and paid a visit to the cellars. You may imagine the duet that ensued *in a very high key* — but as you know I am deaf and De Franck was more intent on the *perch below*, than on the *perch above*, it was, consequently, a long hour (Jane says six) before they were rescued, heartily sick, you may be sure, of the local and the vocal. They swear they will never *ascend* any old ruins again, so I suppose the next time we shall have to *hoist* them out of some old subterranean.

However, the event has supplied a new lay or legend of the Rhine — only in *my* version, after a lapse of half a century, two female skeletons were found on the battlements, with their mouths wide open.*

These excursions have done me good every way, and joined to a *rule* of going out every practicable evening to fish in the Rhine or Moselle by way of exercise, have restored me to some strength. I have prospered in health ever since the great effusion of blood — in fact, had I been well bled at first, all would have been saved. My friends may now be easy about me — and all the rest are well. Jane and Fanny mean to bathe at a bath-house on the Rhine bridge. It is very healthy and pleasant, only the tow-rope of a barge took off the whole roof, and so frightened the female dippers, that some of them ran out and fainted on the bridge.†

* My father subsequently worked up this incident into a very thrilling sketch in the "New Monthly," entitled "The Tower of Lahneck." — T. H.

† The following is a description of this catastrophe in the words of Martha Penny, the Winifred Jenkins of "Up the Rhine." — T. H.

"A nasty grate barge come spinnin down the river, and by sum mismanagement the towin rope hung too low down, and jist ketching the Bath House, wipt off the hole roof in a jiffy! . . . In course it was skreek upon skreek from the other rooms; and thinks I, if tops come off, so may bottoms, and in that case down sinks the floting bath,

The bath man and bath woman, concerned for their subscribers, very wisely *restored* them by carrying them all *in* again — one by one.

I am glad you liked the wine, but you must come here for the next. You may drink my improvement in Art with all my heart — but as to my sketch, the distinctness you object to is characteristic, and peculiar in Spring.

I am as clear as to that, as the atmosphere. De Franck and I verified that you could see the smoke of a pipe *beyond* the Moselle. De Franck made the remark the other day, that it was like "seeing through a glass." In fact I have once or twice neglected my spectacles from not feeling the *want* of them. You must see it to believe it I grant. Why I almost fancy myself an eagle, or at least a Dollond, as I look along the mountainous horizon with the minutest shrubbery defined on it. I recollect, especially last year, when I came up the Rhine I felt almost that I had seen gnomes and fairies — the people at work on the face of the mountains looked so *distinct* and yet so *small*, they appeared literal dwarfs — for want of that medium mistiness which ordinarily signifies distance. The only conviction you had, sensually,

and we 're all drownded creatures as sure as rats. So out I run on to the bridge of boats, jist as I was, with nothing on but my newdity; but decency 's one thing, and death 's another. The rest of the bathing ladies did the same, and some of them, pore things, fainted ded away on the bords. Luckily none of the mail sects was passing by, for xcept won Waterloo blue bonnet we was all in a naturalized state like so many Eves. . . . Thank Gudness, there was no wus harm done; but Catshins says, wen the roof was took off, I ought to have crost myself, and, to be sure, so I ought — as well as said Sanctus Marius, instead of O Criminy!"

of their being so remote was from the silence: you saw, but you could not hear, the blows of their pickaxes, etc. The effect is really miraculous. My eyes seemed well washed with fairy euphrasy; methought, what a pure element it must be that we German fishes now swim in! as good for the lungs as the "Lung Arno." Some of us find it too pure if taken neat, and so mix it with smoke.

N. B. The defunct, lately carried by with "dirges due," was not a schoolmaster, but a butcher, whose widow had borrowed the boys to give éclat. The Spanish general, Spinola, died "of having nothing to do," and I suppose Lent killed the Flesher. That same Lent was a horrid invention, at least for inland towns. I hope it is not the bad fish, but they are dying here on all hands,—two or three children a day. Thank God, we seem in a little Goshen, all well! But we have had an omen, at least equal to a raven on the chimney-pot. The children are just come in from a walk, and a *strange* doctor stopped Fanny, and talked to her in the street!

* * * *

I have never had any of the vulgar insane dread of the Catholics. It appears to me too certain that they are decaying *at the core*, and by the following natural process:—men take a huge stride at first from Catholicism into Infidelity, like the French, and then by a short step backwards in a reaction, attain the *juste milieu.* You see I philosophise, but it is in the air of Germany; only I do not smoke with it.

I cannot help agreeing with Von Raumer about English music; I am deaf and have heard as little good as he; but why sneer at our buying *better?* if we purchased Italian, we paid lately the same compliment to the German. I believe in their "real music," but as to their "real song" I have a creed that the "sickly sentimentality" is as much a characteristic of the best German as the worst English. As for our painters, whom he despises, let him show me a German Turner (except of the stomach), a Stanfield, an Etty, a Stump, a Gump. They are as unheard of as our musicians, except a notorious German, who daubed for George the Fourth. But when were the German artists pictorially great with pen or pencil? Fuseli represented both classes. In their sublimest they introduce the ridiculous, whereas a real genuine Kentuckian in his ridiculous approaches the sublime. I would rather, as to style, prefer the last. Fair play 's a jewel: if you want examples, I'll give them to you out of Goethe himself. We had a specimen of their fine arts yesterday, on a flag carried before a funeral: on one side was a Virgin and Child, both *dark*, mulatto, as if inclining to Lord Monboddo's theory that Adam was *black*, or half-and-half — whereas, on the other side was a bishop, *in pontificalibus*, blessing three little children in a literal washing-tub,* washed as fair as an English mother could desire — as Jane, for instance. This is fact, and it is as fair to judge from it as from the drawings of lap-dogs and poodles at our Society of Arts, an imbecility long since

* This was a representation of St. Nicholas restoring to life the "Three Young Men of Noble Family," who got into a literal pickle, *vide legends passim*. St. Nicholas was the favourite saint with us children, for, on the eve of his day, we used to put our shoes outside the bedroom door, and his Reverence was believed to have filled them in

marked down as a subject for the "Comic" — with that void Aiken, at its head or tail, whom Coleridge used to compare to an "Aching void!" *Apropos* of Art, in the palace here; in the concert-room, there was to have been a series of frescos from the "Last Judgment" of Rubens, very appropriate supposing the orchestra *all trumpets.* But as the laws of *acoustics* only had been neglected, the concert-room was abandoned, and it is now devoted to the sittings of assize, when the frescos would be of some relevance, and accordingly they are *not* there. I have this on the authority of Schreiber, the guide-man, noticed shortly before Raumer, to whom I owe a grudge and will pay it. As the Americans say, if they *poke* their *fun* at me, I will poke again.

* * * *

I am hard at work at my "Comic," somewhat puzzled for subjects, as most of my foreign ones must go to the German book, which I want to make as good as possible.

I do get the "Athenæum," though somewhat more tardily than formerly, and it is a great treat. It *ought* to be very successful. We admired much the articles on Talfourd's "Ion," and Taylor's political book: my mind misgives me they are yours. Pray write as often as you can. Jane desires me to say she longs for Mrs.

the night with the toys, &c., we discovered in them the next day. I believe, but won't confess to any experience, that a child who had been naughty, generally found a rod in his slipper in lieu of the toys. It is almost to be wished that the German tree, had brought over the St. Nicholas' day custom with it as a branch institution. — T. H.

Dilke's promised letter. As for myself, you will not soon have some more last words. But I do live in hope of meeting you bodily this autumn, and would write a whole "Athenæum" (a double one) to *help you out.*

Methinks *fat* as most of the company would be, we should almost talk ourselves into consumptions. Mind, no more Margate! If I chalk all along the dead wall in Grosvenor Place, it would be, "Ask for Coblenz," "Try the Rhine," "Beware of Dublin," "Inquire for Alten Graben!"

We often fancy ourselves in your family circle, and wish you could take a stick to it, and trundle it over here. Pray remember us kindly to everybody, to William and Wentworth, and the rest of the family, "by hook and by *Snook.*" Desire Fanny Staunton to add moustachios to my portrait, and put a pipe in my mouth.

Jane goes all lengths with me in her love, and so does Fanny, and so would Hood jun. if he could, as he should. The manœuvres will begin the last week in August, and then the King will be here; so, dear Mrs. Dilke, mind you keep Dilke in marching order. I have only post time to add God bless you all in my more serious style, which some prefer to my comic, and Jane says Amen religiously, though she has fished of a Sunday. She denies it, and I believe it is an error — she only went to an equestrian play.

Mind the address — as the quacks say — of, Dear Dilke,

Yours ever truly,

THOMAS HOOD.

I forgot to mention that the soldiers have an odd-sounding mode of suicide. As *ball* is hard to get at, they sometimes shoot themselves with *water*, — which blows the head to atoms worse than shot. Now for something in the grand style. One fellow in the true spirit of the *German sublime*, did it with a forty-eight pounder, and went off with *éclat*. How proud some Charlotte must have been of such a Werter!

752, ALTEN GRABEN, 12*th July*, 1836.

MY DEAR DILKE,

You will wonder at hearing from me so soon again, but it is a broken day, and an epistolary one, as I have other letters to write — and perhaps the French letter will be worth the postage; and, above all, I have a positive pleasure in writing to, as well as receiving letters from you. You see I can make as many good excuses for writing, as others for their silence. But the truth is, I have not many correspondents, nor many conversables; so that I select you, both to write to and to talk to on paper — for fear I should die of that most distressing of complaints, a suppression of ideas. I do not, however, though I am in Germany, pretend to open a regular account of debtor and creditor, and expect you to liquidate every letter of mine, as if it were a foreign bill of exchange, by an equivalent on your own side. I know your time is too valuable to be so drawn upon, and so is mine too; but, then, for me to write to you is matter of recreation. You have *too much* of that of which I have *too little* — society: so that if I choose to call on you, or leave my card, *i. e.* letter, I do not peremptorily expect your returning my visits. Now we understand each other; and *should* you ever tire of my billets, you can give me a genteel cut, by returning my last under cover, which ought to be equivalent to "not at home;" or you can get Mrs. Dilke to make spills of them, for I hate my writings to be of no use to any one; a case, I believe, peculiar to my "Plea of the Fairies." I had, I remember, to bid myself for the waste, for fear of their going to the book-stalls. So you can publish my letters if you do not like them, and trust to my buying up the remainders.

We are all well — as well as the heat, that is to say, will let us be. But we never had, as apparently all the world has had, a stranger season. First, a long, cold, wet spring; and then, all at once, out of the ice-pail into the frying-pan, like preserved fish. Our powers of contraction and expansion were well tried. I am, as you may guess, not strong, and wonder I did not become literally *friable.* At mental work I sat in a room (always in shade) with the glass at 80; and at bodily work at a true African heat.

We went one day to see the Royal Iron-works at Säyn, and really, with all the great furnaces and the ladlefuls of glowing red liquid metal, the process going on under a *roof,* the sun seemed to heat the fire, without any great bellows.

One day, while fishing at Lahneck, De Franck and I pursued a trout stream till it ended in what I have several times observed about here, where there is water. There was a sort of earthy cauldron sloping down, almost a regular circle, till you came to a level surface of meadow and water, as the Laacher Zee. The whole country is volcanic — tremendously so, if you think of all the hot springs — a real Solfaterra. Extinct crater, or not, I felt *boiled dry* in it, till I longed to plunge into the clear little stream before me, so cool, so clear; but probably it would have been my death; for, do you know, trout live here in rivers too *cold* for any other fish, and we caught nothing but trout, nor has anybody else. However, in this beautiful picturesque bottom I almost *devilled* myself, without curry or cayenne — in spite of a queer brown holland smock-frock, garnished (as the Germans cannot do even *simplicity* without a flourish) with a flowing brown holland frill! It was one of their sporting costumes, lent me by De Franck; and whilst wearing this, and he in another like thereunto, we had deposited our ordinary coats at a house in the village. And here note, for I wish to be just, that the conservators of our said coats would not, without the greatest difficulty, accept a doit — I ought to say a groschen — for their trouble, although Germans, and *Jews*. I had, perforce, to give it to a poor sick boy, as an excuse for leaving it, and whom I singled out with a sort of Irish philanthropy, to prove we are all Christians. I wish I could hope to give him another little piece of *bad* silver (you know, of course, the *washed*, or rather *unwashed* face of Friedrich Wilhelm on our Prussian coinage), but he seemed destined to abstract a unit from the gross sum of the twelve tribes at present in existence. Set this off against my last picture of the people of these parts, and lament with me that you must go *from* the Rhine to meet *natures* that correspond with its natural beauties. Perhaps I am wrong; I know you think I am prejudiced, but I think I am not. Every day fresh *facts*, not fancies, corroborate my views. You will find a new one in my notice of M. The imposition, I know, was made light of, and made a joke of even, as against the English.

I could quote political reasons for this jealousy, which certainly does obtain, besides more private ones. Namely, under the heads of free trade, probable union of France, Belgium, and England against the Holy Family, alias Holy Alliance, which I guess is a main head and front, besides avarice and envy, and most exaggerated notions of our wealth. I am translating a *serious* tale, illustrative of England, from the "Zeitung," where a lady of Euston Square offers £50,000 *per annum*, a mine in "*Cornwales*," and £20,000 in "East India Actions" (? shares), as a reward for finding her lost child. The lady dies — the King's carriage and all the nobility go to the funeral; the will bequeaths *all her property* to the *finder*, and nothing to the child; and the said child is eventually found by a dog called "Fog"! Imagine a *London fog* finding anything! And these are "Sketches of our Manners," gravely written and read on the Rhine — one of our thoroughfares!! It will make a good chapter in my book as a German exercise!

* * * *

752, Alten Graben, Coblenz, 29*th October*, 1836.

My dear Mrs. Elliot,

* * * *

You will be surprised to hear that Hood* is at this

* In the beginning of October, the 19th Polish Infantry were ordered

present writing, at, or near Berlin — from thence he goes to Küstrin, Frankfort-on-the-Oder, Breslau, Dresden, Frankfort-on-the-Maine, and then back to Coblenz. Mr. De Franck's regiment, the 19th, has been ordered from here to Bromberg, and he proposed Hood's joining their march as a friend of his. As it was his intention to travel for his German book, this affords the best opportunity. He would see parts of the country which are not common to travellers; he would have the advantage of very pleasant companions, and the help of Mr. De Franck's German, who speaks it as well as a native — and Hood therefore very gladly accepted the invitation. The regiment marches fifteen or twenty English miles per day for three days, and then rests one. Mr. De Franck advised Hood to buy a horse to go with them, and when he wished to return, he could sell it and come back by *diligence.* He was so fortunate as to meet with a good one, with new saddle, bridle, and all, for *seven pounds, ten shillings!* As he could not start with them, Mr. De Franck took the horse with him, and they arranged to meet at or near Eisenach. I must tell you that all the officers very politely expressed much pleasure at his going with them. The Captain desired the Quartermaster to arrange quarters for him with De Franck. The Colonel, who has trans-

to march to Bromberg, and my father was induced, by the invitation of his friend Franck (and indeed of all the officers of the regiment), to march with them. My mother's letter is put a little out of date here, in order not to interfere with the continued narrative of my father's letters. These were almost the last of my father's days of health, and henceforward — although there have been occasional mentions of illness before — the letters will record the gradual but sure decline of it. — T. H.

lated his "Eugene Aram" into German and is a very clever man, sent him a handsome message and invitation. Knowing that Mr. Dilke could not leave London for longer than five or six weeks, it had been settled that I should go with Hood as far as Eisenach, and they would not suffer us to alter this; so leaving them here, Hood and I left for Frankfort on the 11th of October, and reached Eisenach on the 13th. We stayed a night there, and went to Langen Seltzers the next morning, expecting to find Mr. De F., but his battalion was quartered in a village near, and we had to go on there. We found him in the house of a Saxon peasant, or rather farmer, for they seemed well to do, and had five or six fine cows. We had their two best bed-rooms — good sized, and nicely furnished — only we were obliged to go through one to the other. The first had two beds for Mr. Franck and a brother officer, and the inner one, which was also the sitting-room, had one for us: this was rather unpleasant, but if I had been a Princess I could not have commanded any better, so I treated it in the best manner I could. Our friend had been out and shot a brace of partridges in the morning, and the Polish officer, his comrade, undertook to superintend the cooking them for supper. I had brought tea with me, but had some difficulty to find a substitute for a teapot, and the luxury of teaspoons was quite unknown, and Hood*

* My father was very ingenious in this way, and had a knack of "cutting and contriving," of which we possess many evidences. While in Germany, he bought a small toy theatre for us, and then (and subsequently at Camberwell, during an illness) drew, painted, and cut out the characters and scenery for a tragedy (Paul and Vir-

carved one out of a bit of pine wood. For supper, they brought us a brown dish of potatoes, boiled in the skins, another dish of boiled eggs, some butter, and a large brown loaf, so the birds were a nice addition. After supper, the host and his wife came to inquire if we had been comfortable — they were unused to entertain such people, but they had done their best. The man then produced a bottle of spirit (very like Scotch whiskey, with a peat flavour even, made from rye), and offered a glass to each, first shaking hands all round. The wife, in the course of the evening, had brought her baby in her arms, and a beautiful little fat thing it was; and Hood desired Franck to tell the father how much we admired it — that it was so fat, we could not ask for all, but would like to

ginia), a spectacle (St. George and the Dragon), and a pantomime. The figures were very clever, the groups and processions capitally arranged — and the dragon *was* a dragon! Some of the scenes, such as the planter's house, and the cottages of Margaret and Madame de la Tour, are gems of effect and colour. Two moonlight scenes are very good too — the grave of Paul and Virginia, and the Palace in St. George, where a (tinsel) torchlight procession by water wound up the play. The whole, however, cannot be described, and must be seen to be appreciated. On high days and holidays this theatre used to be brought out, and my father used to perform the pieces to the delight of the little friends (and big ones too) who were present. He used to extemporise the dialogue, which was considered by the elders, who were better judges than we children could pretend to be, very lively and apt. His stage management, properties, and machinery were capital, and I can still remember the agony with which I used to see the wreck in Paul and Virginia break up by degrees, and the bodies of the lovers washed in over the breakers. In addition to these means of evening entertainment, he had a magic lantern, for which he painted a number of slides, some humorous, and some pretty ones — a flight of doves and swallows with a hawk, and a little cottage in the snow, with a "practicable" regiment marching over a bridge. — T. H.

have a part of it. We thought the man's answer very ready: "Tell the gentlemen, that I speak like the mother to King Solomon, I cannot suffer him to take a part, I would rather present him the whole of it!" As you may suppose, this was all very new and amusing, and we were very merry, only Hood complained at times of pain in the side; still we thought he would be better in the morning, and that it proceeded from over-fatigue. But his night was very restless, and when he rose, the pain was so great that we found he would not dare to venture on horseback; so we made a fresh arrangement, to go and stay at Saxe Gotha, at a quiet inn we had called at on our way, and that he should again meet the regiment on the next Tuesday at Halle, supposing him to be better for care, rest, and nursing. This all turned out to our wish; the pain proceeded from cold in the muscles of the chest, and he was soon well.

On Sunday, at twelve, I left him to return here, for I was to have been with the Dilkes at Coblenz, on that day. He saw me off from Saxe Gotha — but when the diligence arrived there, it was full, and as six passengers were there who had taken places, the conductor placed us "extras" in two "post waggons" as they call them, and Hood went away quite pleased at my going so comfortably. But alas! this was not to continue; after two stages they brought out an *old*, *old* diligence, in which they placed five gentlemen and myself. At Vach, where we supped, having quickly finished mine, I went out to get into the coach, and found a smith mending the wheels, and listening with all my German ears, heard the conductor ask if he was sure it was strong. This was enough for me — but I was too timid to communicate all this in bad German to the others; so I sat nursing my fears "to keep them warm," in most profound silence — suffering a womanly martyrdom. Of course I was not surprised, though dreadfully frightened, when the crash came. About eleven o'clock, when we had got to the top of a steep hill, and so, fortunately, were going slowly, the wheel came off and we were turned over! The young man opposite me scrambled out (we were uppermost) at the window; he did *not* tread upon me, but this was my luck, not his care, for he evidently only thought of himself. As soon as he was out, some one looked in at the window, and holding up my hands, I begged him to help me, but I soon repented this; for, seizing hold of my wrists, he began to pull me out "by force of arms" in spite of my entreaties, which being in English of course he did not understand. I really thought he would break them, for my whole weight was hanging, and I could not find anywhere to fix my feet against at the side. At last he dragged me out upon the top, and there I seemed likely to remain, for he went to help out the rest, and I stood trembling, bruised, and crying in the utmost distress, when I heard a voice from the road say, "Don't be alarmed, let me assist you down." "Thank God! that 's English," I said, and I was almost ready to jump into the gentleman's arms for very joy, as I was afterwards compelled to do for very help, for it was only by his lifting me from the edge, that I could reach the ground. He then went to search for my bag, which held my passport and my shawl. It was, most fortunately, a lovely moonlight night: darkness would have added much to my horror. I found I had a blow on the back of the head, and one on my right shoulder, but I came off better than others; one poor man was sadly cut about the face and head, and another had his arm very much hurt. My English friend now having found my bag and shawl, proposed placing me in a britzka, in which a German and his valet were travelling, but who had stopped to assist. But the old gentleman did not or would not understand, and I said very proudly in German, that I would rather stand there than trouble him. Upon this he was very pressing, and insisted on my getting in, but the diligence being near in which the Englishman was a passenger, I very soon exchanged my seat for the only vacant one there was in it, and went all the rest of the way in it to Frankfort. The other unfortunates were taken on in post waggons, and were *twice overset again* — not arriving at Frankfort until four o'clock — we got there by one.

I went from Frankfort to Mayence that evening, and on Tuesday morning came in the steamboat down the Rhine. It was a beautiful day; and though too rapid, I think the Rhine is much finer to come down, you see it with better effect, than to go up it.

* * * *

You of course have heard of our grand review. There were such preparations for it, and so much talk beforehand, and every village round Coblenz, as well as the Stadt itself, so crammed with military that we did expect something "prodigious," but the weather was miserable, and we were a *leetle* disappointed; still it was such a sight as I never witnessed before, and shall not again. The Lager, or Camp, was erected at the end of August; but the three or four grand days were about the middle of September. The Crown Prince was here three days to review them; but I thought the two days' "sham fights," after he left, by far the most interesting. The Camp was erected on the large plain on the other side of the Rhine and Moselle, between here and Andernach. There were booths for the sale of fancy goods, for refreshment, and for dancing, theatres, horse-riding, &c., and one large one called the Officers' Booth, where they dined always. In front of these tents was a range of kitchens for the soldiers at short distances from each other, a quarter of a mile in length. Behind these were the tents for those troops who could not be disposed of in towns or villages. To those who had only seen at a theatre the representation of a "tented field" this was a beautiful sight, and the lovely green hills that bound the plain on all sides added to the fine effect of the scene.

We engaged a carriage early, knowing the Dilkes were coming, and were so lucky that we paid for the four days, what others paid for one; but poor Mr. Dilke's illness quite spoiled the enjoyment, though they insisted on our going, as we had promised to take a young lady with us. It was unfortunate, too, that what we had reckoned on as an amusement, viz., that we live in the street that leads to the bridge, turned out a source of annoyance to our poor friend, on account of the noise of the carriages and troops going in and out. On the last day but one, Hood and I and Fanny went to see the taking of Bassenheimer, a village seven or eight English miles off. The stupid people of Coblenz having seen the troops reviewed in order, and the Crown Prince, did not care to go to see this, so ours was the only party present. We followed what seemed the successful and advancing army, but on gaining the brow of a hill our troops began to retreat, and we saw the enemy coming out of a dark fir wood, and steadily marching up the ascent. Our situation was very advantageous for seeing the manœuvres, so we drew a little to one side and allowed them to pass us: it gave me a very excellent notion of a battle: the tramp of the feet, the measured beat of the drums, and the firing of the skirmishers was truly exciting. I wish Hood* was here to give you a description, for on talking it over with Franck, he was astonished to find how clearly he had seen it all, and pointed out how one side lost the vantage ground, and ultimately was conquered by that oversight.

Mr. de Franck told us that sometimes the soldiers get so excited the officers are obliged to interfere, or it would be fighting in good earnest. When we were setting out to return, we saw a man lying on the road

* This review, no doubt, was the origin of a game of military manœuvres my father subsequently made for us. He got some common wooden toy soldiers, and painted them proper colours, putting feathers, epaulettes, and all other necessary accoutrements for officers, band, and privates, with colours and tents for each regiment. The whole formed two armies, which acted against each other by certain rules, not unlike chess, and the game was won by the general who took the best position. The two armies were supplied with cannon and caissons, baggage-waggons, and all requirements. The field was supplied with bridges, churches, villages, and forts — all little models. The game was a most ingenious one, and afforded us much amusement, and was greatly admired by my father's friends who saw it. This is another instance of the trouble and time he spent in finding amusement for his children. — T. H.

side, with a surgeon attending him, and we found he had been shot through the arm, near the elbow, with a stone. The men stuff grass and earth into their guns (though of course against orders) to make a loud report, and sometimes they even put in stones. On hearing that he must wait till they got a cart to take him to the hospital, we offered to bring him, which they gladly accepted. Hood mounted the box and they placed the poor man by me, giving me drops to put on sugar to keep him from fainting. The road was very bad, and he suffered sadly from every jolt of the carriage. I never had so miserable a ride from nervousness and anxiety at seeing him in such pain. We heard afterwards that the *grand* people here thought we ought not to have taken him in, and that we had degraded ourselves, as he was only a private. The officers were of a different opinion; but said they were sure the other party would not have condescended to inquire about him at all, when they had seen he was only a common soldier. So much for the pride of the "Vons" — in our country, thank God! it is a matter of course to afford help in such a case. We have only once heard of the poor man since, as they will not admit strangers or even answer messages at the hospital, for fear of the men's friends sending them money. Mr. de Franck called once to inquire for me, he was then in bed, and his arm swollen to a great size — I have now no means of hearing more of him.

* * * *

We have had some snow lately. I am afraid this will retard Hood's progress, for he will not venture on more than he can feel secure about getting back again, for every step he takes is further north.

* * * *

We have great hopes of returning next year to England, if it please God to continue Hood's health, which of course so much depends on, indeed, all of comfort and success! The hope of seeing my dear friends and native land again, renders the prospect of the next winter here not quite so cheerless. I fear we shall miss our friend Franck very much, both his society and his many friendly acts, and also his assistance in speaking German, for we are both of us rather dull in acquiring it. I quite pine after English books, and fear when I return I shall feed too greedily, like a famished man, and so not benefit till time gives me a more healthy appetite. What a loss the musical world has suffered in the death of poor Malibran: I was very sorry to hear of it, she was a beautiful singer, and an admirable actress. Hood has been to the Opera at Berlin, and saw "Undine;" it was very well done he says, and all the Royal family were present. The theatre here is wretched, and the actors too bad to laugh at even.

* * * *

With best love to you all, believe me to be ever, my dearest Mrs. Elliot,

Yours affectionately,

Jane Hood.

The following are extracts from my father's letters to his wife, during the march.

GOTHA, 18*th October*, 1837.

MY OWN DEAREST AND BEST,

I send you a packet for Baily: the "Love Lane" is longer by some verses, so send the present copy: so much for business, and now for the pleasant.

We parted manfully and womanfully, as we ought. I drank only half a bottle of the Rhine wine, and only the half of that, ere I fell asleep on the sofa, which lasted two hours. It was the reaction, for your going tired me more than I cared to show. Then I drank the other half, and as that did not do, I went and retraced our walk in the Park, and sat down in *the same seat*, and felt happier and better. Have not you a romantic old husband? To-day I had some pain, but I had written hard, and I resolved at dinner, out of prudence, and to set you at ease, to ask for advice, when good fortune engaged me in English conversation with a young German physician, a capital fellow; and over a bottle of champagne between us I frankly asked his advice and stated my symptoms. He jumped at once at the cause, and asked if I had travelled long in one position, &c. I gave the history of our journey, and he said it was nothing but what I had supposed, a cold in the pectoral muscles from *that* night in the coach. I am to wear flannel on the chest, and that is all; there is nothing to apprehend. As this coincides with my own views, I hope it will set you quite at rest on the subject, and that you will thank me for putting it out of doubt. He was a nice fellow and we are to meet again at Berlin. I go off to-night at seven, and have little time. I think you will like the "Desert Born."

I hope you got home safe and well, and found all so.

Kiss my darling Fanny and Tom for me over and over. Kindest love to the Dilkes if they are with you. I have a world to say to them and you (my next will not be so hurried). I must keep my terrestrial globe of talk to some other time. Take care of yourself.

Kiss the dear children for me, and believe me,

Ever yours,

THOMAS HOOD.

23rd October.

MY OWN DEAREST AND BEST JANE,

I feel quite happy, and more for your sake than my own, that I have nothing but good news to communicate.

I got to Halle yesterday rather late, four or five in the afternoon. There was a strict examination of passports at Erfurt, and mine was refused *a visé* or *frizzé* as Heilman calls it; I believe because it was in French,—the Dummkopf! I found Franck domesticated (I ought to say quartered, but it would sound like *cutting up*) in *Butcher Street*, the very place for filling one's cavities. After some good beer, bread and cheese, by way of dinner, and a rest, we went and settled all the passport affair right, and then went to head-quarters. My reception was very gratifying indeed, they all seemed really glad to see me, and Franck's captain was particularly friendly; and I quite regret my loss of German, as he is very merry, and likes to talk. There were some gentlemen from Merseberg, who had known some of the officers when the battalion was formerly quartered there, and all was jollity. They were very friendly too, and I felt quite at home, and moreover, supped on the famous Leipsic larks, things that Martin of —— Street would lick the lips of his heart at. Finally, I packed up my trunk, &c., went to bed, and slept soundly and dreamt (don't be jealous for we cannot command our dreams, I wish I could!) but it was of little Tom, God bless him. I rose with the larks, was well up to my time, marched to the muster, mounted my nag, and here I am, at a quarter past one, writing to you, after completing not only my first march, but a hearty dinner. Luck turned at last, for I rose without any pain, for the first time, and consequently in good spirits. I am delighted with my nag. Franck has got him into such excellent order, I was only off him twice, but thank goodness without hurting myself, as it was merely dismounting according to the regular mode when we halted. Tell Fanny he walks after Franck, and knows him like a dog: I expect to be equally good friends with him, by feeding him with bread. Fanny herself might ride him, and I only fear I shall be sorry to part with him at last. I rode so well as to pass muster for a trooper, and *did* the turnpikes. At one village a man said, "There goes the doctor!" The morning was beautiful, the road good, and straight as a line, over the immense plains near Leipsic, where so many a battle has been fought. For some distance I rode between the captain and a gentleman in plain clothes: it turned out he had formerly been a soldier in the battalion, and is now a Professor, and there was I the author turned soldier! I did wish you could have gone with us, the first halt was very amusing, such miscellaneous breakfasting, and a boy with a large tin of hot sausages, sold all off in a minute to his surprise, and regret that he had not brought a whole barrow full. The colonel passed in a carriage: I did not see him, but he stopped Franck to ask if I was there, and sent his compliments. Tell Fanny I was introduced to Minna's father. Minna is not going to leave Coblenz yet, so that she can have her with her sometimes, before she goes. I assure you I found myself getting better every mile, and when we got here about ten, felt so fresh, indeed, not even stiff, that I could not believe the march was over.

From Gotha to Halle was somewhat tedious in a *beiwagen* — without any adventure save one. At supper, for we did not leave till nine, there were two gentlemen, one of whom talked with me a good deal in my bad German; but to my surprise when we had gone some miles he addressed me in English. We sat together in the coupé and gossipped nearly the whole night on England, Bowring, Campbell, &c. He told me he had been an *emigré* from Germany on account of his politics, which had brought him into great trouble, and had held an office at the London University, but having settled his differences with Government is now a Professor at some college in Prussia. Perhaps Dilke will know who he is. I have had good quarters as yet. Bill of fare to-day: roast pork, ditto goose, with apples, good soup, good beer, pickled cherries, celery roots in slices, as large and round as turnips, lamb's milk cheese stuck full of carraways. I should like to see *your* face at the last article. I have no more to say in the victualling line except that Franck caught Heilman ramming matches into his cayenne pepper by mistake for a fire bottle.

And now, dearest, it delights me to hope and think that whilst I am writing, you are at home safe and well, and are just now sitting down to dinner, or ought to be with the pretty little pair; perhaps with the pretty big pair too. You know who I mean! It was fine weather for you, and it was in favour of your impatience that you would travel quickest, nearest home. I hope you enjoyed the Rhine from Mayence. I shall long eagerly to know about you all, whether the Dilkes have left, and how he was, &c., and how you bore your solitary journey. I have thought of you continually, and enjoy by sympathy beforehand the comfort you will feel in reading this, a *true* and not a flattering picture of my mind, body, and estate. I feel really as well as I say, and have now no doubt of getting *very* much better if not quite restored by this trip, with other advantages to boot. (There is a bunch of comforts for you, like the posies chucked in at a coach window.) We drank your health in beer (excuse the liquor). I ramble on how I can, having to take a sleep, and then go in the evening to meet the others, perhaps to play at whist, half-penny points. We are in a pretty little village, and among people the reverse of Rhinelanders. The sudden change from marching soldiers, &c., is quite laughable; look out of window, and there is not a trace of military, not even a cap; all are indoors snoozing, &c. In the evening we shall swarm like bees.

Franck will write to you next, as I shall be busy, but I determined to show you to-day by a long letter how well I was after my march. I shall also write a few lines at the end of this to Fanny, who, I hope, helps and pleases you as much as she can. If the Dilkes are not gone, give my love to them, and say all that is kind. I left in a sad hurry, and had not even time to thank Mrs. Dilke, without whom I should never have been launched. Tell her I shall be as grand over my march, as if I had crossed the Simplon. If you write of your journey faithfully to your mother, the break-down and all, I suspect it will be "vardict, sarve 'em right! Hood and Jane are both gone mad together!" The officers who were in love seem reconciled to their fate. I have found "my own Carlovicz" again — only time to shake hands, but expect him this evening. Wildegans is well again, but gone forward two hours further than us. He was with me all the way nearly. It will be our turn next I guess for a long spell, but I could have gone much further to-day than we did. I have promised the captain to get fat under his command.

I fear you will have no more long letters till the "Comic" is done; but am I not good for this one? I am quite repaid by the anticipation of your pleasure in it. I fear you will have to copy what I send you of MSS., for fear of their miscarrying. I sent you a packet from Gotha.

* * * *

My dear Fanny,

I hope you are as good still as when I went away — a comfort to your good mother and a kind playfellow to your little brother. Mind you tell him my horse eats bread out of my hand, and walks up to the officers who are eating, and pokes his nose into the women's baskets. I wish I could give you both a ride. I hope you liked your paints; pray keep them out of Tom's way, as they are poisonous. I shall have rare stories to tell you when I come home; but mind, you must be good till then, or I shall be as mute as a stockfish. Your mama will show you on the map where I was when I wrote this; and when she writes will let you put in a word. You would have laughed to see your friend Wildegans running after the sausage boy to buy a "*würst:*" there was hardly an officer without one in his hand smoking hot. The men piled their guns on the grass, and sat by the side of the road, all munching at once like ogres. I had a pocket-full of bread and butter, which soon went into my "cavities," as Mrs. Dilke calls them. I only hope I shall not get so hungry as to eat my horse. I know I need not say, keep school and mind your book, as you love to learn. You may have Minna sometimes, her papa says.

Now God bless you, my dear little girl, my pet, and think of your

Loving Father,

THOMAS HOOD.

EXTRACT.

POTSDAM.

From having gone through woods, full of old stumps and roots of trees, without a fall, I begin to pique myself on my horsemanship, but yesterday got into a bit of a caper. I was anxious to inquire at the post-office of Belitz, so had to get before the others, which I all but effected, when, just entering the town in a narrow street, I was obliged to wait with my horse's nose just against the big drum, which he objected to pass; but I contrived to keep him dancing between the band and the regiment. I was more lucky than a captain in Coblenz, whose horse ran away with him slap through the band, all of whom he upset, breaking their instruments to the tune of 300 dollars damages. I am glad I did not know this at the time.

We rise at four, and march about five or half-past: it is moonlight earlier, but then becomes dark, so I march till I can see the road, and then mount; after about three quarters of an hour we halt for a quarter of an hour, and then on again to the general rendezvous, overtaking or passing other companies on the road, for we are quartered sometimes widely apart. At the rendezvous we halt and breakfast — a sort of picnic — each bringing what he can: if I had been searched yesterday they would have found on me two cold pigeons, and a loaf split and buttered. I have learned to forage, and always clear the table at my quarters into my pockets.

It is an amusing scene when we sit down by the roadside; some of the officers, who have had queer quarters,

bring sketches of them; one the other day had such a ruinous house for his, that his dog stood and howled at it. At the inn at Kremnitz, I had dinner, supper, bed and breakfast for 7 good groschen, about 11 pence! Think of that, ye Jewish Rhinelanders. Many of them moreover returned the common soldiers the five groschen the king allows for their billeting, and gave them a glass of schnaps besides. They are a friendly, kind people, and meet you with the hand held out to shake, and say "Welcome." I like the Saxons much. Then we marched to Wittenberg, where a Lieut. J——, an old friend of Franck's, made us dine with him at the military Casino. He spoke French, and I found him very intelligent, and somewhat literary, so we got on well. He asked me if we English had not a prejudice against the Germans, and I assured him quite the reverse.

He seemed pleased, and said, "To be sure we are of the same race" (Saxons). He took me over the town, famous as one of Luther's strongholds. His statue conveyed the very impression I had from a late paper in the "Athenæum," a sturdy friar, with a large thick-necked jowly head, sensual exceedingly, — a real sort of bull-dog to pin the pope's bull. From thence we went to Pruhlitz to our quarters, which were queerish; Franck was put in a room used as the village church, and I in the ball-room; we were certainly transposed. Our second quarters were at Nichel near Truenbritzen. We arrived after a march of eight hours and a half: think of that for me! and I came in all alive and kicking. We got at it over wide barren heaths, and plenty of deep sand. Our billet was on the Burgomaster, or schultze, and his civic robe was a sheepskin with the wool inward, the usual wintry dress in those bleak parts. The lady mayoress a stout, plump, short-faced *mutterkin*, with a vast number of petticoats to make amends for shortness. I told my host I was an English burgomaster, so we kept up a great respect and fellowship for each other. You would have laughed to see Bonkowski hugging and kissing the Frau — it is reckoned an honour — and the husbands stand and look on; we shook hands all around, and then dined; I was not too curious about the cookery, and ate heartily. Every time I came to the window, a whole group in sheepskins, like baa lambs on their hind legs, pointed me out to each other, and took a good stare, so I suppose Englanders are rarities. At leaving, the Burgomaster inquired very anxiously about me, and being, as he thought, in the way to get information, he said he had heard of *Flanders*, and wanted to know if it was money like *florins!* There was a Worship for you!

*   *   *   *

We had but two beds, one for me, and one for Bonkowski, and Franck was on the straw.

Thence we went to Schlunkendorf (what a name!) near Belitz: quartered at a miller's, very clean and wholesome, but only two beds, so Franck was littered down again. I wanted the host to give him corn instead of straw by mistake, and then come and thrash them both out together. I forgot to say the little captain called on me at Pruhlitz to see how I was, and took tea with us. Last night I called on Bonkowski, who was opposite to us; I found him flirting with the Frau. I told her I had come 50,000 miles, was married at 14, and had 17 children; and as I was in yellow boots, and Mrs. D.'s present of a robe, and really looked a Grand Turk, she believed me like Gospel. We made a Welch rabbit for supper, and then played loo till bed-time for pfennings; I had a young officer for our third instead of Bonkowski. This morning I rode over from Schlunkendorf to Belitz, Heilman taking back the mare, where I found your welcome letter, and started by diligence to Potsdam, where I am, having just eaten a capital dinner — chiefly a plate of good English-like roasted mutton — and a whole bottle of genuine English porter. I am to brush up here to see them parade before the king to-morrow morning.

Then a day's rest here, and then to Berlin. After the parade, a party of us are going to Sans Souci, and so forth, sight seeing. Franck hopes to introduce me to the Radziwills at Berlin; I have no pain, and really wonder how I *march*. But I had made up my heart and mind to it, and that is everything; it keeps me, I think, from falling off my horse, I am so determined to stick to him, and keep my wits always about me: in fact I quite enjoy it, and only wish I could return so, 't is so much better than being jammed up in a diligence, and, says *you*, "less dangerous!"

Pray tell my dear *good* Fanny that at Schlunkendorf, there was a tame robin, that killed all the flies in the room, hopped on the table, and the edges of our plates, for some dinner. I am delighted with her keeping her promise to me.

My project is to go with the 10th Company to Custrin, and then home by Frankfort on the Oder, Breslau, Dresden, Frankfort on the Maine, Mayence, Coblenz, where God send I may find you all well.

I forgot to say I composed a song for the 19th, which made them all laugh. I send it for you.

SONG FOR THE NINETEENTH.

The morning sky is hung with mist,
  The rolling drum the street alarms,
The host is paid, his daughter kiss'd —
  So now to arms! to arms! to arms!

Our evening bowl was strong and stiff,
  And may we get such quarters oft,
I ne'er was better lodged, — for if
  The straw was hard, the maid was soft.

So now to arms! to arms! to arms!
  And fare thee well, my little dear;
And if they ask who won your charms,
  Why say — " 't was in your *nineteenth* year!"

BERLIN, *October 25th.*

The country round Berlin, the Mark of Brandenburg, is bitter bad, deep sand almost a desert: I don't wonder the Great Frederick wanted something better. Some parts of our marches, through the forests, with the bugles ringing, were quite romantic, and the costume of the villagers, when they turned out to see us pass, really picturesque. I have now made five marches, and am not fatigued to speak of. I am sworn comrade with most of the officers; one rough-looking old captain told me when he got to Berlin, he should have his Polish cook, and then he should ask me to dinner, promising me an "*overgay*" evening, which I shall take care to get out off. By-the-by, when we were at the burgomaster's, I saw said captain, striding up and down in a great fume before the house; it turned out he was to sleep in the same room with a man, his wife and *seven* children! which he declined. Finally, I believe, he was put in the schoolroom in an extempore bed. We are often short of knives, spoons, and forks, but the poor creatures do their best and cheerfully, so that it quite relishes the victuals. I shake their hands heartily, when we part. Yesterday I had a nice dessert of grapes, sent over to me by Bonkowski, and they are scarce in these regions.

Carlovicz one night got no quarters at all: it is quite a lottery. You should have seen Wildegans riding on a baggage waggon between suttlers! Tell Tom that Franck comes to pat my horse, and she spits all over him sometimes, for she has rare yeasty jaws; and yesterday I had the prudence to take myself to leeward after spangling the captain's cloak all over! She eats rarely, and will sell well I dare say, but I shall be sorry to part with her. When I find myself on horseback, riding through a long wood with a regiment, it seems almost like a dream; your mother will no more believe it than your upset. You have subjects enough now for the Elliots with a vengeance, and so shall I have! I wish I *could* wish the Dilkes may be comfortably in Coblenz by my return. As they are not wanted, they would see the vintage; God bless them any way, and say everything kind for me. I really think they might stay longer in Coblenz, quiet and cheap enough, and recover thoroughly, against their winter campaign of company; I long to see them again ere they cross the sea.

I have rambled on to amuse you, and left little room to say all I could wish to yourself; but you will find in your own heart the echo of all I have to say (rather an Irish one, but a truth-teller).

* * * *

I seem to have scarcely had an inconvenience, certainly not a hardship, and it will ever be a pleasant thing for me to remember. I like little troubles; I do not covet too flowery a path. By-the-by I have some dried flowers for my flower-loving Fanny, gathered at odd out-of-the-way places; I will show her where on the map when I return.

It was singular in the sheepskin country, whilst the men were all so warmly pelissed, to see the women in their short petticoats, their legs looking so cold. I suspect I pass for very hardy, if not fool-hardy, I slight the cold so; but it seems to me a German characteristic, that they can bear being sugar-bakers, but can hardly endure what I call a bracing air.

* * * *

Bless you, bless you, again and again, my dear one, my only one, my one as good as a thousand to

Your old Unitarian in love,

T. H.

P. S. If Desdemona loved Othello "for the dangers he had passed," how shall I love you? With my utmost *diligence*, or rather so much more than my heart can-hold, that it must get a *beiwagen!* And with that earnest joke, good bye.

BERLIN, *October 29th.*

MY DEAREST LOVE,

Here I am safe — but my march is over! The Prince Radziwill has invited Franck to stay two or three weeks here, so he of course stays. As he was the pretext for my journey, I cannot well go without him, but had planned to return by Dresden and Leipsic. To-day, however, it snows; and for fear of bad roads, &c., I think I shall come direct. Moreover, owing to the hurry I have none of my papers or lists with me, so that I find it difficult to do anything with the "Comic." You may look for me, therefore, in a fortnight from the date of this. I hope the Dilkes will not be gone. I shall not write again. I am very well, and busy going about. I saw the Cadet school here yesterday morning. I swig away at good London porter. Don't you envy me?

Last night I was at the opera — "Undine" — the whole royal family present; it was very well done, and I really longed for Tibbie, it was so full of fairy work. Nearly the whole of the 19th were there, and Wildegans says he regrets not to have heard the comments of the men. I have been with him to the exhibition of pictures this morning. Then we took leave, and it made me quite down to say Good-bye to so many, and probably for ever. He desired me to say everything that is kind to you, Fanny, and Tom. I was introduced to the Colonel last night, at the opera. We have a great joke amongst us: half the officers having a day or two's leave, stay here behind the regiment; they lunch with me sometimes, and we call it "eating the horse." I suppose I shall get rid of both him and his price before I leave.

I have met with no disagreeables here, which will please you, and shall reserve all stories for our *tête-à-têtes*. In a fortnight you may expect me.

Tell my dear Fanny I was very much pleased with her letter, and so was her friend Franck. I gave her love to Wildegans and Carloviez. I parted with Wildegans yesterday, about two o'clock. I reckon I shall never see him again. He desired everything kind to be said to you, and said he should never forget us, and spoke of the children, "*kleine* Tom and Fannie *la petite*."

God bless you all three, dear ones!

BERLIN, *November 2nd*, 1836.

MY OWN DEAREST AND BEST LOVE,

I do not know whether this will reach you on your birthday, but I hope so.

* * * *

I have been very busy sight-seeing, and very gay. The day before yesterday Franck brought me an invitation from Prince William Radziwill, the head of the family, to dine with him at three o'clock. I was run for time, having to get dress-boots, &c.; and to crown all, a coach ordered at half-past two did not arrive till three, nor could I make them understand to get another. Thank heaven, the dear Princesses were long in dressing, for it would have been awful to have kept them waiting.

They say no man is a prophet in his own country, and here literature certainly came in for its honours. The Prince introduced me himself to every one of his family, who all tried to talk to me, most of them speaking English very well. Some spoke French, so I got on very well, save a little deafness. The Prince placed me himself next to him at dinner, on his right hand, and talked with me continually during dinner, telling me stories and anecdotes, &c., and I tried to get out of his debt by some of mine. There were present Prince William, Prince Boguslaw Radziwill, Prince Adam Czartoriski, Prince Edmund Cläry, Count Wildenbruch (whom I had met before), Count Lubienski, Councillor Michalski, Hofrath Kupsach, Captain Crawford, R. N., Princess Cläry, Princess Felicia Cläry, Princess Euphemia Cläry, Princess Boguslaw Radziwill, Princess Wanda Czartoriski, and Miss von Lange, lady-in-waiting. So I was in august company. (Franck was obliged to dine at the Duke of Cumberland's.) I was quite delighted with the whole family; they are all excellent. I stayed till seven. We were very merry after dinner. Franck came in, and the Princes kept telling me sporting anecdotes about themselves and him. Prince William proposed to call on me and see my sketches, but I told him I had none, and then begged his acceptance of my books, which I am to send. The Princesses asked me to send them this year's "Comic." Both the Prince Radziwills shook hands with me at parting. They (the Princes) have since spoken of visiting me, but Franck declined it, on the plea of my being so far off; for the place was so full, not a bed was to be had when I arrived at that end, and I am in quite a third-rate hotel, at the opposite quarter.

I have more particulars to tell you when we meet, but I knew you would be pleased to hear of this. The Duke of Cumberland asked Franck who "that gentleman was who marched with his regiment," and was surprised to hear it was me; he had been told it was an officer. Prince George spoke in such very handsome terms of me, that I left my card for him. As he regretted not having had the last "Comic," Franck presented one of his. It is a sad pity, but the Prince is quite blind; a fine young man, and very amiable. I do not know whether I shall see any of the Princes again before I go, but I expect I must call to take leave. They had even read "Tylney Hall!"

*　　*　　*　　*

Since writing the above, I have been unwell, and could not meet Franck as I promised at the Exhibition. I think principally it arose from a sudden change in the weather, from really severe frost to rain. Only yesterday we were walking in the fish market, where the huge tubs of jack, carp, &c., were almost frozen hard, but to-day the streets are covered with genuine *London*-like mud. I have seen Franck, however, at the café where I dine, and he told me Prince William called on me yesterday, and the other Princes to-day, also Count Wildenbruch. This is really most flattering attention. I sent to-day to one of the Princes a written account of Franck's tumble into the Lahn, which I expect will make them laugh, as I had highly embellished it. Franck is gone again to-night to the Duke of Cumberland's. We only meet by snatches. He and a young lieutenant, Von Heugel, are all I see now of the 19th. The latter and I are very good friends: he is quite young, and having leave as long as Franck's, and more leisure, we go about together a good deal. You should hear the lamentations of Franck and myself, that you are not here, — it is really amusing.

Yesterday I was in the Musée, and saw some wonderful pictures: the "Titian's Daughter," for instance. I should like to be one of the attendants for a month. There were some curious antique pieces I will describe when we meet. Altogether I have had a most happy time of it, and in health and every respect have reason to be highly gratified. I am now all right — a little good port wine, which all the officers here recommended me to take to-night, has cured me, and here I am writing to you with the spirits of a lark, in the hope that after a couple or three days, every hour will bring me nearer to all that is dearest to me on earth.

* * * *

The following letter was written, after my father's return from Berlin, to his friend, Mr. de Franck, who was then with his regiment at Bromberg. My father missed him sadly on many accounts, and indeed I think, after he left, Coblenz became very dreary and tedious to him. They were fellow disciples of Izaak Walton in the "gentle art of angling," and after his friend's departure, my father found his pleasant fishing rambles had lost their greatest charm. They had spent so many happy days with rod and line at Lahneck, and by the side of the Moselle, &c., that the old haunts seemed very lonely and deserted after Mr. de Franck left. The frequent address of "Tim says he" between them, arose from the following dialogue which my father had picked up somewhere.

The characters were supposed to be a thoughtless Irishman in difficulties, and his more prudent servant, and the conversation ran thus: —

"Tim!" says he.
"Sir!" says he.
"Fetch me my hat," says he,
"That I may go," says he,
"To Timahoe," says he,
"And go to the fair," says he,
"And see all that 's there!" says he.
"First pay what you owe!" says he,
"And *then* you may go," says he,
"To Timahoe," says he,
"And go to the fair," says he,
"And see all that 's there!" says he.
"Now by this and by that," says he,
"— Tim, hang up my hat!" says he.

This so tickled their fancies that "Tim says he" was a far more frequent preface and salutation than their own proper names. The origin of the nickname "Johnny," I have not been able to trace.

752, Alten Graben, Coblenz, *Dec. 2nd*, 1836.

Tim, says he,

It was odd enough I should have my accident too as if to persuade me that German eilwagens are the most dangerous vehicles in the world — but about four o'clock on the third morning, after a great "leap in the dark," the coach turned short round, and brought up against the rails of the roadside; luckily they were strong, or we should have gone over a precipice. There we were on the top of a bleak hill, the pole having broken short off, till we were fetched by *beiwagens*, to the next station, where a new pole was made; but it delayed us six hours. Here I got the first of my cold, for the weather and wind were keen; the night journey from Frankfort to Mayence in an *open* coupé confirmed it. I could not help falling asleep in it from cold. So I came home looking well, and as ruddy as bacon; but the very next day turned *white* with a dreadful cough, which ended in spitting blood; but I sent for the doctor, was bled, and it was stopped: but I am still weak. To make things better I had not sent enough for the "Comic," and was obliged to set to work again, willy-nilly, well or illy. I have not been out of doors yet since I came home, but shall in a day or two. The Rhine and Moselle are very high — the Castor Street is flooded — the weather being very mild — but I guess cold is coming, for I saw a fellow bring into the town to-day a very large wolf on his shoulders. He was as fat as a pig. I found all well at home. Tom stared his eyes out at me, almost, and for two days would scarcely quit my lap. He talks and sings like a parrot. I should have liked to see your Grand Hunt (a Battue), but for sport I would rather take my dog and gun and pick up what I could find. The night procession must have looked well. Poor Dilke went away very unwell, but the last account of him was better. I did not get home soon enough to see him. I am going to give him a long account of my march. I think the horse sold very well, but cannot fancy what you will do with the saddle, unless you put it on a clothes-horse when you want to ride. Don't forget in your next to let me know the fate of the cheese. I guess it got "high and mity" enough to deserve a title. Oh! I do miss the porter at Berlin! Schumacher's is to let again, and the beer we get is "*ex-crabble!*" I hope next winter to taste it in London, but can form no plans till my health clears up more. I must beg you in your next to give me the list of the officers. I was to have had it before we parted, as I begin my German book with the march. How do you find your quarters? Are there any Miss A——s at Bromberg? By-the-by, I undertook a letter from Lieutenant B—— to deliver here, and sent it by Katchen, who says the mother came in and made a bit of a *row*. But I cannot well understand what she said in German. Perhaps there has been a cat let out of the bag, the young lady having left the letter lying on the table in view of the mamma.

How is Wildegans? and do you ever see him and Carlovicz? My kind regards to both, and most friendly remembrances to all you see, not forgetting *my* captain. How you will delight in settling down to your drill duties and parades after so much gaiety! I quite envy you: a few raw recruits would be quite a treat! You do not tell me whether you had any trolling with Prince Boguslaff: all our old fishing-stands by the Moselle are under water. I hope to get out a "Comic" early in the spring, and the books for Berlin; but I shall not know how to get anything over before, as I guess land-carriage cometh very dear, and they must come *viâ* Ostend till the Rhine-boats run again. Perhaps my painter will come out early; as Jane has told you I am to be "done in oil." I have now no news — how should

I have? for I have at least been *room*-ridden. I shall take to my rod again as soon as the season begins; but I shall miss you, Johnny, and your "wenting in."* I must promise you a better letter next time. This is only a *brief* from,

Dear Johnny,

Yours ever truly,

JOHNNY.

Fanny and Tom send their little loves.

COBLENZ, *December 15th*, 1836.

MY DEAR WRIGHT,

Now for a slight sketch of my march. Our start was a pretty one. We were to go at six, Jane and I, by the coach, and were to be called by four. Everything ready, but not all packed. I woke by *chance* at half-past five, our servant — hang her German phlegm! — being still in bed. Now, as all mails, &c., here are government concerns, you pay beforehand, at the post-office, fare, postilions, turnpikes, and all, which makes it very pleasant to lose your place.

By a miracle — I cannot imagine how — Mrs. Dilke helping, we somehow got Jane's bag and my portmanteau rammed full, and caught the coach just setting off. A fine day, and a fine view of the Rheingau, for we went round by the Baths to Frankfort-on-Maine, but "dooms" slow, for it is hilly all the way, and they walked up, and *dragged* on slowly down.

* Mr. Franck had so forgotten his English as to make little mistakes at times, and once said he "wented in" somewhere. Of course this gave my father an opportunity for *inwenting* endless fun. — T. H.

Started in the evening-coach from Frankfort for Eisenach. Myself taken very ill in the night; but had some illness hanging about me brought to a crisis by being stived up, all windows shut, with four Germans stinking of the accumulated smoke and odour, stale, flat, and unprofitable, of perhaps *two* years' reeking garlic and what not, besides heat insufferable. I was for some-time insensible, unknown to Jane, and, coming-to again, let down the window, which let in a very cold wind, but delicious to me, for it seemed like a breeze through the branches and blossoms of the tree of life. But it was the cause of a severe cold on the chest. We slept at Eisenach; next morning posted to Langen Seltzers, the head-quarters. * * *

I shall soon begin on my German book with "wigger." I have material prepared. Minor adventures on the march I have not given, as you will see them there. I pique myself on the punctuality of my brief military career. I was never too late, and always had my baggage packed by my own hands ready for the waggon. It was almost always dark at setting out, and I had to lead my horse till I could see. After half an hour, or an hour, we took generally a quarter's rest, for a sort of after-breakfast; then made for the general rendezvous, where we piled arms, and all fell to work on our victuals,—a strange picnic, each bringing what he could; and we made reports, and some showed sketches of their last night's quarters. On the whole, I was very fortunate. Some were regularly hovelled, in pigeon-houses or anywhere. It was a lottery. On the march I rode by turns at the head or the tail of the companies, talking with such of the officers as could speak French. They were, one and all, very friendly, and glad of my company. I almost wondered at myself, to find that I could manage my horse so well, for we had queer ground sometimes, when we took short cuts.

I assure you sometimes I have almost asked myself the question, whether I was I, seeming to be so much out of my ordinary life,—for example, on horseback, following, or rather belonging to, a company of soldiers; the bugle ringing through a vast pine wood to keep us together, or the men perhaps singing Polish songs in chorus, for this is a Polish regiment chiefly.

About a year ago I had a military cloak, at the contractor's price, from Berlin, but without any idea of a march. Thanks to it, and my horse, having been a captain of engineers', with its saddle-cloth, &c., I cheated the king of all the road-money, for they let me pass all the toll-houses as an officer. I was taken alternately for the chaplain and doctor of the regiment. It did me a world of good, but the finish marred all again. I was disappointed at not going to the end with them, but as De Franck stays, I could not well proceed; and I have since heard he has been stopped three weeks more, to go on a grand hunting party into Austria. I am going to set to work to learn German during this winter, as I know I shall be able to turn it to account. I am reading the papers, but they are not worth reading.

I shall be very happy to see Mr. L—— and show him all the *countenance* I can in Coblenz as a portrait-painter, by letting him take my own, but, for my part, I never got any good of my face yet, except that it once got me credit for eighteen pence at a shop, when I had gone out without my purse. If he has not yet seen the Rhine, he will find the "face of nature" very well worth his attentions, and I shall have much pleasure in offering him such hospitality as we have here,—for it is not quite English in its fare, this good town. But a change is sometimes agreeable. I had a change of it on the march, and I cooked our supper of Welsh-rabbits one night, but though it was good Stilton cheese, no less, the two German officers we invited express, would n't eat it. It ran a near chance of being thrown away, *because it was turning blue.* I must tell you of a good joke. I sent De Franck's servant with my passport to a country Burgomaster to be *visé,*—he brought it back with a message that "I could not be '*frizzé,*' without coming in person!" Encore. They use little fire bottles very much here,—one morning at four o'clock we were an immense time getting a light, the bugle had sounded long ago,—at last we found him with a bundle of about fifty phosphoric matches, trying them all by turns in our little *phial of Cayenne,* very much bothered that they would not catch fire. And now, dear Wright, adieu, with kind regards,

Yours, ever truly,

THOS. HOOD.

752, ALTEN GRABEN, COBLENZ, 26*th Dec.*, 1836.

MY DEAR DILKE,

I intended to write to you long ago, but, as usual, I have been laid up in ordinary, a phrase you must get some Navy Pay Officer to translate. My marching in fact ended like Le Fèvre's (it ought to be Le Fever) in a sick bed — my regiment came to a regimen! Oh, Dilke, what humbugs of travellers you and I be now, that we cannot compass a few hundred miles, but the leech must be called in at the end! I came home, looking ruddy as a ploughboy, and, excepting some signs of my old local weakness, better apparently than since I have been here; but almost the next day after my return, I turned white, with a most unaccountable depression, which ended in a fit of spitting blood as before. Dr. S—— was immediately sent for — I was bled, and there was no return.

Now I cannot believe that such a poor crow as I can have too much blood. I suspect this time it was a touch on the lungs, which were never touched before, being indeed my strongest point. I attribute it to our unlucky accident of the coach — at four o'clock of a cold, windy morning. However, I am nearly right again, but weak and low — rather: your kind letter has just arrived with its good news, quite equal to three cheers, one for Dilke, one for the "Comic," and one for myself. I was afraid the first would be worse for his homeward journey. I must and will think you set off too soon, and as a prophet after the fact, you had plenty of mild fine weather before you, for it only snowed here for the first time yesterday, Christmas Day! I am heartily glad to hear of so much decided improvement, but it will be a weak point always and require great care; — even at the expense of having a fell of hair like a German.

If he cannot get it *cut at home*, he deserves to have his head shaved for that last expedition. What would

Dr. S—— say, only I can't tell him. I hope *you, Mrs.* Dilke, preached a good sermon on it, and you will do well to read him daily a morning lesson out of the Bible, showing how Samson lost all his strength by going and having his hair cut. What an epitaph must I have written, if he had died through *that* little outbreak of personal vanity: —

"Here lies Dilke, the victim to a whim,
Who went to have his hair cut, but the air cut him."

I certainly do not agree any more than Dr. Johnson as to his being a *Cyst*-ercian; from the great tenderness, the evil did not seem to me to be so deeply seated as Dr. B. supposed, but nearer the surface; I have now great hope of him — barring barbers — and especially that leaving Somerset House; the change will perhaps add to his years, and let him live a *double number*, provided always he don't come up the Rhine again. I am always happy to see friends — but really I *do* wish you had not come, for now we have nothing so agreeable to look forward to, and not much at present to look back upon! I wonder if the visit will ever be returned — shall I ever go *down* the Rhine and drop in at Lower Grosvenor Place?

I live in hope of the first part at least; I try to fill up my own cavities instead of the sexton's by every care I can take; for instance, I am sailing on Temperance principles. I drank your health, and the compliments of the season to you yesterday, in a glass of Jane's ginger wine; and at night, being Christmas, indulged in a glass of — lemonade! As for you, Maria, having lost your sides, you must expect to be always middling, but no more spasms! So huzza for us all — who knows but our united ages may become worthy of a newspaper paragraph, some forty years hence.

I am glad you relish the "Comic" so well: indeed, I always try that it shall not fall off, whatever its sale may do — that the fault may be the public's, not the private's. But it seems doomed never to be early — thanks to that slug-a-bed, Katchen, and her German phlegm, it was some three weeks after it should have been out.

In the meantime, I will give you some particulars of my excursion. You have heard how well I got through my first day's ride — it was a fine morning, and we crossed part of that flat which surrounds Leipzic — what an immense flat it is! An ocean of sand literally stretching beyond the reach of the eye. It seems to have been intended for the grand armies of Europe to decide their differences on. That is to say, if Nature or Providence ever intended to form convenient plains for wholesale butcheries, of which I have some doubt.

However, it is classic ground to the soldier, as several great battles have taken place in the neighbourhood. The next morning, I packed up and started at four, and after rather a longer spell got to Brenha, where I found my quarters at a sort of country inn and butcher's shop rolled into one. I only breakfasted at Brenha — spending the rest of my time at a château of Baron B——'s, with De Franck and the Captain — the old Major-domo, the image of a Scotchman, doing the honours. He sent down to invite me, and thenceforward I boarded at the château, and only slept and breakfasted at the inn. I had the prettiest girl in the place for my waitress — and told her I was a prisoner of state on parole with the regiment, which interested her in my favour, I suppose: anyhow it brought up the mother — dram bottle in hand — who sat herself down, *tête-à-tête* at the table, and seemed determined to hear all the rights of it: but I grew very English, and her curiosity could get nothing out of me. At the château we lived like fighting-cocks, and drank a very good wine, made on the estate, as good as much of the Rhenish.

We had a sort of under-steward for our host, and for our waiting-maid, an ugly, grisly female, with the addition of an outlandish head-dress, and a huge frill — stiff, and *fastened behind to her cap*, so that she was in a sort of pillory. The pretty girl at the inn did not get half so much of my attention. The fare — poultry, jack, carp, beetroot, neat's tongue. I saw in the farm-yard some very fair pigs — one with a stiff neck — his head regularly fixed on one side; some excellent Polish fowls; and in a long stable a range of fine-ish cows, with a long solid bench before them, where each had a circular hollow scooped for it like a bason. I have seen tables for human beasts, in Berkshire, with the dishes and platters, scooped out in like fashion — not a bad plan for sea-faring furniture — not over cleanly, perhaps, but fast and not breakable. There was also a garden and a fish-pond in it.

The next day being a rest, we spent at the same place, and we went trolling, the steward giving us leave, in a mill-stream, where we only caught one little jack before dinner, who had tried to swallow the bait, a carp as broad as himself. We brought both into the house, as they were, by the way of a curiosity, but leaving tackle and all in the passage, during dinner, we hooked the favourite cat to boot, who had taken the bait too. Our bad sport in the morning procured us leave for the afternoon, in the *garden pond*, a sort of preserve, where we immediately hooked a good large jack. As soon as the line went off under the weeds, I pulled out my watch to give the fish eight or ten minutes to pouch the bait, while De Franck stood still as a statue with the rod; the captain up at his window wondering what solemn operation was going on. At last we got him, a good jack; then a second, a third, and a fourth, the face of the steward lengthening to each catch, in the most laughable manner. He evidently thought we should "distress the water," as it is technically termed. Jack are much esteemed, you must know, in inland Germany, and the old man was quite glad when we packed up our tackle. He was comforted at last to find three were so little hurt, that they might be thrown in again. But he told us, half in joke, half in earnest, when we came again he should set a watch over all his ponds.

Three years since there were four thousand trees blown down on the estate by a storm, they stopped all the roads in the neighbourhood, which took fourteen days in clearing; and some of the trees are not yet removed.

They must have had some such treats in Germany elsewhere, I guess, during the late hurricanes. At the inn I had one dinner, one supper, bed twice, and two breakfasts, for ten groschen, or one shilling. But these bye-places are poor, and a little money goes a great way. Here I not only found soap for the first time in Germany, but a place in the *bason* expressly for holding it. The Saxons seemed generally good sort of people. Our next march took us across the Elbe to Wittenberg. A Lieutenant J——, an old crony of De Franck's, met us on the bridge, and insisted on our dining with him, so we got leave, dined at the Casino, and J—— showed me the lions of the place.

As to Luther's statue, I could not help thinking of Friar John, in Rabelais, as a brother of the same order. Thinks I to myself, so I am to thank that fellow up there for being a Protestant. I had remarked at Wittenberg the peculiar tall glasses, a full foot high, with a glass cover (no stems), and afterwards at Berlin I saw Luther's drinking cup, or vessel, made after the same jolly fashion. J—— showed me his residence, now a College, where he said a good deal of mysticism prevails. J—— drove with us, in a hired carriage, to our quarters, about an hour's ride through deep sand to Pruhlitz, a very tiny village. We passed, by the way, a well miraculously discovered by Luther when he was dry, by a scratch of his staff in the sand — he looked more like the tapper of ale barrels. In our quarters I had for a wonder, a *four-post bed* with the old feather beds below and above, and as the bed was made at an angle of thirty-five degrees, I slept little more than I should have done on a "Russian mountain," always sliding down and getting up again. Hereabouts this slant was quite the fashion. Partridges are so plentiful about Leipsic and Wittenberg, as to be three groschen the brace. Next morning we got to the Mark of Brandenburg. We went over sands, and such desolate, bleak, bare heaths, I expected on every ascent to come in sight of some forlorn sea-coast (we took often short cuts across country, rendezvousing in the high roads). Our march lasted eight and a half hours, having a grand parade (as rehearsal) on the way, and were quartered at last at Nichel, near Treuenbritzen, so called as the only place that stood *true* to Frederic the Great.

When we arrived here, the whole population had turned out to see us, as military do not often appear in such parts. The females look very picturesque — for the single wear black head-dresses, the married ones, quite a game of *rouge et noir.* I don't think Cook could have been more wondered at by the Sandwichers, than I was by the Nichelites. A party waited in front of the house, and pointed me out whenever I came to the window, and stared with only the glass between us, as heartily as if they had really been sheep and not merely skins. The Captain of the 11th company (mine was the 10th) called politely to see how I was lodged. * * * I was much amused in the evening to see the gaunt hogs trotting home of their own accord, from I know not where — each going into his own quarters as regularly as we did — and the geese the same, though some next door houses were infinitely to appearance more selectable than their neighbours.

I saw a goose wait for a long while at a house, where no door happened to be open, till at last she was admitted. I will give you a recipe for our dinner. First make some rice-milk rather watery, and stew in a few raisins. Then cut a fowl in pieces, six perhaps, and make a broth with it. Pour the first dish and the second together, and the mess is made. We had two beds for three; so De Franck slept on the straw. Next morning we got to Belitz; from here we rode across to Schlunkendorf, quartered with De Franck and another at a miller's. Millers', by the way, are the best quarters everywhere, though we got but two beds, and so De Franck was littered down. I went out after dinner, and could see nothing but a sandy waste with a windmill. In my yellow boots and figured robe (Mrs. D.'s present), I was not at all out of costume, for such an Arabian-like scene. Next day being a rest, I took advantage of it to push on to Potsdam to see all I could. Here ended my actual marching with the regiment, for the next morning the King came to Potsdam to review it. He was much pleased; but as an instance of his love for military minutiæ, and correct ear, when they were giving him cheers, the huzzas and the drums did not time exactly together, and he exclaimed "What beating is that?"

Everything about Potsdam smacks of the Great little Frederic, but nothing is more striking than the superabundance of statues. They *swarm!* — there is a whole garrison turned into marble or stone, good, bad, and indifferent. They are as numerous in the garden as the promenaders; there is a Neptune group, for example, without even the apology of a pond. The same at Sans Souci — in fact, everywhere. The effect, to my taste, is execrable, or ridiculous. Solitude and stillness seem the proper attributes of a statue. We have no notion of marbles mobbing. I saw, of course, all the apartments and relics of Frederic. The chairs torn by his dogs, his writing-table, &c. The Watteaus on the walls, containing the recurring *belle* Barberini, pleased me much; he seems to give a nature to courtliness, and a courtliness to nature, that make palace-gardens more like fairy-land, and their inhabitants more like Loves and Graces than I fear they be in reality. I was much interested by a portrait of Napoleon when consul (said to be very like), over a door in the palace. It had a look of melancholy as well as thought, with an expression that seemed to draw the heart towards him. There must have been something likeable about him, to judge by the attachment and devotion of some of his adherents; but I could not help believing before the picture, that when younger, he had been of a kinder and more benevolent disposition than is generally supposed.

One of the other curiosities was the present king's bed — a mere crib. I visited the Peacock Island, of which I thought little; and two of the country-seats, the Crown Prince's and Prince Charles's. The first in the style of an Italian villa, with frescoes, in the medallions of which are introduced portraits of personal friends, &c.; but the German physiognomy does not match well with the Italianesque. The public are admitted into the gardens — even when the Prince is enjoying himself in them with his parties: this is very, almost ultra, liberal; but it seems to me a German taste to enjoy nothing without this publicity. At Prince Charles's (he is attached to the sea, and wished to be a sailor) I saw some annuals on his table, and an English caricature; also English prints and pictures hung in the rooms. He is partial to us, and I entered my name in a book he keeps to know of his visitors. I saw some fine pictures in the gallery — Titians; a most miraculous *living* hand of flesh and blood, as it seemed to me to be, in one of them.

I entertained some of the officers here to luncheon; they dined by invitation with the Guards, who gave them a dinner, first for the king, and secondly for themselves. I saw here the Russian colony, living in cottages *à la Suisse.* I saw, of course, the famous mill that beat Frederic in a battle, like Don Quixote; and I sat down at Frederic's table where he worked, with a statue of Justice in sight through a window at the opposite end of the room — "a conceit! a miserable conceit!" — that he might always keep justice in view. An acted pun! As his favourite dogs were all buried with a tombstone apiece, very near Justice's feet, there óught to have been some *meaning* there, too; but I could not find or invent it, unless that Justice had more to do with dead dogs than with living ones.

The garrison church, externally, looks like an arsenal, 't is so be-stuck with helmets, flags, and military trophies, carved in stone; but in the interior it is worth one's while to go into a dark narrow tomb, just under the organ, only to reflect on the strange chances of finding Frederic and his father so near, and yet so peaceable, as they lie side by side — *not* "lovely and pleasant in their lives, but in their deaths not divided."

* * * *

And now, my dear D., with kind regards to Mrs. Dilke,

Believe me ever

Your faithful friend,

THOMAS HOOD.

On returning from Berlin, my father settled down to complete, as far as possible, the matter and drawings for his German book. In one of my mother's letters to England, she says, "You will be glad to hear Hood intends seriously to study German during the winter, and I don't mean to let his purpose cool. He talks of seeing more of Germany in the spring." (Here my father seems to have been at his old tricks again of embellishing my mother's letters, for there follows in his own handwriting). "At present Germany has seen *him*. As at Berlin there was London porter, reasonable Cheshire cheese, to say nothing of *caviare*, smoked goose breasts, and other relishes; he says he regularly 'filled his cavities.' After the discipline his stomach underwent in such villages as Schlunkendorf and Nichel it is so much improved in its tone, that I have very little of my old trouble, and it *was* a trouble, in suiting it. He swears that he eats 'würst' even with a relish. I wish he had marched a year ago, and almost regret with Mr. Dilke that he is not in the army. I mean to make him a present of a walking-stick on New-Year's day, and to make him trot out on errands."

The German book "Up the Rhine," progressed favourably, the "Comic Annual" coming out as usual. I can just recollect the actual finish of the latter. My father always wrote most by night, when all was quiet and the bustle of the day and the noise of us children stilled in sleep. This year I recollect being waked by hearing my father and mother in the next room, packing the little box of drawings and MSS. to send off by steamer to England. When they found I was awake my mother came in and rolled me up in a huge shawl, installing me in an arm chair; we then finished up with a merry supper (though it must have been nearer morning than night) my father, relieved from the anxiety and worry of his work, brightening up through all his fatigue, and joking and laughing quite cheerfully. Each following year did these finishing suppers take place, to celebrate the completion of the "Comic Annual."

CHAPTER IV.

1837.

At Coblenz.—Letters to Mr. Wright, Lieut. de Franck, and Dr. Elliot.—Leaves Coblenz.—Settles at Ostend.—Letters to Mr. Wright, Dr. Elliot, and Mr. Dilke.

IN the beginning of 1837 my father finally made up his mind to leave Coblenz. Among other reasons, the difficulty of sending backwards and forwards was really serious. "A month to côme, and a month to go," as he writes to Mr. Wright, "makes a serious difference in time to me, and throws out all my plans." In these days of easy railway locomotion, when there is a line almost over even those primitive wilds he travelled through on his march, this time seems fabulous. It is curious to think how all these increased facilities for travelling must have civilised those remote places,—such as Schlunkendorf and Nichel,—and transformed, I will not say improved, the Schultz and his fellow-villagers of the sheepskin robes into very ordinary German peasants, with fewer outlandish characteristics, and with possibly less honesty.

752, ALTEN GRABEN, COBLENZ, 13*th January*, 1837.

MY DEAR WRIGHT,

I have no doubt but the Count you are doing some

cuts for, is the same that Prince Radziwill mentioned to me, as engaged on a work on modern German art. The Prince alluded to the excellence of our *wood-cutting.** You would do well to send the Count some of your *best specimens;* I saw some wretched German woodcuts in the Berlin exhibition. I think the name I recollect was something like Raczynski. I should not be surprised if seeing the Comic had suggested you to him as good wood-engravers. The Germans cannot cut; and if they could make fine cuts, couldn't print them. And yet Albert Dürer, a German, was the founder of the art. I am hard at work at my German book. You will soon have a box. Some of the subjects are larger than usual, and must be printed the long way of the page. Have the goodness to make a polite message to Messrs. Saunders and Otley for me, saying, that till I return to England I cannot well undertake any such arrangement as they propose; but that when I come back I shall be open to offers of the kind. Indeed, for the next six months my hands are full.

I have no time to write more, except to present all good wishes and seasonable compliments to yourself and Mrs. W. Pray remember me kindly to all friends, not

* Those who remember the rudeness of the Comic cuts, or even of "Up the Rhine," will smile at this. I don't suppose Messrs. Linton or Dalziel would allow their apprentices to turn out such blocks. The art appears to have been bound in German swaddling-clothes from Dürer's time until Bewick released it, since when it has made strides worthy of an ogre in seven-league boots. I take this opportunity of publicly expressing the thanks of my sister and self to the engraver, who has cut the illustrations for this work with such great spirit and fidelity. — T. H.

forgetting poor Ned Smith. Did I name a book for Harvey? But I trust to you, who know my wishes, to rectify all casual mistakes and omissions.

I am, my dear Wright,

Yours ever truly,

THOMAS HOOD.

I shall write a chapter on German Draughts (of Air), and their invention of cold-traps. I have a stiff neck, that goes all down my back, and then comes up the other side, thanks to their well-staircases and drying lofts in the attics.

752, ALTEN GRABEN, COBLENZ, *April* 23*rd*, 1837.

MY DEAR JOHNNY,

Are n't you glad to hear now that I 've only been ill and spitting blood three times since I left you, instead of being very dead indeed, as you must have thought from my very long silence. I began a letter, indeed, a long while ago; but, on hearing of the setting off of the box, I waited for its arrival, and a precious wait it was. Only a month and three days, and my box was still longer in going to London. Hurrah for German commerce! It must thrive famously with such a quick transit! One might almost as well be in America.

I had a sharp brush with the Customs' officers after all, for they wanted to unpack it at the office, which I would not stand. I think I scared Deubel, I was in such a rage; but I gained my point. You know last year they offered to send an officer to the house, and even declined to see it at all; so I told them. There was a full declaration of every article, and I was charged for "*plumbing*," by which I understand the putting of *leaden seals* on, but there was no trace of anything of the kind. To make it worse, I have since ascertained that the scoundrels had already opened it at Emmerich. This has been such a sickener to me that I have made up my mind to leave this place, with no very pleasant recollections of its courtesy towards strangers.

However, I shall have my revenge: the materials of my book are in London, and so let the Rhinelanders look out for squalls. I hope you will like the tackle; it all came safe; and Wright assures me it is the very best made, and at the wholesale price. I send the Prince's and Wildenbruch's at the same time. The bad weather for fishing hitherto will make the delay of less consequence. Did you ever know such hot and cold, such snow and rain? It has been killing work; we were all well "gripped;" and a nasty insidious disease it is, leaving always its marks behind it. I have got all my books (save one, which is out of print) for the Prince, in the newest fashion of binding.

Tim, says he, I laughed heartily at your description of the fishing at Bromberg, for you seemed in a whimsical dilemma enough; and so, after wishing with all your heart, soul, and strength to be within reach of salmon, you were frightened at them when you had them at hand!

I should be rather nervous for my tackle myself. It would have been no use writing to R——, who knows no more about it than I do: nor have I any practical salmon-fisher of my acquaintance — they are chiefly

Scotch and Irish. But I am pretty certain of this point, that there is nothing peculiar in it from other fly-fishing, but that all use stronger tackle, larger bright flies, big as butterflies, and that you must play with the fish a wonderful deal more, — say half or three quarters of an hour, — to wear them out. There is a famous winch and line coming with this. If I were you, I would get up some sort of a German rod extempore, put this winch on it, and make the experiment before risking your good rod. For myself, Johnny, I must give up all hope of ever wetting a line at Bromberg; not only are my marching days over, but I fear I shall never be able to travel again. I am now sure that this climate, so warm in summer and so cold in winter, does not suit my English blood. Inflammatory disorders are the besetting sin of the place. Witness poor Dilke. And at my last attack Dr. —— told me he saw the same thing every day. The man who bled me, and there are *several* bleeders here, told me he had attended eighty that month. Moreover, I had been not merely moderate, but abstemious; at one time only drank Jane's ginger-wine, and at my last attack was actually only taking two glasses of wine a day. We even get good English porter now at the Trèves Hotel, *and I dare not touch it!*

This low diet does not at all suit me. When I was a boy I was so knocked about by illness (and in particular by a scarlet fever so violently that it ended in a dropsy) that as I grew up I only got over it by living rather well. Besides, as all doctors know, studious pursuits exhaust the body extremely, and require stimulus at times, so I have made up my mind to decamp. My present idea is *per* Cologne and Aix to Ostend or Antwerp, when I shall be able to get over to England in a few hours at any time, if necessary; and should I get strength to travel, I can see something of Belgium and France. I rather incline to Ostend on account of the sea air, which always does me great good. I shall regret the children not completing their German here; but the difficulty of intercourse (which neutralizes all my efforts to be early with my books) and the climate forbid it; and, in addition, I have quite a disgust to Coblenz, or rather its inhabitants. I have begun German myself, through L——, but that must be at an end. I find him as a German Jew better than the Jew Germans of the place. I have not seen the General, "cos why?" I have only crossed the door three times, perhaps six, since I came from Berlin. But I shall call some day before I go. When my plan is once arranged I shall go at once. Towards the end of this month, I suppose, I shall trouble the chub again for the last time. I have some famous large chub flies by the box — some like small cockchafers. I am not sure whether my chest will stand the casting. It is miserable work, Tim, to be such a shattered old fellow as I am; when you, who are in years my senior, are gallivanting about like a boy of nineteen! The artist who is coming out to take my portrait will have a nice elderly, grizzled head to exhibit! What! that pale, thin, long face the Comic! Zounds! I must gammon him, and get some friend to sit for me. *Àpropos*, I sent up two months ago a box full of sketches of my Rhine book; and I had managed such a portrait of D—— in a Rhenish spare bed! I have drawn, too, the captain, who gave me leave to make use of his jolly red nose, Mr. Schultz, Mrs. Schultz, and all, not forgetting the maid in the pillory-ruff at Burg-Kremnitz. D'ye know, Johnny, I half suspect the Rhinelanders opened my box going down, and were not best pleased at my sketches of some of the dirty dandies hereabouts, which perhaps makes 'em so uncivil. Should all happen that I have wished to the Coblenzers in general, and the Douane in particular, during the last ten days, they will be far from comfortable. Only imagine that I blessed everything for them down to their pipes. They have the worst of the French character without the best of the German. I have no news to tell you about them; how should we pick up any, for we are not on speaking terms with any one in the place, save the two teachers. Nor have I been to the Military Casino, so that I cannot answer your inquiry how the young ladies take the loss of the 19th.

I have just asked L—— if there is any local news. He knows nothing except that this last winter there have been *more* balls and parties than usual, so that the ladies have not kept their faith to the 19th.

As to the breaking off the *verlobbing* with Von B. we have not heard one word about it. How should we? Perhaps it is not true, but has only been reported to quiz you, and make you fancy you have a chance again. But I will drop that subject, or I shall make you as savage as you were one night with me and Wildegans, and even with yourself, till I expected you would call yourself out. Oh, Tim, she enjoyed hitting you over the heart, like the man who had a donkey, with "a bit of raw."

She is learning English, of course for your sake says you — but I forget! I see you in fancy twisting your moustaches and pouting. Mrs. N——, through L——'s means, is reading some of my Comics.

I guess they will puzzle her pretty considerably. Also Mrs. A—— has had them. She and Captain A—— have been living at the Weisser Ross for months, and he is a member of my club; but we have not met, and they are now going. I am not sorry to have missed them, for I saw them pass, and they not only look queer people, but awfully Scotch! Besides, we have had our share of luck in picking up friends on that side the water.

Since writing the foregoing, Tim, I am a little better; but was n't I in luck, after spitting blood and being bled, to catch the rheumatism in going down-stairs. I ordered leeches on my foot, and the wounds bled all night, so I was uncommonly low, as you may imagine. I suppose I shall get out some day. This morning I was going to have a ride for the first time, but it clouded over, and I gave it up. What a precious season we have had — eight months' winter. But now the ice will be broken up, and you will be blessing me for not sending your tackle. It has had to wait here almost a week for a frach-wagen, which only goes on Sundays. I had little or no news from London by the package, but I have heard that poor Dilke is in a very precarious state: he does n't rally well, and the least illness flies to the old place. The last account, though, was a little better.

What do you think, Tim, of a black man, who by dancing and singing *one* little song called "Jim Crow," has cleared, in London and America, 30,000*l.*! There 's one string to your bow for you! I never heard of the history of the bit of Stilton that went on to Bromberg. The Cheshire we send makes Welsh rabbits well — don't forget to try it. Also you will find some ginger for ginger-beer. I send a box of lozenges for "Ganserich," for the cold drill mornings. I shall always be glad that I saw you as far on your road as I could; but when I look back and think how very little I have stirred out of the house ever since I came from Berlin, that march seems to me a dream.

I do not think that the book about it will come out before the next Comic. I have been so delayed, the spring season for publishing is over. You'll be sure to have it. I have drawn you just as you came dripping out of the Lahn, and I mean to try some way or other to commemorate Wildegans. Tom Junior does not forget any of you. The other day he pointed to that old fat major or colonel of the 29th, who walks about with a thick stick, and laughed, and said: "There is Franck."

He says "Franck bought Bello — Bello is Tom's dog" — and he always toasts Vildidans and Tarlyvitz when he gets a drop of wine. He talks a strange jumble of English and German, and English according to the German Grammar. "That is hims," "There is you's chair," "Will you lend it for me," &c., &c. Fanny is very well again, and very good; Jane is as usual; she is now drinking porter, at which I look half savage. Only think, porter and Cheshire cheese, and I dare n't take *both!* I must n't even *sip*, and I long to *swig*. Nothing but water. I shall turn a fish soon, and have the pleasure of angling for myself. I am almost melancholy, for I never had any serious fears about my health before; my lungs were always good. But now I think they are touched too. I 've had a sort of plaister on my chest which will not heal; but I won't bother you with my symptoms. In spite of all this, I ordered this morning a new fishing-jacket — a green one; so you see I mean to show fight, and keep on my legs as long as I can. But one must reckon the fishing calendar a month later; those that used to spawn in May will do it in June, I expect. Of course they would not come out while there was snow. I meant to have got some gudgeons this month, which is the prime, or ought to be the best season — but this is all gone by. I have such difficulty in writing, I cannot send you so long a letter as I should wish: it is some exertion to me at present to think of any thing: I am obliged to keep myself quiet.

Moreover there is so little news stirring that it is not easy to fill up a letter. Mind and give my remembrances most kindly to every one of my old comrades, and pray thank them for thinking of me. I only wish I could put myself under our Captain's orders again, and have to trouble your Quartermaster.

It will be a pleasant subject for life for me to think upon that same march — for though I was not on speaking terms with many of your officers, I was not the less friendly. Do not forget my best respects to the Colonel, whenever you see him, — nor my compliments to the Major: I suppose Carlovicz is not with you, but send our regards to him — and tell him Tom is an excellent master to Bello — indeed more attentive to him than to me even — for at the least scratch at the door, whatever play he is engaged in, he breaks off to go and let in his dog. Say everything kind to Wildegans — he and I ought to insure each other's lives. I hope he likes the Brombergian quarters.

I cannot give more particular messages, for the names are very difficult to spell — but I trust to you not to omit my compliments to every officer of my acquaintance in *our* regiment. I must, however, especially name my own quarter-comrades Von Bonkowski, and Von Heugel, of whose attentions I retain a grateful impression, often recurring in memory to Hagelstadt, Burg Kremnitz, Nichel, and Schlunkendorf. Pray give me all the regimental news when you write. I shall not leave here till June — and, at all events, you shall hear from me before I move. We have our lodgings till 15th July, but shall not stay so long as that; and now, old fellow, God bless you, and send you all sorts of luck, and happiness, and sport, and promotion — everything you wish. May you pull out salmons, and may salmons pull you in, but without drowning you. I say, Tim, says he, if I was at Bromberg would n't we have fun; but that 's over. So as Mahomet said to the mountain — "why if I can't come to you, why you must come to me." Farewell and Amen, says, my dear Johnny,

Yours ever truly,

THOMAS HOOD.

Rather better to-night.

Your box leaves here with this — acknowledge receipt of all.

752, Alten Graben, *Saturday*, 29*th April*, 1837.

My dear Franck,

I quite forgot to ask in my letter for what I wanted. If you can spare it then, not otherwise, please to send me the book the old clergyman gave you on the march, of military songs.

I mean that where he says his sweetheart is his belt, his knapsack, his firelock, &c., &c.; if you have it not, tell me the name of it.*

* I give the literal translation of this song, and the comment on it, from "Up the Rhine." Would not Mr. Theodore Martin translate it well? — T. H.

"It smacks of the very spirit of Uncle Toby and Corporal Trim, and seems written with the point of a bayonet on the parchment of a drum.

"LOVE LANGUAGE OF A MERRY YOUNG SOLDIER.

"O, Gretel, my Dove, my heart's Trumpet,
My Cannon, my Big Drum, and also my Musket,
Oh, hear me, my mild little Dove,
In your still little room.

"Your portrait, my Gretel, is always on guard,
Is always attentive to Love's parole and watchword;
Your picture is always going the rounds —
My Gretel I call at every hour.

"My heart's knapsack is always full of you,
My looks they are quartered with you;
And when I bite off the top-end of a cartridge
Then I think that I give you a kiss.

"You alone are my Word of Command and Orders,
Yea, my Right-face, Left-face, Brown-Tommy, and Wine,
And at the word of command, 'Shoulder arms,'
Then I think you say, 'Take me in your arms.'

I have heard from London, and am happy to say Dilke is considerably better, which is a very great relief to us. All concur in advising me to quit this; in fact, I feel sure that another winter and summer here would kill me between them.

So we are going — that's *decided* — on the 1st of June — a week earlier if we can get all our arrangements made. I am better, and feel quite pleased with the thought of leaving Coblenz, of which I am heartily sick — for it has nothing now to make us regret it, but the mere beauty of the scenery. We shall go to Ostend for the sea: if we do not like it to Bruges, Ghent, or Brussels, for as I do not expect to come to the Continent again, I mean to see a little of Flanders and France, should I be strong enough, while there; and then we are so near we can pass over to England in a few hours whenever we like.

Dilke says he will not swear he *won't* come over to see us, though he had such bad luck in his visit to us here. There is a gentleman coming out shortly with the Comics, so I will send you one, and one for Prince Charles, if you like to send it. By the time you receive this I hope you will have your box quite safe. Don't

"Your eyes sparkle like a Battery,
Yea, they wound like Bombs and Grenades;
Black as Gunpower is your hair,
Your hand as white as Parading-breeches.

"Yes, you are the Match, and I am the Cannon;
Have pity, my love, and give Quarter, —
And give the word of command, 'Wheel round
Into my heart's Barrack Yard.'"

forget to toast some of your cheese, it makes famous Welsh rabbits. We sup on them four nights a week. I suppose, Johnny, all my fishing will "suffer a sea change," and I must adapt my tackle for flounders, soles, whiting, cod, and mackerel.

As to wittles and drink, Coblenz is worse than ever. There is no Bavarian beer now, and no Westphalian hams! Deubel pulls a very long face at our going, and no wonder, for there are lists of "lodgings to let" as long as your arm. I never saw so many before. I am riding out every fine day to gain strength, and bid good bye to the views. We don't take Katchen with us, who has been trying hard to go, as well as to be made residuary legatee as to all our things here — modest impudence!

Tim, says he, I saw a fight between men here the other night for the first time. It was good fun, two to one; and did n't they pull hair like *gals*, and then haul him down, and give him a good unfair beating while he lay on the ground! And did n't he go away, wiping his bloody nose, for good as I thought, but came back again with three or four allies; and the others, at least one of the others, was ready with a mighty big bit of wood; and did n't the women squall, and run out to see with candles, though it was hardly dusk; and did n't they screech like a knife on a plate, and lug the men about! Then the fellows all gobbled like turkey-cocks — such explosions of gutturals! You know what thick voices the common people have. And then they began to fight again; and a lot of men, women, and children bolted up all sorts of streets, *sauve qui peut.* I don't know how it ended, so I won't say.

And now, old fellow, God bless you. I will write again with the Comic when it comes. The Dilkes desire kind remembrance to you; so does Jane, and Fanny ditto, and Tom ditto ditto. Don't forget me to all the 19th, including the staff, and believe me, from my top joint to my butt,

My dear Tim,

Yours very truly,

THOMAS HOOD.

752, ALTEN GRABEN, COBLENZ, *April* 29*th*, 1837.

MY DEAR DOCTOR,

Many thanks for your kind letter; it positively did me good. But you seem seldom to put pen to paper without that effect, whether in letters or prescriptions. I wrote a very brief notice of the state of my health to Mr. Wright.

The Germans drink low sour wines, and have a horror here of anything that *heats* them in the way of drink, such as Spanish wine, &c. Yet, in spite of this care, they are subject to inflammatory attacks very commonly. The grippe here took that character very decidedly.

Fanny was obliged to have leeches on her face. Tom's was highly inflamed, and had a great discharge from his nose and behind his ear, which were very sore. Mr. Dilke's attack here was attended with strong inflammation. We have heard only yesterday of an English lady obliged to have leeches; in fact, there are standing advertisements in the town papers where leeches are to be had cheap. I *know* of three barber-surgeons who bleed; there may be more. The one who bled me in

February is only just set up, and he told me he had bled eighty that month; one may say two hundred and fifty, between the three operators, with safety. Inflamed eyes are extremely common here, and there is a peculiar inflammation of the whole face called the "rose." I dare say the causes may be found in the very great changes of temperature here, both abroad and at home. The sun is *very* much warmer than in England, and the winds are much colder.

It is dangerous to pass from the sun into the shade. Then in the houses their mode of building is the worst possible. This one is a fair sample. Below, a passage right through the house, with front door to the street and back door to the yard, always open till after ten at night. From the middle of this passage a well staircase right up through the house, terminating in the garrets, where the high roofs are full of unglazed windows or holes, for the special purpose of creating draughts for drying linen. On this stair, or open landings, all your room-doors open; so that you step out of a close stove-heated room into a thorough draught of the street air. I tried it once by thermometer: the room was 60°, and outside 45°. The winters are very cold, and doubly so in these comfortless buildings. I used to fancy the Germans never cut their hair, by way of defence against cold in the head, but I saw two fight the other day, and the hair was of the greatest feminine use, namely, to pull at. My last attack of spitting blood came on the moment after going down the stairs; and the first time I came up them again I caught the rheumatism, and had leeches on my foot, which bled all night. So I am somewhat reduced, and the diet here is anything but nourishing. Take for example the present bill of fare: no fish ever, no poultry now, no game of course, never any pork, veal killed at a week old, beef from cart-cows, and plough-bullocks, which when cold is as dry and almost as white as a deal board. The very bread is bad, poor wheat mixed with rye and inferior meals. The people are poor, and the ground is wretchedly over-cropped. It is a beautiful country indeed to the *eye*, but I shall not regret leaving it. There are no books within reach, and no society, which I need not to care about, for the torpidity or apathy of mind in these people is beyond belief. German phlegm is no fable; but you will have a book about them next half-year with plenty of sketches. The communication, too, with London is so vexatious and slow (it takes above a month) as to be a serious evil to me. I had resolved on a change on this account alone, when my last illness clenched my decision. We are going to Ostend, where I shall be not only within reach of England, but hope to be benefited by the sea-air, which always did me the most marked good. I have tried in vain to master German, partly from its difficulty, and partly from having only the intervals between my attacks for all I had to write or draw. But Fanny talks it fluently, and Tom understands it perfectly as well as English. Fanny is very well now; and Tom a fine hearty fellow, full of fun, which his motley jargon makes very comic. The "*Jane*," too, wears very well. For myself, I keep up my spirits on my toast-and-water, which is all I drink, save tea and coffee, and seem rallying again. I have a sort of appetite, too, if there were anything worth eating.

I really cannot do as the invalids do here. Mrs. Deubel, our landlady, as the first luxury on recovering from the grippe, comforted her inside with a mess of dried bullaces in sour wine! Head only tells half the truth, for instance, of the breeches maker, who ate a bowl-full of plums; but he does n't hint that he swallowed all the stones. I *know* that 's their way of eating cherries! I could tell you some strange stories. The mortality here has been great, but of young children it is painfully so all the year round. And no wonder — the other day a mother called in a barber-surgeon to save expense. The child had a rash — he put ice on the head — turned the red spots blue and black, and it died.

When we are at Ostend you will perhaps be tempted to come over, and see us and the country.

The cities in Belgium are interesting, and all within easy reach. I think I shall make a strange sitting to an artist, who wants my portrait for next year's exhibition!

I look more like the Rueful Knight than a Professor of the Comic.

Pray tell Mrs. Elliot that the man at Moselweis, whither we went by moonlight, who had only a bit of plum tart in his house, failed subsequently, as might be expected, but another has taken the gardens, and they are as popular as ever. I hope it has not given her a taste for White Conduit House, and the like. But it was a sample of our German manners and amusements.

I have not learned smoking yet; but hate it worse than ever, since I see its effects on the mind and the person. However, should I leave Germany, I have introduced angling and am the Izaak Walton of the Rhine, Moselle, and Lahn.

I shall write a less selfish egotistical letter when I get to Ostend, to tell you how it agrees with me, as well as some little anecdotes, &c., I have not now time or space to get in; besides being a little weary of holding my pen. I flag at times rather suddenly, of course from weakness. Jane promises to write too, when settled, in answer to Mrs. E.'s kind letter, to whom she sends her kind regards with mine; and Fanny begs to mingle — not forgetting Willy.

I am, my dear Doctor,

Very truly yours,

THOS. HOOD.

I was ordered lately a sort of slow blister on the chest, which would only stick on by help of strips of adhesive plaister.

The grippe seemed to cause a great deal of this humour here.

It has been a nasty malignant disease, infinitely worse than the influenza as we used to have it in England. The people have a great horror of what they call a nervous fever. They say the French brought it from Moscow. But I suspect the sour wines here are very bad, *per se*.

752, ALTEN GRABEN, COBLENZ, *May 4th*, 1837.

MY DEAR WRIGHT,

* * * *

As regards "Up the Rhine," I am glad you liked the

drawings; you are right about them, they will require *engraving*, and I should like them well done. They are not like the Comic cuts, mere jokes; but portraits and fac-similes of the people, &c., and should be correctly done. I hope to make it altogether a superior book. I shall have another set of good ones to send you; which you may show to Harvey if you like. I had a rare bother about the box with the customs. It had been opened at the frontier; and they wanted to open it again here. But I had them — some wet had got in, and the blocks were almost wet, and one of the bindings was a little stained by damp. I admire the style of the Prince's books. I did not venture any more than you to open the Prince's things, they seemed so well packed, but sent them off as they were. And Franck's are gone, too, with a bit of cheese! It is very good, and toasts capitally. Ain't it provoking for me? — by chance we can get porter here just now, and I dare n't touch a drop of it with my cheese! I 'm on toast and water, though very low and weak. But I am getting better; and, as the weather improves, shall ride out. I am delighted to think of leaving here; it is a beautiful country, and living is cheap; but I am worn out by these repeated attacks and delays, with anxiety to boot; and it is most dismally dull here now. No one to converse with, and I cannot see a book or know what is going on in the literary world — the "Athenæum" excepted; that *is* something. But the worst of the "Athenæum" is, it makes me long to read some of the books it reviews. Then the diet is so wretched for an invalid, and the domestic comforts few. The country is anything but the land of corn, wine, milk, and honey one would think to look at it; and the people are hateful — I mean unbearable — to Englishmen. They hate *us* I am quite convinced. I have given up any idea of colouring my sketches, except perhaps a bit here and there, as the caps in some carnival figures to show they are the tricolour.

It is quite a comfort to us that Dilke is better; he is an old man though, he says. We were uneasy about him. He says that, in spite of his sorry Rhenish trip, he won't swear not to visit us at Ostend. Now that would be quite a practicable distance for you, and it would do us both good. I have some projects I could concert with you there. I fancy already that I sniff the sea, and feel it bracing me. I once literally left my bed for the first time to get into the Brighton coach, and the next morning but one I was walking on the *shingles*. The sea is *life* to me. I propose to quit *here* about the 1st of June, — sooner if I can.

We talked with our landlord to-day about going. His naturally extra-long face grew still longer. He complained bitterly of the state of trade, want of money, &c.; and unluckily for him, though when I first came to Coblenz I could hardly find a single place; there is now a list in the paper, as long as your arm, of lodgings and houses to let. I have been trying to learn German, but it is very hard; I am too deaf to catch the pronunciation, and when I do, can't imitate it. And the grammar is hard, and the construction too. The Germans are fond of long-winded sentences; and as the verb comes at the end, you're very much bothered. My teacher is a Jew, a Doctor of Philosophy, and talks English, so I hoped for some conversation; but wherever we set out it ends in buying, selling, and bartering. He is going to leave Coblenz in about a month. We went all of us to tea there the other day, and ate up all their Passover cakes but two, and they must not just now eat anything else.

My fancies now are rather piscivorous, — I am thinking of skate, brill, turbot, dabs, and flounders, and even what Jane once resented so, a red-spotted plaice. I have at times quite longed for oysters, fancying they would agree well with me — they are considered so nourishing. Dilke would call me a humbug if I say there 's little nourishment on the Rhine, but so it is, and it gets worse. Last year Bavarian beer was to be had, none this; Westphalian hams ditto. And yet, oh yet when I look at the Rhine, it *is* a lovely country, and I love the beautiful. I shall see all I can before I go, as I can carry all the scenery vividly in my mind.

We have missed De Franck much. By accounts from him he likes Bromberg; it is a superb place for fishing; but after wishing for salmon, they are so large there he 's afraid to attack them on account of his tackle. I expect there will be some droll work there. There are enormous fish in their lakes, and all the party are unused to our tackle: the Germans fish by main force. We have a sea fish here, they call a *May* fish, comes as high as this, but we do not expect it this season; it is a very inferior sort of bass.

* * * *

I am glad to hear you liked my letters on copyright: I have got the "Athenæum" with the second part. I think, remembering T——, I let off the booksellers pretty easily. I was glad at having such a subject in the "Athenæum;" when I get nearer I hope to be in print there more frequently; for here, things I should like to have my say on are gone by before I can come at them. Ostend will be next best to being in London. I have some thoughts of beginning a new series with next Comic if I can hit on any novelty to distinguish it. I have a dim idea of one in my head.

The heat here is sudden, and would try us all if we stayed through June. Jane, who has conquered a little German for household use, will have to learn a new jargon. They talk, I believe bad Dutch and French, and I expect English also. The cities are very interesting, and easy to get to — famous pictures to be seen; so, if you contemplate coming, I will reserve my visits to them for your company. I have lots of funny things to tell you. When Dilke was here I did not get a single gossip with him, he was too ill to talk or be talked to; and when better I was away at Berlin: so I should also stand some chance here of dying of a suppression of ideas. Jane is hearty in health now: Fanny very good, reads a good deal, and remembers it to good purpose. As for Tom, he is a fine, funny, spirited fellow, with a good temper, and very strong. Yours that I remember must be getting into big boys. My godson ain't much the better for his godfather's Christian looking-after, is he? And mine are away from their godparents among Roman Catholics and Jews. Fanny makes crosses of wax, and Tom is very fond of Passover cakes. Our maid is a Roman Catholic, but the easiest one I ever saw. She confesses only once a year, and very seldom goes to mass, from sheer indolence. She is the most phlegmatic being I ever saw.

" Should the whole frame of Nature round her break,
She unconcerned would hear the mighty crack — "

provided it did not hurt herself; a fig for German philosophy — it 's all selfishness.

Pray give our kindest regards to Mrs. Wright, and the same to yourself. I do now live in hopes to see you before long, and so remain,

My dear Wright,

Yours ever truly,

THOMAS HOOD.

Pray don't forget to remember me to E. Smith, and recommend to him, in my name, to hold his shoulders instead of his sides when he laughs. Did I ever tell you that there is a young man over the way so like you we call him "John Wright." N. B. I will try to fatten my face up for Mr. Lewis against he comes! Tell B—— to beware of falling out of gigs during a commercial crisis, or people may think he 's *broken.* God bless you! Kind regards to Harvey and all friends.

At this time we finally quitted Coblenz, travelling down the Rhine by successive day's stages. The railroad was then only just commencing, which has since afforded such increased facilities of speed and comfort. It is to be regretted that so little was known of Germany and Belgium in those days. My father's constitution was as unfitted for the miasmatic swamps and mists of Ostend, as for the alternate extremes of heat and cold at Coblenz. But for his exile to these countries — an exile which he underwent for the faults of others — he might still be delighting the world with the later fruit of a genius that had barely attained its maturity at the time of his death.

39, Rue Longue, Ostend, *June 28th*, 1837.

My dear Wright,

You will see from the above address that we are not only safe here, but settled, after a prosperous but slow journey; nothing lost or broken but a little bottle of marking-ink, so that it was luckily performed, with the advantage of fine weather to boot. Our exit from Coblenz was worthy of the entrance: the farce did not, like many modern ones, fall off at the end. We had a famous row with our landlord. He rushed up his own stairs, and shouted from the top, "Dumme Engländer!" and then Jane had a scrimmage with him. R——i played the Italian traitor to both sides all the time. Finally, just on the gunwale of the packet, as it were, they gave us a finishing touch; for Jane called to pay a bookseller on the road, and he made her pay for a number more than she had had.

As for Katchen, she cried at the parting point — partly, I suppose, because we did not take her with us (for she told all her friends she intended it), and partly because she was bidding farewell to good wages and to *enough to eat* — a case, by her own account, rather uncommon with servants in Coblenz. We had a fine trip down to Cologne, lodged comfortably, and took a coach to Liège, with an old coachman, oddly enough, of the very family we were going to visit. Next night at Imperial Aix, and the following one, after a long pull, and a fine, but tremendously hot, day at M. Naglemacher's at Liège. He has a beautiful country seat an hour's drive from the city; but I was so exhausted with heat and fatigue I could scarcely speak, and kept my room all the evening, but rested there, and enjoyed the two next days extremely.

There are beautiful grounds, rhododendrons, hill, wood, and all quite to my taste, with a superb view. Moreover, one of the most amiable and accomplished families I ever met with. The lady paints in oils beautifully. I really took them for good Dutch pictures. A delightful sweet girl about ten made Fanny very happy, and Tom raced about like a young Red Indian, till he was half baked in the sun.

The Nagelmachers all speak French except Mademoiselle, so that Jane had to sit very like the matron of the Deaf and Dumb School, but she made up for it with our friend Miss Moore. We parted sworn friends with the Nagelmachers; ate and slept wretchedly at a dirty inn at Tirlemont; and the next night reached Brussels, where we rested the Sunday, too tired to stir out, except the children, who went to see St. Gudule. Besides, it was wet weather. I started next day with a new coachman for Ghent. Slept at Ghent, and thence by trackshuyt (or barge) through Bruges to this place, where we arrived at seven in the evening in good style rather as to fatigue, after such a long pull with children, luggage, and bad health. I ventured to drink a glass of porter on leaving Brussels, which helped me up amazingly, as for four or five months previously I had not positively touched wine, beer, or spirit, till that hour. I then thought I might have held the curb too tightly, but there was no more porter to be had all the rest of the way. Jane, of course, is fatigued very much, but no more than was to be expected.

To do poor Fanny and Tom justice, they were models for grown travellers, ate and drank whatever came before them, slept when tired, waked all alive, talked and made friends with everybody — waiters, maids, coachmen, and all — so much so, that the coach was loaded with large bouquets of purple and white lilac, and other flowers: got into no scrapes except from exuberant fun, and came in at the end as fresh as larks, though almost roasted from sitting in the coach with their backs to the sun and no blinds.

Give my remembrance to all, and come as soon, and stay as long, as you can, Jane begs to say ditto, as I feel sure it would do me good, body and mind, to see friends.

Yours, ever truly,

THOS. HOOD.

39, RUE LONGUE, OSTEND, 30*th June*, 1837.

MY DEAR WRIGHT,

Do not forget to write yourself, whenever you mean to come, that we may meet you at the landing-place, and I trust it will not be long before we have that pleasure; and have the kindness to bring with you the articles mentioned at the end, chiefly books. I hope Mr. and Mrs. Dilke will come to see us in our new quarters, or we shall die of suppressed jokes, stories, and arguments we were to have had on the Rhine. We are just recovering from the fatigue of our journey — poor wretched travellers that we are — and I begin to enjoy myself as well as my weakness will permit.

We have now been here a week, and I have exposed myself to the sea-breeze to judge of its powers; and, as it has had no evil effect on my lungs, I begin to hope they are not very unsound, and that in other respects for sea-side enjoyment there cannot be a better place.

The Esplanade is very fine, and the sands famous for our brats, who delight in them extremely. We munch shrimps morning and night, as they are very abundant, and quite revel in the fish. I have dined several days on nothing else, and it is such a comfort to think of only that strip of sea between us, quick communication by packets, and posts four times a week, that I feel quite in spirits as to my work, and hopeful as to my health. I am very weak, but otherwise as well as can be expected from such repeated attacks.

But I have moved only just in time, for I feel convinced the Rhine was killing me: between hurry, worry, delay, tedium, disgust, the climate, and the diet, and the consciousness with all these disadvantages, of no very great improvement besides in health. I write a long letter by this same post to Dr. Elliot, with further particulars that I may have the benefit of his advice, how to live and keep alive.

I have now the comfort of thinking, that whatever I may do will not be long in reaching you, whether blocks or MS. It will even be possible here to see the proofs; not that I undervalue your kindness in that respect, but the German book would have unusual difficulties as to names, words, &c. I shall see some of the Germans here, as some come for bathing; and I propose, if strong enough, to take a trip, by-and-by, through the old Flemish cities, which are well worth seeing. Perhaps we may get together to one or two of them, as the communication is easy.

Bring with you such of the German cuts as are engraved, and arrange for as long a stay as you can, as it will do me good to converse a little about old times. The first news we had on arrival here was of the King's death, a kind old friend of mine. I do not mourn for him visibly, for it is too hot for blacks; and the English here, who are all blacked at top, or bottom, or in the middle, no doubt take me for an extreme Tory or Radical. The King and Queen of Belgium come here in a fortnight; so that I shall be the neighbour of royalty, as they will live in our street, only three or four doors off. I am rather tired from writing at length to Elliot; and, moreover, feeling you are to come soon, I do not care to pen what I would rather say personally. So, with kind regards to Mrs. W., in which, with love to yourself and the boys, Jane and Fanny join, not forgetting my godson in particular,

I am, dear W.,

Yours ever truly,

THOS. HOOD.

Tom, whom I have told of your hand,* expects you,

* This is an allusion to an accident which happened to Mr. Wright's hand while he was out shooting. — T. H.

and even anticipates your appearance. You would laugh to see him walk with one arm trussed up like a fowl's wing, as he expects to see you.

OSTEND, *June 27th*, 1837.

MY DEAR DR. ELLIOT,

* * * *

I will now give you a sketch of our departure from Coblenz. Beautiful as the Rhine is, I left its banks without the slightest regret. Coblenz I was particularly delighted to turn my back upon, for it was associated with nothing but illness, suffering, disgust, and vexation of spirit. I left not a single friend or acquaintance with a sigh, Lieutenant de Franck being at Bromberg since October, and everything I had to do with the people, especially at the end, was attended by circumstances of a kind almost to disgust one with human nature. The history of our last ten days would present only a series of petty robberies, just short of open force: lying, dissimulation, treachery, "malice, hatred, and all uncharitableness."

First, a shopkeeper took a shilling, or its German equivalent, and swore it was only sixpence; then the work-girl stole a handsome book, a recent present from London to Fanny; then came a bill for half-a-year instead of a quarter; then our maid grumbled because, as we were going away, our tradespeople no longer tipped her; and then our landlord, knowing our witness was at Bromberg, flatly denied a verbal agreement, and wanted to make me repair, &c. As a sample of his conscience, he demanded sixteen dollars for whitewashing. I sent for a man, who offered to whitewash the whole place for four and a-half, and the rascal himself took six. He, moreover, conducted himself so that I threatened him with a gens d'arme, whereupon he retreated, and vented himself by shouting, "Dumme Engländers! Stupid Englishers!" from the top of his own stairs.

Between our broken German and his broken French it made a tolerable farce. Then a civil functionary and his wife condescended to call and beg some of our furniture and our stock of wood! In fact, they cheated us to the water's edge; for Jane called to pay a bookseller a door or two from the packet office, and he made her pay for a book we had never had. And, finally, Jane only discovered yesterday, that at the very last of the packing the maid (not the old thief that you saw, but another) had abstracted a new un-worn worked collar. This is but a sample of the usual style. In short, with cheating and downright thieving, I doubt whether we have economised much. At least we might have lived in England in the same style (i. e., without carpets and other comforts, according to the national custom here) for the same money.

It is not pleasant, nor even a pecuniary trifle, to pay from twenty to thirty per cent. *on your whole expenditure*, for being an Englishman — and you cannot avoid it; but it is still more vexatious to the spirits and offensive to the mind to be everlastingly engaged in such a petty warfare for the defence of your pocket, and equally revolting to the soul to be unable to repose confidence on the word or honesty of any human being around you.

In aggravation, I am persuaded that the English are no favourites with the natives.

They are too independent to be servile, and, when not abject to German despotism, the natives are Frenchified and Buonapartists. The proud poor barons detest the English for their superior wealth; and talk who may of intellectual Germany, I have found none of their mental acquisitions or ability. You will not be surprised to hear, that so soon as I found we were out of Prussia, I threw up all our caps, hats, and bonnets, with a mental vow never to enter the Prussian dominion again.

Our entrance into Belgium was auspicious, on the very finest day of the season.

The Belgian Douane opened a box or two, mistaking me at first (what an unwelcome compliment) for a Prussian, but passed all the rest. I could have smuggled very easily; but a genuine Prussian, I understand, gets well overhauled; and he deserves it, as their own system is so rigorous. At Cologne we were so lucky as to get a return coach to Liège, and the driver happened to be an ex-coachman of M. Nagelmacher's; so that we had no difficulty at all. Madame N. had a German governess from near Coblenz; and (does n't it sound like prejudice?) she was as disagreeable as her countryfolk. We had a laughable description of her dignified descent to the kitchen to fetch her supper, and her dignified marches up again if it was not ready, for she would not condescend to ask for it of the servants. The latter all called her the Proud German. Here (at Liège) we had two days' rest, then slept at Tirlemont, rested another day at Brussels, slept at Ghent, and came on here by the canal boat. I saw nothing, being fatigued, of any place we passed through. But the cities are all highly interesting, and at easy distances; so that, when I get strong enough, I shall go round to them. Brussels seemed a nice little city to live in. We like the aspect of this place; the sands are capital for the children, who are as happy as can be with their shell baskets.

I ought to tell you that little Tom is a capital traveller, ate, drank, and slept heartily, was always merry, and chatted and made friends with everybody. All the coachmen, waiters, maids, &c., were in love with him; so that our trouble was less than might have been expected with such a youngling. We had a very narrow escape from damp sheets at an hotel at Aix, which advertises itself as a connection with the Emperor's bath; and really the bed linen seemed just to have come out of it. So we slept without, and the chambermaid had the conscience not even to show herself in the morning.

In my state such a mishap as a damp bed would be serious. I could not help remarking that we paid the dearest frequently at the worst hotels, as well as the best, the middle ones being most reasonable, and in essentials most comfortable.

I found the wide green landscapes of Belgium very refreshing; and the rich clover, fine corn, and handsome cattle in the meadows, partake something of the air of a Land of Promise, after the delusive sordidness of Rhenish Prussia. The extreme cleanliness, too, as, for instance, between Bruges and Ghent, was a delicious feature after the German filth. But to enjoy them, people should come from the Rhine to Belgium instead of *vice versâ*, the general route of our tourists, who go to Antwerp instead of Rotterdam, and thence to Brussels. It is no slight relief to hear English and French, and even Flemish, instead of that detestable gabble of gutturals, which may account, perhaps, for the German partiality to turkey-cocks. The people here are notoriously favourable to the English, and seem civil, good-humoured, and obliging. They also look healthy. I walked into the market on purpose to observe them, and saw only ruddy faces, polished by the sea-air. If they cheat us, which I do not yet know, they do it with more civility and a better manner, which is something *per contra*.

Our servant took a fancy to Tom, and has brought him a little family relic, a china cup and saucer for his especial use; and our landlady actually thinks for us, and keeps adding little articles of comfort for our use, though I never saw lodgings so completely furnished, even to umbrellas! In my own little room I have a chamber organ, should I get weary of grinding my brains. And the kitchen, little as it is, is complete, even to an eight-day clock. In fact, I feel we are very lucky, for some old occupants have already applied for our apartments, which speaks well for the people of the house, and the place is filling, and every day lodgings get scarcer.

There are a good many English and some foreigners. We shall have a few Germans by-and-by to bathe, so that I shall have an opportunity of seeing how they behave when away from home. Our friends, Mr. Wright, and probably Mr. Dilke, and probably Mrs. Dilke, are to come over to visit us shortly, so that we may have cards now with AT HOME upon them; it is indeed but a step across compared to our late distance; and I felt it quite a comfort to reflect, as I stood on the sand, that there is but the sea and a few hours between me and England, in case of extremity. I am none of those who do, or affect to, undervalue their own country, because they happen to have been abroad. There is a great deal of this citizen-of-the-worldship professed now-a-days — in return for which I think the English only gets ridiculed by foreigners as imbeciles and dupes. Overweening nationality is an absurdity; but the absence of it altogether is a sort of crime. The immense sums drawn from England and lavished abroad is a great evil, added to other pressures at home. We read that last year the Romans were starving on account of the absence of the English, deterred by the cholera; and if such be the effect of their absence on a foreign capital or country, it must be injurious in as great a degree in their own. The Spitalfields weavers starve; and the waiter at the Belle Vue at Coblenz rides his own horse in summer, and in winter in his sledge in a cap of crimson velvet!

We are luxuriating on fish: it composes (with vegetables) my dinner as often as not.

For six cents we get as many shrimps as we can eat, so that in addition to always dining, which was not often the case in Coblenz, I always breakfast.

I sometimes, since I have been here, find myself irresistibly attacked by sleep in the afternoon; but I attribute it to the morning walk and the sea air, as it has been breezy weather, though fine, ever since we came.

I was never so strong or so stout in my life as after a

six weeks at Hastings, when I went to recover from a rheumatic fever. I sailed daily fair or rough; steering the boat myself, and drank always on my return a large bowl of milk, with bread and butter by way of lunch.

Perhaps if I find the sea air affect me favourably, I had better try the boating again, which gives it in an intenser dose. Up to this point (and at my last walk it blew almost a gale), I have not felt any bad effect from the sea air, being out at least two hours each time. We think of bathing for Tom and Fanny. They visibly are better already for the coast.

Indeed Tom looks quite handsome with his bronzed little face and white teeth, and Fanny has acquired a good colour; and there is no keeping them from the loaf. We are all in mourning here for the King; that is to say, we wear such black as we happen to have,—myself not included, for I feel the heat so that I dress as lightly as I can. I have no doubt I pass for something extreme therefore in my politics, as the mourning is very general here with the English. But, like an old man, I give up to ease all dandyism, fashion, or forms that might interfere with my comfort, and go in dishabille of green and white.

Indeed the two last years have been as twenty to me in effect, and I almost feel as if on the strength of my weakness I could give advice, and dictate to young men who were born no later than myself. However, I hope to see you again before I am quite grey and childish; and in the meantime pray accept my felicitations on the satisfactory settlement of your brother, with my heartfelt thanks at the kind interest you have taken in me, and every best wish I can think of towards you and yours, down to the last little unknown. Jane unites with me in kindest regards to Mrs. Elliot and yourself, and Fanny begs me to add her love, which is echoed by Tom.

I am, my dear Doctor,

Ever truly yours,

THOMAS HOOD.

39, RUE LONGUE, OSTEND, 13*th July*, 1837.

MY DEAR WRIGHT,

* * * *

We find ourselves very comfortably settled now. If you come, there is a spare bed for you, and another for the Dilkes; so that if you should come together there is room for all. I am looking anxiously for your coming, as I think it would do me good, and give me spirits to finish off in style the books for this year. There are four mail packets come every week, and one Company's steamer. We have had famous weather, not one unfair day since we came; but if you prefer bad weather you can wait for it, though I think it will be late this year.

There are still a few things I should like to have: Talfourd's speech on copyright, Tegg's remarks on ditto, and Lamb's Letters. I could perhaps make an article for Dilke of the latter, and weave into it some anecdotes, &c. of Lamb I was collecting before. It is published by Moxon.

I cannot make up my mind to write any particulars to you, as I look forward to the pleasure of telling them. I get the "Athenæum" regularly here on the Wednesday;

and have been introduced to two people here, Colley Grattan and — but the other I will show you, and then surprise you with his name.

I wish I could end here without having worse news; but our *debût* here has not been in all respects lucky. Poor Jane has had a terrible sore throat, so much so, that I was obliged to call in a doctor; who gave her two grains of calomel only, but which seemed to revive all she had taken in her former illness, and in consequence she had her mouth in a dreadful state. A warm bath will carry this off, and we have one within a door or two; but she has had a relapse with her throat, probably from coming down too soon. I am assured it is *not* an affection belonging to the place, which they say is very healthy, and the people look so. Grattan has been here some years, and speaks well of it too. Poor Tom has had a most severe pinch with the street door, and has lost the nail of his finger; but let 's hope this is all the footing we have to pay here.

And now, my good fellow, come as soon and stay as long as you can; and tell B—— not to make me quite such an *Exile of Hearin'*. And mind do not write to me any of your *poste restante* but to the address at the head of this. It will save postage if you bring your next yourself. I cannot help thinking that perhaps, as the French say, you *are* here next Saturday, in which hope I sign and *resign* myself, dear Wright,

Yours very truly,

THOMAS HOOD.

Saturday will be St. Swithin's day, so bring your umbrella. *That* puts me in mind of an impromptu on poor William the IVth:—

"The death of kings is easily explained,
And thus it might upon his tomb be chiselled—
'As long as Will the Fourth could *reign*, he *reigned*,
And then he *mizzled*.'"

I am contemplating an ode to Queen Victoria for the "Athenæum." You may tell Dilke I think Janin's last paper a capital example of political criticism. I own I am curious to see T. Tegg's "Remarks on Copyright;" so don't forget it. Pray poke up Dilke: and should he have any qualms about coming, scrunch them in the shell! You would do me a world of good among you; and I have never had a palaver with him yet. And it would not hurt *him*. Besides, he went to Margate some summers back, and it "ain't to compare" with this for selectness and sea. I suppose, and hope, he is tolerably well. Unless you come soon, let me have a bulletin, rather clearer than those about the King. Why can't the Queen make me Consul here? I don't want to turn anybody out, but can't there be nothing-to-do enough for two? The King and Queen of Belgium are coming here. I rather think the Dilkes, who are very fashionable, are hanging back till they hear the Court is here, which makes Jane and me jealous. Mrs. Dilke need not bring a bit of soap with her, as they use it here; it is quite a treat to see the clean faces and hands. I *could* kiss the children here about the streets—and the maids too. I think the German men kiss each other so because, thanks to dirt, there is no *fair sex* there. Flemish contains many words quite English to the eye. Over the taverns here, you see "Hier verkoopt *Man Drank*." As we entered here, just under the words "man drank," sat a fellow with a tremendous black eye, quite as if on purpose to prove the text by illustration. But I am forestalling our gossip, so good bye. Pray attend to the business part of this letter, and do not neglect the pleasure part either.

Pray congratulate Moxon for me on having an article on his sonnets in the "Quarterly," where I never had a line though I write odes!

39, RUE LONGUE, OSTEND, *Saturday*, 10*th Sept.*, 1837.

MY DEAR WRIGHT,

I received yours this afternoon. Your account of your brother's family, and still more of the funeral, is very gratifying, and contains all the comfort that one could have under such an affliction: it must have soothed your feelings very much to witness such an unusual demonstration. A man is not all lost who leaves such a memory behind him. I am heartily glad your reflections have such a scene to rest upon, connected with him, to set-off against some of the bitterness of the deprivation.

You may be at ease about me, my health has not delayed the Comic; but I was so forward with the cuts, I thought it worth while to wait to send them *all* at once instead of by detachments; and accordingly I shall despatch them to you next week. What a comfort to think that they will not have to be six weeks on the way! It makes a vast difference. I except the frontispiece. Did I understand you that Harvey would do one? His pencil is worth having — that there may be something artist-like; but if any doubt of delay say so at once, as I should in that case prefer knocking one off myself. With regard to the two setters, do it by all means; the motto, "Together let us range the fields," is the best. Have it drawn according to your own idea of it. You will find in the box a list of the mottoes, and the blocks will be numbered as before. I am in good spirits about it, as the "Comic" will, must, and shall be earlier than common this year. I will send an announcement in time for the Magazines. And now for the fishing plate. I did not know there was such a hurry, so laid it aside; but I will take it up again. If I do it, it will come by *one of next week's* posts. I do not know of anything more we want per parcel, unless you have a spare copy of the "Tower Menagerie." Do not forget two or three copies of "Eugene Aram" unbound, and one or two of last "Comic." But you had better see the Dilkes, for we have strong hopes of their coming out, and they would perhaps bring what we want.

Don't think of any beer; we get good here now. The poem in the "Athenæum" about Ostend confirmed us in our hopes. I suspect it is written by Sir Charles Morgan (Lady Morgan's hub.), who has heard them talking of it. I wish they may come, as there is a chance now of their enjoying themselves; and I should like to talk over German matters with him.

By the way, we have heard from Franck, who has been off into Silesia with recruits. He sent the money for the fishing-tackle; and our banker at Coblenz advised me that he received it, and sent it off on the 12th of last month; but it has never reached here yet. I suspect that post-office at Coblenz has kept it, so that they have even done me after leaving them. They tricked me once before. * * * For my part, I say, hang party! There wants a true *country party* to look singly to the good of England — retrench and economise, reduce taxes, and make it possible to live as cheap at home as abroad. *There* would be patriotism, instead of a mere struggle of Ins and Outs for place and pelf. Common sense seems the great desideratum for governors, whether of kingdom or family. I suspect the principles that ought to guide a private family would bear a pretty close application to the great public one; their evils are much of the same nature — extravagance, luxury, debt, &c. Thanks for your recipe: I may try it some day, but I am shy of stimuli. I do not suffer either under lowness of spirits; now and then I feel jaded rather, and indulge perhaps twice in a week in a single glass of sherry: my appetite is better than it used to be. I always eat breakfast now; so if I can but conquer the lung-touch, or whatever it is, I shall do. I think I have got a fair set of cuts, and have some good stories for the text of the "Comic;" so that I am going on quite "as well as might be expected."

Are the other German cuts done? I have a hint to give you about the cutting the "Comic," — not to cut away my blacks too much, as they give effect. I am not sure whether some of the German cuts do not want black, but perhaps they *print* up more. I am so pleased with your ideas of the fables, I think I shall do them next after the German book, with nice little illustrations.

Jane is getting dozy, and so am I, for it is twelve o'clock; so I must shut up. Tom is very well, and talks of "Mr. Light and Jim Co." Oysters are in here; that is to say, they send every one of them up to Brussels. I think I'll petition the King about it. My swallow seems disposed to migrate on that account to the capital.

Hang their shelfishness! confound their grottoes! I own I did look forward to the natives, but one cannot have everything in this world. As the 'prentices say, "I'm werry content with my wittles in this here place!" Our kindest remembrances to yourself and all yours. God bless you.

My dear Wright,

Yours ever truly,

THOS. HOOD.

There is a clergyman wanted (Church of England) for this place, salary £130 per annum. There's a chance for a poor curate! Tell Dilke of it. It's a fortnight since I heard of it; perhaps it may be gone.

39, RUE LONGUE, OSTEND, 16*th October*, 1837.

MY DEAR WRIGHT,

According to promise to B——, I sit down to write to you to-day.

* * * *

On the subject of my health, I feel somewhat easier, as it seems to give me better eventual hope. God knows! It has been a great comfort to me, and gone somewhat towards a cure, to feel myself within distance, and have such posting and sending facilities. The receipt of the "Comic" cuts in three or four days actually enchanted me. Altogether, in spite of illness, I have done more this year. I feel I only want health to do *all*. I do not lose time when I am well, and am become, I think, much more of a man of business than many would give me credit for.

Now for your main subject; and I wish with you, we could talk it over instead of writing. There are so many points I should like to know something about. Such an idea as a periodical it would have been impossible at Coblenz to entertain for a moment. Indeed, some months back I should at once have rejected the notion from sheer mistrust of my health. But I have now more hardihood on that score, and shall turn it well over in my mind. I have no doubt in the world that such a thing well done would pay handsomely, but I do not yet see my way clear. For instance, it is hardly possible for the first of January, seeing that the "Comic" and the German book have to be done. Then there must be *two* numbers of the new work, for I would not start without a reserve in case of accidents, or the whole craft would be swamped in the launching. Moreover, the idea is yet to seek, as much, indeed all, would depend on the happiness of that. There is no end of uphill in working with a bad soil. Now I am not damping; but one must look at the probabilities and possibilities, and count chances. As for coming often before the public, — as I mean to do that anyhow, it goes for nothing. Nor am I afraid of its running the "Comic" dry, fragmentary writing being so different, that what is available for one will not do for the other.

So I shall seriously keep my eye on it, in the hope of some lucky thought for a title and plan. Such an inspiration would decide me at once perhaps. In such a case we must have a consultation somehow, as writing not only is unsatisfactory, but takes up so much time.

Please God I be well the year next ensuing, the "Comic" will take up but one-quarter of my time, and I must have some work cut out for the rest. I fancy the fables for one thing, but that would be light. I do not think I fall off, and have no misgivings about over-writing myself; one cannot do too much if it be well done; and I never care to turn out anything that does not please myself. I hear a demon whisper — I hope no lying one — I can do better yet, or as good as ever, and more of it; so let's look for the best. Nobody ever died the sooner for hoping. I do not know that I can say more on the subject; it *must* be vague as yet. Of course, January is the most important; but if it *cannot* be done, I have no doubt of February, health being granted. But I would a thousand times rather talk over all these things instead of writing of them. I am glad to get rid of the pen and ink if I can, out of school-hours; and there is a sort of spirit of freshness about *vivâ voce* that on all joint affairs is much more invigorating than scribbling.

We are getting into the Slough of Despond about the Dilkes. No word from them since we wrote. It will be a disappointment if they do not come, as our hopes have been strong enough for certainties. And now, my dear fellow, I must close, for I am so tired I shan't add anything but Good night.

Yours ever,

T. HOOD.

21st November, 1837.

MY DEAR WRIGHT,

In a hasty note to B——, I made an angry piece of work, which yours received to-day does not serve to unpick. I complained that, for want of *reporting progress*, I was at a loss to adjust any matter to the finis, and behold the fruit.

Had I known that the Song from the Polish and Hints to the Horticultural made some twenty-two pages instead of sixteen (as I reckoned by guess), I should hardly have written two unnecessary articles.

They were, in fact, the drop too much that overbrims the cup. But for them I should have come in fresh; but through those, and, above all, the nervousness of not even knowing if those two articles before had been received, I half killed Jane and half killed myself (equal to one whole murder) by sitting up *all* Saturday night, whereby I was so dead beat that I could not even write the one paragraph wanted for preface, whereby five days are lost.

I suppose there was a gale at Dover, for what you had on Saturday ought to have reached on Friday. I guessed the "Hit or Miss" well enough, as I can count lines in a poem, but prose beats me, having to write it in a small hand unusual to me.

Of course my sending a short quantity would cause a fatal delay, and I was hardly convinced even with the two superfluities that I had done enough. It is a nervous situation to be in, and I do not think you allow enough for the very shaky state of health that aggravates it. I am getting over it by degrees; but at times it makes me *powerless* quite. It is physical, and no effort of mind can overcome it — I could not have written the end of preface to save my life. Indeed, Sunday I was alarmed, and expected an attack.

I am rather vexed the "Concert" will not be in, as I like it. I think such *short* things are good for the book. Had it been in the palmy days of the "Comic," I should have given an extra half sheet; but now I can't afford anything of the kind. However, I am not sorry to have two articles to the fore. Should the re-issue be decided on, the "Concert" will do for the first number, with a prose article I have partly executed. I think it is a very likely spec, and the best that can be done under circumstances. There is a tarnation powerful large class, who can and would give one shilling a month, and cannot put down twelve shillings at once for a book. I know *I* can't, and you would hesitate too.

I suppose you have heard of Dilke's opinion of the monthly thing. I quite agree with him, that because it *has been* done, is rather *against* than *for* the chance. The novelty is the secret. *Non sequitur* that something *like* ——'s would do, because *his* has done.

Whether *I* could not make a hit with a monthly thing is another question — but the more UNLIKE *to his* the thing is, the more chance. Now I do not despair of finding some *novelty*, which for the same reason as the re-issue of the "Comic," it might be best to do monthly: but as you must know, that all depends on a happy idea, granting a *new* and lucky thought, I should start on it directly, and I shall keep it in mind, for I shall want something to fill up my leisure with.

We looked to have an account of the Guildhall Dinner — pray send the *fullest* one. I think I can make use of it even yet. We don't see the "Times" now Grattan's gone away.

However, one against the other, we don't miss them. As I expect a longer letter from you to morrow, I shall shorten this. On the other side I repeat the end of the preface, for fear of the first edition not reaching you. It was sent *viâ* Calais; and please note, and tell me, when it arrived.

You will understand "Potent, Grave, and Reverend Signiors" to face the opening of preface, as if addressing them.

Take care of your cough, lest you go to Coughy-pot, as I said before; but I did *not* say before that nobody is so likely as a wood engraver to cut his stick.

TUESDAY, 21*st November*, 1837. (New style.)

Pray send off a *very* early copy to Devonshire House.

It is only fair, as I have abused you, that I should thank you for seeing the "Comic" through the press at all. I forgive all your errors beforehand, as I know mistakes will happen. Pray accept, then, my sincere and earnest thanks for the more than usual trouble I fear I have given you, for I could not guide you much in the cut-placing. God bless you.

Yours, dear Wright,

Ever truly,

THOS. HOOD.

39, Rue Longue, Ostend, *2nd December*, 1837.

My dear Doctor,

I have several times been on the point of writing to you; but firstly came a resolution to try first the effect of the place on me; secondly, the Dilkes; and, thirdly, the "Comic." Indeed, an unfinished letter is beside me, for (some time back) there seemed to be a change in the aspect of my case, to which I can now speak more decidedly.

I have done the "Comic" with an ease to myself I cannot remember.

We are also very comfortable here. Fanny is quite improved in health, getting flesh and colour, and Tom is health itself. Mrs. Hood, too, fattens, and looks well. I have got through more this year than since I have been abroad. I wrote three letters some months ago in the "Athenæum" on Copyright, which made some stir, and I have written for a sporting annual of B——'s. Also in January I am going to bring out a cheap re-issue of the "Comic" from the beginning, so that my head and hands are full. I know it is rather against my complaint, this sedentary profession; but in winter one must stay in a good deal, and I take what relaxation I can; and, finally, "necessitas non habet leges." I am, notwithstanding, in good heart and spirits. But who would think of such a creaking, croaking, blood-spitting wretch being the "Comic?" At this moment there is an artist on the sea on his way to come and take a portrait of me for B——, which I believe is to be in the Exhibition; but he must flatter me, or they will take the whole thing as a practical joke. Of course I look rather sentimentally pale and thin than otherwise just at present. I must take a little wine outside to give me a *colour*. I have a little very *pure* light French wine, *without brandy*, which I take occasionally. I got it through B——, but do not drink a bottle a week of it — certainly not more. One great proof of its being genuine is, that it is equally good the second day as when first opened. French wine is cheap here: it only cost me, bottles and all, under fourteen pence per bottle.

We had an agreeable fillip with a visit from the Dilkes, accompanied by his brother-in-law and sister, who have a relation at Bruges. It put us quite in heart and spirits, for we are almost as badly off here as in Germany for society. Not but that there are plenty of English — but such English — broken English and bad English — scoundrelly English!

To be sure, I made an attempt at acquaintance, and it fell through as follows. Coming from Germany with my heart warm towards my countrymen, and finding there was even a literary man in the same hotel, I introduced myself to Mr. G——. He came here afterwards with his family, and we were on civil terms, exchanging papers, &c., till at last they even came to lodge underneath; but we never got any nearer, but farther off from that very neighbourly situation — in fact, we never entered each other's rooms, and they left without taking leave. There was no possible guess-able cause for this; but from what I have seen, and since heard, I rejoice that it "was as it was." So I determined to stick as I be. The intercourse is so easy, we see a *friend* occasionally; for instance, Mr. Wright has been across to see us. There is also a possibility of seeing an English book now and then. Nay, there is a minor circulating library two doors off, but Jane and I had such reading appetites, we got through the whole stock in a month, and now must be content with a work now and then — say once a month. But we go on very smoothly, and as contentedly as we can be abroad. Almost every Fleming speaks English more or less, and our lodgings are really very convenient, and our landlord and lady very pleasant people.

He is not an old man; but was a soldier, and marched to Berlin; and he is a carpenter *by trade*, but paints, glazes, and is a Jack of all trades. I have in my own little room a *chamber organ*, and I discovered the other day that he had made it himself, and he quite amuses me with his alterations, contrivances, and embellishments of the premises. He dotes, too, on children; and Tom is very fond of him, and of his wife, too, but declares he will not dance any more with Madame, because "she fell down with him in the gutter, and kicked up her heels."

He gets a very funny boy, with a strange graphic faculty, whether by a pencil or by his own attitudes and gestures, of representing what he sees. I have seen boys six years old, untaught, with not so much notion of drawing, and he does it in a dashing, off-hand style that is quite comical. His temper also is excellent, and he is very affectionate, so that he is a great darling. Fanny goes to a day-school, and is getting on in French, and improving much. So that I only want health at present to be very comfortable, and for the time being, I am better where I am than in London. I have as much cut out for me as I can do; and am quiet here, and beyond temptation of society and late hours, living well, and cheaply to boot. I seem in a fair way of surviving all the old annuals — most of them are gone to pot. My sale is nothing like the first year's, but for the last three or four it has been steady, and not declined a copy, which is something. The re-issue promises well.

If I were but to put into a novel what passes here, what an outrageous work it would seem.

This little Ostend is as full of party and manœuvring as the great City itself — or more in proportion. I verily believe we have two or three duels per month.

There have been not a few about the minister at the Church — both parties having a man to support — and one gentleman actually fought three duels on the question.

Some of us are very dashing, too; but it is a very hollow *Ostend-tation.* But I like the natives; they are civil and obliging, and not malicious, like the Rhinelanders. The English benefit them very much, and they seem in return to try and suit them. Indeed the prevalence of speaking English amongst the very lower class does them credit, and reflects disgrace on the "Intellectual Germans" of the Rhine, who do not even speak French, which here is very general also. I believe this to be a very prosperous, happy, and well-governed country.

Their kitchen-gardening, I forgot to say, is very excellent.

The vegetable market is quite a sight; much of it better, and all as good as English.

And now I take warning to close. Jane is very anxious to explain to Mrs. Elliot that she has not been unwilling, but unable to write. I have written you but a stupid desultory letter, but hope you will get the "Comic" about the same time, and that it may prove more amusing.

I am still rather languid, and have had to write besides on business: but having a spare hour or two, and something decided to say on my health, would not defer longer. I am unfeignedly glad to hear of your professional success, and also find from Dilke's report that I have to congratulate you on your brother's connection with Mr. C——.

Pray give our kindest regards to Mrs. Elliot, and Fanny's love and Tom's, which is always overflowing to "Willie;" and God bless you all as you deserve.

I am, my dear Doctor,

Yours ever truly,

THOS. HOOD.

EXTRACT FROM A LETTER TO C. W. DILKE, ESQ.

December 4th, 1837.

Jane and I were very much concerned to hear so bad an account of Mrs. Dilke. We hope none of it is attributable to her trip. I can now sympathise in degree, leeches and all; but it is perhaps as well to have it, if possible, set to rights at once. Pray beg that she will send us word how she goes on. Jane laughed heartily at her description of the journey to Calais. But it served you right. Here our mail, charged with letters, with business public and private to forward, will stay in port if the weather is bad; but you, only for pleasure, must *set out* on a day you were not to be *let out* upon, by your own confession, as if the devil drove you, and for what hurry? Why to wait at Dover for the worst fog ever known!!! Werdict: "Sarve 'em right!"

* * * *

Please to thank Mrs. Dilke for her kind message to me; and tell her not to be bothered with indexes, &c., to the "Athenæum." I cannot help wishing for her sake that the little Doctor might be proscribed again, he might do much more good to her than he will, I fear, to Spain.

What three hundred-power donkey wrote that tragedy in last "Athenæum?"

A Polly-puss.

CHAPTER V.

1838.

At Ostend. — Illness. — "Hood's Own." — Mrs. Hood to Mrs. Dilke. — Portrait Painted by Mr. Lewis. — Letters to Mr. Wright, Lieut. De Franck, and Mr. Dilke.

I INSERT the following letter from my mother to Mrs. Dilke as an example of the illness and harass under which most of my father's works were completed.

39, RUE LONGUE, OSTEND, *Feb.* 24, 1838.

MY DEAR FRIEND,

I write a few lines, for I am sure you have all been sadly vexed and uneasy at the last account I sent to Wright, and the non-appearance of anything for "Hood's Own." On the Wednesday morning we sent for Dr. B., in hopes that he might suggest something serviceable. All Tuesday Hood had been in such an exhausted state he was obliged to go to bed; but I was up all night, ready to write at his dictation if he felt able; but it was so utter a prostration of strength, that he could scarcely speak, much less use his head at all. The doctor said it was extreme exhaustion, from the cold weather, want of air and exercise, acted upon by great anxiety of mind and nervousness. He ordered him port wine, or said he might safely drink a bottle of Bordeaux, but this would not do; and the shorter the time became, the more nervous he was, and incapable of writing. I have never seen Hood so before; and his distress that the last post was come without his being able to send, was dreadful. When it was all over, and since, I have done all I can to rouse him from vain regrets, and to-day he is better.

*   *   *   *

I will not attempt to describe our harass and fatigue from days of anxiety, and nights of wakefulness and sitting-up.

*   *   *   *

I have nothing to tell you new, and am, with love to all,

Yours affectionately,

JANE HOOD.

After the post was gone — and the pressure therefore removed — my father recovered, as will be seen in the following letter.

39, RUE LONGUE, *Feb.* 28, 1838.

MY DEAR WRIGHT,

The books per *Stewardess* arrived in port Monday night, but are not delivered yet, thanks to that folly the Carnival, which plagues other houses besides the Customs. In Coblenz it was kept up by the tradesmen. Here it is the Saturnalia of the lowest class. They have been roaring about the streets all the two last nights, our servant no doubt among them. She applied to be out two whole nights running (how your wife will lift up her eyes!), and insisting it was the custom of the place, we could not refuse. She masqueraded, too, as a broom-girl. The first night she got her mask torn, and to-day, after her second night, can hardly crawl with a swelled foot — maybe from a fight, nobody knows what, but it has given me quite a disgust. Neither Germans nor Flemings ought to Carnivalise — though the Germans have one advantage. I have heard very good singing in parts from the common people about Coblenz, but never did I hear such howling and croaking as here. They beat our ballad-singers in London all to sticks.

Now I think of it, was there ever a Flemish singer of any celebrity? I do not recollect one. How Rooke would enjoy "Amalie's" popularity in Ostend! Shall I send him over a Flemish Rainer Family? It would be at least a novelty. Murphy seems *done up* lately; but his very style, full of long mazy sentences, is quackish, and seems purposely mystified. I have thought of two cuts for him. Low Irish, with pots and sacks, looking out for a "shower of *Murphy's*;" and "the prophet a little *out*," *i. e.* caught in a shower without his umbrella. I think he does n't understand the *Pour* Laws.

No local news, only another bloodless duel at Bruges. I have hopes our frost has gone — I noted some wild geese yesterday going back to the "nor'ard," and every one of them is a Murphy. Give my kind regards to everybody — I can't stop to enumerate, my head is so full of "My Own." Take care of yourself, and when you dine, don't leave off hungry — leave off dry, if you like. I am, dear Wright,

Yours very truly,

THOMAS HOOD.

In this spring Mr. Lewis came over to paint the picture which forms the frontispiece to "Hood's Own." The likeness was an excellent one.

OSTEND, *April* 5, 1838.

MY DEAR WRIGHT,

I have just received "Hood's Own," and it looks like a good number. The cuts come capitally, including Scott's, which is a great acquisition. I am satisfied in print with the Elland article and Grimaldi: I had partly written some verses for the latter, but luckily did not risk going on with them, or all might have hitched. It was not my fault but my misfortune, for I had been finishing the Elland article all night in bed, and was copying out the Murphy when the last minute arrived for the mail. I did afterwards hope you would guess the case, and "take the very bold, daring, presumptuous liberty," perhaps, of getting the ghost off the stage as you could. I have read of one, that would not go off, being hustled away by the performers. But bygones must be bygones; it might have been worse. There are better than two sheets of a "Comic Annual." I was shocked to see no more advertisements, and parodying a note of B——'s, I might write "I am not the man to say *Die*"—but, by the Lord Harry, you must get me fresh advertisements; *that* will give me fresh vigour to work on the letter-press and cuts! By the way, as you say, the notices get very frequent and favourable; they ought to be saved, as it might be advisable to print them some day in an advertisement, as they did formerly with the Athenæum. A thing that gets frequent and favourable notices ought to move, if properly pushed. Has B—— done anything abroad? Brussels is particularly full, — Paris, — America. — There are plenty of English to buy *cheap* books, and with so many cuts, it cannot be pirated. I do not think the field has been even yet properly beaten, and the one-shilling book is the very thing where a twelve-shilling one would not do.

For the next Number, I propose "Hieroglyphical Hints," — a paper on the dismissal of the yeomanry with the old "Unfavourable Review," that you had a hand in turning into a libel on Mrs. Somebody and her close carriage. I think of writing something from a black footman on the Emancipation question.

* * * *

I get my papers very irregularly. For instance, I have not yet had last Sunday's "Dispatch." This is bad, and might be very unfortunate, as in the charge against me of plagiarism. Pray tell B—— to blow up that "d——d boy that puts papers in the wrong box," and please then desire said boy to row his master for sending wrong advertisements. I mention this for B——'s sake, as well as my own, because he must be badly seconded in other cases as well as mine.

I am quite satisfied and pleased with your arrangement of No. 3, and only regret, my good fellow, I have to give you so much extra trouble. Do go out of town and refresh! Poor Rooke! How Amalie's nose is put out of joint! for of course you will now sing nothing about Herts, Essex, Middlesex, and Kent, but "This is my eldest daughter, Sir!" Take care of her now you have got her, at last. Some infants are squatted on, like the "spoiled child."* Mind, and whenever Mrs. Wright looks fatigued and sedentary, take care to hand her a chair. Now and then, a child is turned up with a bedstead, but that could not happen, if the maids slept in hammocks. Mind how you nurse her yourself. Never toss her up unless you are quite certain of catching her, a butter-fingered father might become wretched for life in a moment. Don't let her go up in your study among the wild young men. What do you think of her for our Tom? Don't give her a precocious taste for lots o' daffy; or a box at the Opera. You ought to know better than dream of operatising, yourself such an invalid. I have never d——d or t——d out since at Ostend, and am going, to-morrow, for the first time, but only to my doctor's, and if any-thing happens, he will be at hand.

How do *all* the boys like the Gal? Poor things! I never knew a *dozen* brothers, but *one* sister managed to tyrannise over 'em all. Have you got a dictionary name yet? If I might propose, I should say christen her "Mary Wollstonecraft," as the supporter of *Female Wrights!*

You must not be out of heart about your cough,—of late years the spring has brought an almost certain influenza in England as elsewhere. Easterly damp winds are the cause. I have been teazingly coughing, and Jane is wheezy, but what proves it to be *influenzial*, is that Tom, Junior, is as hoarse as a crow. How

* One of the cuts in "Whims and Oddities," engraved by Wright. —T. H.

should we weak ones hope then to escape! For he is a young horse for strength, and indeed, has adopted from "Nimrod's Sporting," the name of "Plenipotentiary!"

There is a genteel blot, as the clerk said, on my scutcheon. That comes of foreign paper. Jane, at the other side of the table, is grumbling at it too. Thanks for the fishing-tackle, — all right, — and gone to Bromberg. I wish the Prince Radziwills would go to the Coronation and bring Franck with them. But, no! Prussia, and Russia, the two great enemies of England, are to colleague together in a family party instead. There is a great conspiracy there, or I 'm mistaken, but it will fall through, — say I Murphy'd it. For Mrs. Wright's benefit, I must tell you now, the finis of our maid, Mary. She insisted on two whole nights' leave at the Carnival, as being customary, and came home each morning between seven and eight, so done up she could hardly stand. At last, one evening there came by a jolly, roaring, set of Carnivalites that quite set her agog the moment she heard the *singing*, if it might be called so! She *took* leave *instanter*, came home next morning, jaded to death, and had occasion to *take some soda!* Of course we paid her off on the spot, and have since learned she used to *persecute* a waiter we called *Cheeks* (ask Lewis about him), and go out on the sly, and drink brandy-and-water with him. She was seen at the Carnival with petticoats up to her knees, bare-legged and be-ribboned, in the character of a broom-girl. Won't Mrs. Wright bless her stars there is no Carnival in England? Greenwich fair is next to it as performed here. And even the respectable people join in it, the tradespeople and all, and the children of the gentry go about in character, — some of the *banker's* here did, for example. By the bye, did I ever tell you of an incident the other day. There was going to be a grand religious procession, and a fine gilded car, or chariot containing a figure of the Virgin, which was to be filled with angels, represented by children with spangled wings, &c., and our landlord, who was engaged in preparation for it, came to borrow Tom *for an angel!* Just fancy Jane's great horror and indignation, — I could hardly appease her by suggesting that it was a compliment to his good looks.*

And now, I must shut up: I will send as much and as often as I can. Give my comps. to B——, and tell him to get a whole No. of advertisements. Seriously, we must both stir our stumps, and I do my best. What would he say now the Copyright Bill is coming on again, to reprinting my letters as a pamphlet, as proposed before?

What would n't I do if I had health and bodily strength? Pray for that when you pray for me, for without it, what a clog to one's wheel!

And now, God bless you and yours, including Miss Wright — only think of a *mile* of daughters! there is a family of Furlongs coming to live here, whereof *eight* are daughters — 8 furlongs = 1 mile.

* I confess I shed some "natural tears" at being denied a chance of wings. When the procession did come off, I remember, the harmony of the car was not exemplary, for the angels were all "fallen" to fisticuffs, like a lot of little Benicia Boys and girls, or Hee-nans and She-nans. — T. H.

Give my kind remembrances to all friends of ours, and believe me,

Dear Wright,

Yours ever truly,

THOS. HOOD.

Two more commissions! *What* a bother I am; but would you let somebody inquire where to get it, and send me two packets of *vaccine matter* by the stewardess next Saturday, and a German grammar for Fanny, with plenty of exercises for young beginners; and pray thank E. Smith kindly for the seeds he was *sow* kind as to send. Is anybody coming out a Maying?

39, RUE LONGUE, *July* 3, 1838.

MY DEAR WRIGHT,

I was disappointed at not receiving the "Hood's Own" per *Liverpool*, not from eagerness to see the dear original's reflection, but I was anxious to see how the Introduction read. I have seen it partly in to-day's "Athenæum," and it reads decently well. I shall want a* "Progress of Cant," and also some old "London Magazines" from J. H. R. I am struggling to get early this month with my matter so as to give you as little trouble as possible. The weather has been up to to-day very

* This was a large outline etching, caricaturing all the humbugs of the day. Some of the figures are worthy of Hogarth — and the hits are felicitous to a degree — for instance, the stout parson, with his flag "No fat livings," in close proximity with one inscribed "The Cause of Greece," — or the banner of the pious barber, "No Person is to be Shaved during Divine Service," wherein an unlucky rent robs "shaved" of its "h." — T. H.

so-so. I have had only one sail, and it did me such manifest good, that I quite long to get to sea again, but either there is no wind, or rain with it. You will be glad to hear I am getting better slowly. I wish, my dear fellow, you may be able to give as good an account of yourself. Pray send me a full and particular *bulletin*. And, in the meantime, please to present my best thanks to Mrs. Wright for the cane, and tell her it is quite a support. I seem to walk miles with it.

* * * *

Did I give you the history of a steamer built at Bruges? They quite forgot how she was to get down the canal, and they will have to take down the brick-work of the locks at a great expense — some 1500 francs instead of 25; all along of her width of paddle-boxes. Well, the other day, 10,000 people assembled to see her launched; troops, band, municipals, everybody in their best; and above all Mr. T——, the owner, in blue jacket, white trousers, and straw hat. So he knocked away the props and then ran as for his life, for she ought to have followed; but, instead of that, she stuck to the stocks as if she had the hydrophobia. Then they got 200 men to run from side to side, and fired cannons from her stern, and hauled by hawsers, but "there she sot," and the people "sot," till nine at night, and then gave it up. She has since been launched *somehow*, but in a quiet way quite; she looked at first very like an *investment* in the *stocks*, and I should fear her propensity may lead her next to stick on a *bank*. The only comfort I could give, was, that she promised to be *very fast*. To heighten the fun, the wine was chucked at her by a young lady who thought she was going; I know not what wine, but it ought to have been *still* champagne.

And now, God bless you and yours, take care of yourself, and mind and send us an account of how you feel, and what your doctor says of you. The vicissitudes of such weather try us feeble ones. I am anxious to know whether you think your new doctor's course has produced any marked effect. Don't B—— mean to come, or don't he not? If he and Mr. S—— would make the trip together, it might be pleasanter, and we have accommodation for two, and especially a *tall* one for B——, for whom an accommodation bed ought to be like an accommodation bill — the longer it runs, the better. When you see Rooke, pray thank him handsomely in my name for "Amalie" — though I do not quite find the airs suit my compass. What Jane has said about F—— please to make me a partner in — and tell E. Smith that our *Sandy* soil has *Scotched* the flowers, so that he would n't know them for his seedlings. But Jane is very proud of them, as they are very good for Ostend. Our festival of Kermesse has begun, and will continue for a fortnight, and then we are to have the King and Queen next month, when your royal gaieties are over and gone. What does Dymock think of being cut out of the pageant? I suppose he will pretend that he "backed out." I shall try if I cannot have a verse or two about the Coronation. I went to know if any distinction was shown to Art, Science, or Literature on the occasion. Was the P. R. A. there? Had the live Poets admissions to the Corner? What became of the V. R. at the Prussian ambassador's? He seemed only to compliment Frederick William with initials. How wonderfully well the mob behaved; but then, to be sure, they are not Tories! I am glad they cheered Soult.

And now I must shut up, and believe me, dear Wright,

Yours ever very sincerely,

THOS. HOOD.

39, RUE LONGUE, À OSTEND, *July* 3, 1838.

I SAY TIM,

If you are dead, write and say so; and if not, pray let me hear from you. Perhaps you were killed at the taking of Spandau — or are you married — or what other mortality has happened to you? or have you had the worst of a duel — or taken a fancy to the Russians and gone to St. Petersburg? Perhaps some very great "Wels" has pulled you in — or have you been to Antonin?

The chief purport of this letter is to inquire about you, so you must not look for a long one — but we are getting uneasy, or rather too uneasy to bear any longer your silence — fearing that in the unsettled state of Prussian and Belgian relations, the intercourse may have become precarious.

I sent you a box containing your fishing-tackle, a "Comic," some numbers of "Hood's Own," and the sporting plates, which I calculated ought to reach Bromberg about the 20th of April. It was directed to Lieut. von Franck, 19th Infanterie Regiment, Bromberg en Prusse, with the mark 

I paid the carriage to Cologne, and sent a proper declaration of the contents. Jane, at the same time, wrote per post to announce it, with an especial request for an acknowledgment of its arrival; so that we begin to fear that neither the box nor the epistle has reached its destination: pray write and let us know; because, in case THE *case* has stuck at Cologne, I will write from here, and you send inquiries for it from *there*, *i. e.*, Bromberg.

We are going on as usual. I am getting better, but slowly; my monthly work, and the very bad season, having been against me. I shall be better when I get to sea, but till last week I have been unable to boat it; we have had fires within the last ten days. Springs are, I suspect, going out of fashion with black stocks. Jane and the 'kin' were on board with me, and I wish you could have seen the faces and heard the uproar they made. It was an ugly, long, narrow craft enough, for a short sea; three lubberly Flemings for a crew, and myself at the helm. Jane groaned and grimaced, and ejaculated, and scolded me, till she frightened the two children, who piped in chorus. Tom, like a parish clerk, repeating after his mother, with the whine of a charity boy in the litany, "Oh, Lord!" &c. &c., and then very fiercely, "Take me home — set me ashore directly! Oh, I 'll never come out with you again!" and so forth. So we have parted with mutual consent, so far as sailing is concerned, which is very hard, as I cannot take out any other ladies without Jane, the place being rather apt to talk scandal, — and one of our female friends here is very fond of boating. For my own part, I have been lucky enough to get a capital little boat, built under the care of an old English shipmaster, and his property — all snug, safe, and handy — so that I mean to enjoy myself as a marine.

In the meantime, Jane has made a voyage to England and back, which I shall let her relate. She had fair weather out and home, and prefers a dead calm to a living storm. I suppose I must take to sea-fishing, as there is some fresh-water fishing, but the canals are too much of thoroughfares to my taste, who enjoy the contemplative man's recreation — only with one companion. I sometimes wish for the Lahn.

It was odd enough — but on our return from Bruges fair in the barge, an English family came with us on their way from Coblenz, where they settled in the Schloss Strasse just before we left. He gave the same account of the people as I do, and was a fisherman — but caught nothing but dace.

England is all alive now with the Coronation. Why did you not egg on one of the Prince Radziwills to visit Her Majesty *viâ* Belgium, with yourself in his *sweet.* I read the other day that some of the 30th were coming to Luxemburg. When our railroad shall be finished, it will only be two days' post from Cologne to this — and I have just taken my lodgings for another year — *Verbum sap.*

We expect several guests this summer from England — one of Jane's sisters and a daughter amongst the rest — and we know *a* FEW *people* here — but the majority are not worth knowing, being of the scamp genus.

We still have an undiminished liking to the place,

which suits our quiet "domestic habits," though it is notorious as dull, amongst the *notoriously* gay.

We know enough to be able to get up a rubber when we feel inclined, besides "taking our three." I get excellent Bordeaux here, and bought a cask with my Doctor, only thirteen or fourteen pence English per flask, whereof on the last 23rd May, I did quaff one whole bottle out of a certain* Bohemian Goblet to my own health, not forgetting the donor of the said vessel, which has a place of honour in my sanctum.

What a bore it is, Johnny, that you are not in the Belgian service; most of its garrisons are near, it would be but a holiday trip to come and see you. Were I, as I once was, strong enough for travel, I should perhaps beat you up even at Bromberg *viâ* Hamburg. But I shall never be strong again — Jane got the verdict of our friend Dr. Elliot, that the danger of the case was gone, but that as I had never been particularly strong and sturdy, I must not now expect to be more than a young old gentleman. But I will be a boy as long as I can in mind and spirits, only the troublesome bile is apt to upset my temper now and then. We are all a little rabid at present, for after having fires far into June, the weather has just set in broiling hot, and the children do not know what to make of it.

* This is a large Bohemian glass goblet, of white glass, clear as crystal and without a flaw, decorated with amethyst medallions, and bunches of flowers. The shape is graceful, and it was highly prized by my father as the gift of Franck, who brought it from Bohemia. If I remember rightly he purchased it of the gipsies, who engraved the flowers. — T. H.

The faces of Tom and Fanny are like two full-blown peonies, or two cubs of the brood of the Red Lion. Tom is a very funny fellow. The people of the house try to talk to him, and as they speak very bad English, he seems to think that they cannot understand very good ditto, and accordingly mimics them to the life. You would think he was a foreigner himself when he is talking to them. Fanny is learning German and French, and makes up by her quickness for some idleness.

She is very much improved, and gets stouter, as she was too thin, whilst Tom gets thinner, as he was too fat; as for Jane, all my London friends said she had never looked better, so that I doubt the policy of walking out with her, for it makes me look worse than I am.

You will judge when I send you a proof of my portrait, which is to be in the next number of "Hood's Own," on the 1st July. It is said to be very like.

I have no news to give you; but there are plenty of rumours. Of course you were at the grand review at Berlin. Tell me all the particulars you can, and of your fishing, in which I take great interest, though now but a sleeping partner. I quote at the end of this a few words about Salmon. I expect a friend out here on a visit, who is very fond of the rod. By the bye, I must not forget to tell you, that the other day, which proves there must be some sort of fishing, my Doctor was called out of his bed in the morning by an Englishman, who mumbled very much, and on going to the door, found him with a hook, and not a little one, through his own lip. He had been tying it on by help of his teeth, and by a slip of the line had caught himself, genus *flat* fish. Being a Belgian hook, like the German, with the shoulder at one end and a barb at the other, it would not pull through; but had to be cut out. Lucky he had not gorged it. *My* leaf is full,* so God bless you says,

Yours, Tim,

Ever very truly,

JOHNNY.

Kind regards to Wildegans.

Tom, Junior, sends his love to you and Carlovicz and Wildegans. He said to his mother this morning, "I love you a great way;" so he can love as far as Bromberg. It has just occurred to me, that there may be a reason for your silence I never thought of before. You are promoted and in the first pomp of your captainship, and

Distant Relatives.

too proud to own to us *privates*. If that is not the reason, I can think of no other with all my powers of imagination. Perhaps it is your D—Douane that always bothered my own packages. I hate all Customs, and not

* The other leaf was left for my mother to write on.—T. H.

least the Prussian. I wish all the officers would confiscate each other. Sometimes this hot weather, I should like a glass of Rudesheimer, one of the few things I care for that is Rhenish — Bow, wow, wow!

The next is to Mr Franck, who had been laid up at Posen, and had had his head shaved.

OSTEND, *August* 20*th*, 1837.

MY DEAR FRANCK,

I have been laid up again, but this you will say is no news, it happens so often. A sort of bastard gout, without the consolation of being the regular aristocratic malady, as if I were an aristocrat. By the way, I almost rejoice *politically* in the results of your own illness, you were always an abominable Tory, but now must needs be a moderate *wig*. But as Gray says:

"To each their evils — all are men
Condemn'd alike to groan."

You (to speak as a fisherman) complain of your hair line, and I of my gut, which I fear has some very weak lengths in it. I hardly go ten days without some disagreeable indigestion or other, which is the more annoying as here the victuals are really good. Moreover, I am, in a moderate way, a diner-out; for instance, the day before yesterday, at the Count de Melfort's, whom I had known previously by his book, the only one that ever coincided with *my Views of the Rhine*.

In fact, in spite of keeping quiet, I am a little sought after here, now I am found out. A friend of Byron's wanted to know me the other day, but I was laid up in bed; and now Long Wellesley (Duke of Wellington's nephew), my old landlord is here, and asking after me. Luckily, there are so many lame men here, I am not singular in my hobble, for though I have got rid of the rheumatism these ten days, the doctor gave me a lotion with cantharides therein, that has left me a *leg*acy of blisters. Then again what an abominable swindling season! The winter embezzled the spring, and the summer has absconded with the autumn.

A fig for such seasoning, when the summer has no Cayenne, and in July even you wish for your ices, a little mulled. I have only managed to keep up my circulation by dint of sherry, porter, and gin and water; and nine times out of ten, had it come to a shaking, I should have given but *a cold right hand*. That is one of my symptoms. In the meantime the Belgians are bathing daily, but I observe they huddle together, men and women, for the sake of warmth, at some expense to what we consider decency. As for Jane she is very willing to believe that winter is absolutely setting in, as an excuse for wearing her sables.* They are very handsome, but no thanks to you on my part, considering a hint that I have had, that it is a dress only fit for a carriage! I don't mean, however, to go so *fur* as to set up a wheelbarrow. Many thanks, however, for your views of our old piscatory haunts, which cannot lead one into any extravagance, for here there is no fishing. It is another Posen in that re-

* Mr. Franck had sent my mother a very handsome set of sables. After her return to England, she was so unfortunate as to *lose* all that were not *stolen*, within an incredibly short space of time. — T. H.

spect — but mind, do not go and marry for want of better amusement. Talking of aquatics, a pretty discussion you have got me into by your story of the beavers on the Elbe. I have repeated it, and been thought a dupe for my pains — indeed, I began to believe you had hoaxed me, but only this afternoon I have found a Confirmation of the Baptism in a book of Natural History.

In the Berlin Transactions of the Natural History Society, 1829, is an account of a family of beavers, settled for upwards of a century on a little river called the Nuthe, half a league above its confluence with the Elbe, in a sequestered part of the district of Magdeburg. There! To be candid, I always thought you mistook for beavers the Herren Hutters, or gentlemen who always wear their castors. But why talk of keeping on one's hat to a man, who can hardly keep on his own hair? Methinks instead of sables you ought to have bought of the Russian merchant a live bear, to eat up the little boys that will run after you, as they did after Elisha, crying "Go up, thou baldhead!" Of course the Radziwills, who made you so retrench your moustaches, will be quite content with you now; but I hope you will not slack in your correspondence in consequence, although I must expect to have more *balder*dash out of your own head. As for Wildegans, he will forget that you ever had any hair, and will take you for some very old friend of his father's, or perhaps for his grandfather.

For my own part, as promotion goes by seniority in your service, I do hope you may have an opportunity of taking off your hat to the king, who cannot make anything less than a major of such a veteran. In the meantime you cannot be better off than in the 19th, which has so many Poles to keep yours in countenance; you see how little sympathy I profess, but having fancied you killed, wounded, or missing, in some riotous outbreak, I can very well bear the loss of your *locks*, as you are upon the *key* vive!

Moreover sickness is selfish, and invalids never feel acutely for each other.

The only feeling I have on hearing of another patient in the town, is a wish, that, whilst about it, he would take all my physic. When I can make up a parcel worth sending you, you shall have a copy of my face, to hang on the gallows for a deserter, if you like. Tim, says he, either I shall get over this liver complaint, and be a portly body, or the liver complaint will get over me, and I shall die like a Strasbourg goose. How lucky I should have a decent interval of health for that march to Berlin! I often recall it, Tim, trumpet-call and all, and wish you were one of *our* military.

I do not know how the Belgian question goes on, but would not advise you to attack us, for in case of a reverse, your Rhinelanders are not the firmest of friends to fall back upon. Your Posen Bishop is a donkey for his pains; a Needle, if it enters a piece of work, ought to go through with it. For my part I like fair play. I would have everybody married, and blessed, how they please, Christian or Jew. Privately I really believe marriages between Jews and Catholics would make capital half-and-half, one party believing too much, and the other too little.

I wear no mitre, but if you should wed a Polish Jewess, you shall be welcome to my benediction. But there has been a precious fuss about nothing. You say the Bromberg ladies, old and young, were very kind during your illness, and sent you nourishing food. You have omitted to mention whether they considerately masticated it beforehand. Yes? Of course you will have some fishing at Antonin. Pray present my best respects to the princes. Were I as young as I am old in health, I would come and beat up your quarters at Posen, but my travelling is over, in spite of steam and railroads; so, if we are to meet again in this world, I am the mountain, and you, Mahomet, must come to it.

My domestic habits are very domestic indeed; like Charity I begin at home, and end there; so Faith and Hope must call upon me, if they wish to meet. And really Faith and Hope are such ramblers, it will be quite in their line, so with all faith in your friendship, and a hope we may some day encounter in war or in peace,

I remain, my dear Johnny,

Your true friend,

TIM.

Tom, Junior, sends his love and says, "if you will come he will give you a kiss, *and teach you to draw.*" Vanity is born with us, and pride dies with us; put that into German by way of metaphysics. Give my love, when you see him, to the King of Hanover, and God grant to those he reigns over a good umbrella. I have many messages in a different spirit, which you will be able to imagine, for my old comrades, for instance, Carlovicz. You do not mention "Ganserich," has he *forgotten* to exist; say something civil — as becomes a civilian — to the rest of your militaires on my behalf; you will see the colonel I guess, or are you the colonel yourself? It would be fatal now to your hair to have many go over your head. Have you ever tried currant jelly to it? Thank Heaven you require no passport, or how, as Heilman said, would you get "frizzé?" Shall we send back that hair lock you gave to Mrs. Dilke? No news except local, and you would take no interest in our abundant scandal, as you do not know the parties. To me it is very amusing, there is so much absurdity along with the immoralities; it is like an acted novel, only very extravagant. You know that this is one of the places of refuge for English scamps, of both sexes. But the parson and I do not encourage such doings, we are almost too good for them.

SATURDAY, 6 P. M., *Oct. 10th*, 1838.

MY DEAR WRIGHT,

Take care and do not get drunk with your Prussic acid.

I wish you better health in a glass of sherry. I am concerned to hear you still suffer with your throat, but have hopes of your medical advice, as Elliot concurs.

His offer is very kind, and pray avail yourself of it at need, as I have reason to know he is sincere in his kindly professions. I think also he has *very* great skill. For myself you will be glad to hear that I am at last taking a change I think for the better: partly from better weather, but greatly I think from the occasional use of a warm sea-bath, and partly, B—— says he thinks, I am wearing out the disease. Time I did, says you, or it would have worn me out.

Something perhaps is due to a slight change of system, but I almost flatter myself, there is a change for the better. I have done without my doctor for an unusually long time, partly from being better, and partly from knowing how to manage myself; I have left off Cayenne and *Devils*, and such stimulants recommended by B——. I begin to think as they are supposed to be bad for liver complaints in India, they ought not to cure them in England, and referred to Elliot, who said "No," very decidedly.

But I have no great faith in the principles of my doctor here, though some in his skill, but without the first, the last goes for little. He shook my opinion lately when I had rheumatism, by giving me cantharides in lotion, which favoured me with a sore foot for weeks. It looked like making a job. I now eat well and have much less than before of those depressions, though hurried and well worked. The baths I do think *very highly* of. Should you see Elliot, ask him; you might run over here for a fortnight, they are almost next door and cost little. *Think of this seriously.* I *have not felt* SO WELL FROM THE 1ST JANUARY *as during the last ten days:* accordingly I am getting on, and, at the present writing, have a sheet of cuts, besides those sent, and some tail-pieces drawn. I expect next packet (on Tuesday), to send a good lot; they promise to be a good set, and I find the pencilling come easier, which is lucky, as they are to your mind too. So I am throwing up my hat, with hope of making a good fight.

I doubt whether the first article will be on the Coronation, which is *stalish*, but seem to incline to "Hints for a Christmas Pantomime, personal, political, (not party), and satirical."

The baths I have in the house before going to bed, — no fear of cold. I strongly recommended them for Mrs. Dilke, and suspect they have gone to Brighton with that view; we have been very anxious about her.

I hope to send with this "the Reminiscences," but if not they will be certain to come with the cuts on Wednesday; I am so full swing on the drawings, I hardly like to leave off to write. You say you are short of prose, but there is all "Doppledick." We heard to-day from Franck: he is well, and back, to his great joy, at Bromberg and his fishing; he has at last caught a salmon of eleven pounds. He tells me a sporting anecdote of a gentleman he knows, that will amuse you as it did me. He was shooting bustards, of which there are plenty near Berlin. They are shy to excess, but do not mind country people at work, &c.; so seeing a boy driving a harrow, he went along with him, instructing him how to manœuvre to get nearer. At last, wishing to cross to the other side of the harrow, he was stepping inside of the traces, as the shortest cut, when at that very instant the horses took fright, and he was obliged to run, with the gun in one hand, taking double care between the horse's heels, and the harrow, which occasionally urged him on with short jobs from the spikes. It might have been serious, but just as he was getting tired out, the horses stopped at the hedge; the gentleman, besides the spurring, having his breeches almost torn off by the harrow. Franck wants me to draw it, and truly a flogging at *Harrow* School, would hardly equal it for effect.

Wellesley went back to Brussels to-day; I declined dining with him, but he sent me venison twice, some Wanstead rabbits, birds, and a hare. We have been up the railway to Bruges in forty-six minutes, Brussels in six hours for nine francs! Tell B—— to think of this. Count Edouard de Melfort wrote a book "Impressions of England;" he is a cousin of the Stanhopes: the family are to stay here the winter, and as we like him and her, and they seem to like us, they will be an acquisition for the winter. They sometimes drop upon us, as he calls it, and we drop upon them. As to local news, lots of scandal, as usual; I could fill a whole Satirist with our own town-made. I think the idea of "The Heads" a good one, but do not like the specimen either as to the head, or the style of the writing; and now God bless you. I must to work again, and leave Jane to fill up the rest. Kindest regards to Mrs. W—— from

Your ever, dear Wright,

Very sincerely,

THOMAS HOOD.

N. B. My hand aches with drawing, I am going to bed for a change.

Pray put in again the advertisement of Harrison's Hotel in "Hood's Own," and keep it standing to the end; kind regards to everybody all round my hat. We had a complete wreck, close to the mouth of the harbour, such "a distribution of effects," no lives lost, but such a litter, as Jane would call it. The cook's skimmer was saved, at all events, for I saw it.

There was a soldier shot to death at Franck's last review — putting stones in the guns! The confusion on our rail is great, one may easily go on the wrong line; two of our party at Bruges were actually in the wrong coaches, but were got out in time; I shall make some fun of this. We have had the Nagelmacher family from Liège, and Miss Moore, lodging for a fortnight on the floor below, but they are gone again. How goes on the Amaranth, or off rather? And have you seen the Bayaderes? Our new opposition steamer is come — "The Bruges" —a very fine boat. But how will the fish like the railroad, seeing they now have such facilities for going by land, there will be many more fish out of water; who can calculate the results in future, of railroads to bird, beast and fish — besides man? We have begun fires in my little room, quite snug. Tom is going into trousers for the winter, and is very proud of it. He complained the other day that "Mary washed all the *flavour* off his face."

Well, I must shut up; I have done a good day's work, and leave off not very fagged, but rather cocky, as the tone of this will show. Give me but health and I will fetch up with a wet sail, (but not wetted with water). Who knows but some day Jane will have a fortune of her own, at least a mangle. Has your mother sold her mangle? I admire Harvey's "Arabians" extremely.

November 22nd, 1838.

MY DEAR WRIGHT,

I have no immediate occasion for writing, but hoping that my chance letters may be as agreeable to you as yours are to myself, I sit down partly for your sake and partly for mine own, as it is pleasant to exchange the pencil for the pen. I have just sent you off nine more principal cuts: in my list I have put "Off by Mutual Consent" and "All Round my Hat" as principals, and so you can make them, should I not send you others in lieu by the packet that leaves here on Saturday, when I hope to send you all the drawings, tail-pieces and all; exclusive of frontispiece, which I should be really glad if Harvey would do for me, however slightly, I sending an idea for it, as I am very short of time. The effect of "Hood's Own" has been to somewhat hinder the "Comic," by preventing that quiet *fore*thinking which provided me with subjects, but I have done wonders on the whole.

The "Comic" is always *a lay miracle*, and done under very peculiar circumstances; perhaps being used to it is something, though the having done it for so many years, and having fired 700 or 800 shots, makes the birds more rare, *i. e.* cuts and subjects. But somehow it always *is* done, and this time apparently by a *special Providence.* God knows what I did, for the "Hood's Own" was the *utmost* I could do. Strange as it may appear, although little as it is, it amounts probably on calculation to half a "Comic," as to MS. But I literally *could do no more,* however willing; the more's the pity for my own sake, for it was a very promising spec. For the rest I feel precisely as you do about "My Literary Reminiscences," but the fact is all I have done, I hoped to do in one or two numbers. For instance, the very last time I was thus thrown out.

As usual, I had begun at the end, and then written the beginning; all that I had to do was the middle, and breaking down in that, you had but a third of what I had intended. It was like a fatality. Moreover I never wrote anything with more difficulty from a shrinking nervousness about egotism.

But although declining to give a life, I thought it not out of character to give the circumstances that prepared, educated, and made me a literary man — which might date from my ill-health in Scotland, &c. Should I be as well as I am now, I hope to fetch up all arrears in Nos. 11 and 12: and it may be advisable to give a supplement, as, after December, I shall be free of the "Comic," and it may help the volume of "Hood's Own," with literary letters from Lamb, &c. &c. &c. This is my present plan, and perhaps the 13th No. would partly help to sell up the whole. But advise on this with B——, &c. In the meantime you will have a good batch for next No.: allowing me as long as you can, perhaps the whole first sheet, and more afterwards. This I know to be mine own interest — I would not have B—— lose *on any account*, much less on mine. With letters, &c., I could fill a good deal when I am once clear of the "Comic" — about which I am in capital spirits. I think I have a good average set of cuts, and some good subjects for text. But above all, as the best of my prospects, and for which I thank God, as some good old writer said, "on the knees of my heart," is the, to me, very unexpected improvement in my health, which I truly felt to be all I want towards my temporal prosperity. The change has been singularly sudden for a chronic disease. I wish I could hear as good news of Mrs. Dilke as this, which I beg of you to convey to them. Pray say that as far as I can judge, a radical change for the better has taken place. I have some thoughts, as a finisher and refresher after the "Comic" (both for body and mind), of dropping in on them for three or four days — in which case you will *not* have further advice. I want to talk over the German book with him, which I shall most assuredly soon get through, health permitting, in the course of February or March.

I do most seriously, comically, earnestly, and jocosely tell you that "Richard is himself again," and therefore you need not, Hibernically, have any fears on Tom's account: which last word reminds me of your kindness in going through all mine — for which I thank you as earnestly, as I know you have been engaged on the work. You must occupy yourself much on my behalf, and I can make you no return but to say that I feel it, which I do, very sincerely, or I should not take so much to heart as I do, the good effects of Prussic acid on your complaint, and wish the three drops which would kill any one else, could render you immortal, at least as long as you liked to be alive. But it does seem, or sound an odd remedy, like being revived by the "New Drop."

I am writing a strange scrawl, but my hand is cramped by drawing. Otherwise, "I am well, *considering*," as the man said, when he was asked all of a sudden. Sometimes I feel quite ashamed of these bulletins about my carcase, till I recollect that it is too far off to be of interest merely as a subject. Seriously I believe I am better, and if I enforce it somewhat ostentatiously on my friends, it is because I have achieved a victory unhoped for by myself!

To allude to the battle of Waterloo, I should have been glad to make it a drawn game, but I think I shall escape the Strasbourg pie, after all.

The above was written sometime back, and given up from sleepiness. I have now yours of the 19th. Glad you like the cuts — I think they *are* a good set. To-day, or to-night rather, have sent off three more large, which if you take in "Off by Mutual Consent," will make up the six sheets. Also three more tail-pieces, in all forty-eight and eleven. A dozen more tail-pieces will do. I wish Harvey would do the frontispiece, I am so very short of time. Methinks the lines

> "Mirth, that wrinkled care derides,
> And Laughter holding both his sides,"

would supply a subject. The "Reminiscences" I must send you on Saturday by the "*Menai;*" our post comes and goes so awkwardly.

Thank God I keep pretty well, — a day or two back rather illish, but took a warm bath and am better, wonderfully, considering my "confinement." After the Custom-house stoppage, no fear for some time of any hitch. It only cost three shillings, as the woman says.

I hope Mr. C. will not forget the books I wrote for, by next Saturday's boat. Pray send me proofs, rough or anyhow, of all the cuts you can, as they help me in writing. Do not forget this. Bradbury's proofs will do. It is getting very wintry, and I and the fires are set in — in my little room. You talk of a grand Christening Batch — but what is to be the name of "my eldest daughter, Sir?" Tom exclaimed pathetically this morning, "I wish I had *none* teeth!" He is cutting some that plague him! He draws almost as much as I do, and very funny things he makes. He picks up both Flemish and French. We went to a French play the other night, and I was much amused by an actor very much *à la* Power. It set me theatrically agog again. Perhaps — who knows? — I may yet do an opera with Rooke! In the meantime, I shall some day send you the piece that was accepted by Price, with a character for Liston, for you to offer to Yates. Jane is going to write, so I make over to her the other flap. We were much rejoiced to hear good news of Mrs. Dilke, as we had not had a word. Pray tell Dilke how much better I have been, and take care of yourself, and believe me, with God bless you all,

Yours very truly,

THOMAS HOOD.

What a capital fish a dory is! We had one for din ner t' other day. Good — hot or cold.

OSTEND, *Dec.* 17, 1838.

MY DEAR MRS. DILKE,

As I always came to your parties with a shocking bad cold, I now write to you with one which I have had for three days *running*. But it was to be expected, considering the time of the year and the climate, which is so moist that it 's drier when it rains than when it don't. Then these Phlegmings (mind and always spell it as I do) — these Phlegmings are so phlegmatic, if it 's a wet night, your coachman won't fetch you home, and if it 's a cold one, your doctor won't come; if he does, ten to one you may forestal his prescription. If it 's a sore, a carrot poultice; if an inward disorder, a carrot diet. I only wonder they don't bleed at the carotid artery; and when one's head is shaved, order a carroty wig. The only reason I can find is that carrots grow here in fields-full.

Well, my book is done, and I 'm not dead, though I 've had a "warning." The book ran much longer than I had contemplated, and I 've left out some good bits after all, for fear of compromising Franck and my informants. It has half as much writing again as the "Comic," and I told Baily to consult Dilke about the price, as it has five sheets more paper and print than the Annual.

We thought this week's "Athenæum" much duller than the one before it; it had n't such a fine hock flavour. I read the review six times over, for the sake of the extracts; and then the extracts six times, for the sake of the review. If that is n't fair play between author and critic, I don't know what is. I have been prophesying what will be Dilke's next extracts. We go on as usual at Ostend. Tell Dilke there are some other "friends" staying at Harrison's, a Captain B., *alias* K., and Sir W. J., said to be of large fortune. But what a residence to choose!

I heard also of two young men obliged to fly from the troubles at Hanover; but it turns out that they have robbed or swindled a Chatham Bank. So we don't improve. A Colonel B. has done W. out of 100*l.*, and an English lady, in passing through, did the banker here out of 78*l.* Then an Englishman shot at his wife the other day with an air-gun; and Mrs. F. will not set her foot in our house again, because I gave her a lecture on scandal-mongering; and the doctor has done Captain F. in the sale of some gin; and the Captain talks of calling out the doctor for speaking ill of his wife; and the De M.s are gone;—a fig for Reid and Marshall, and their revolving hurricanes! We Ostenders live in a perpetual round of breezes.

I must now begin to nurse poor Jenny, who has had no time to mend and cobble her own health for soldering up mine. The children, thank God, are very well, and very good, and "so clever!" The other day, Jane advised Fanny to talk to C—— (about her own age) to subdue her temper. "Oh," said Fanny, "she is so giddy, it would be like the Vicar of Wakefield preaching to the prisoners!" Tom has taken to his book *con amore*, and draws, and spells, and tries to write with all his heart, soul, and strength. He has learned of his own accord to make all the Roman capitals, and labels all his drawings, and inscribes all his properties, TOM HOOD. He is very funny in his designs. The other day, he drew an old woman with a book: "That's a witch, and the book is a Life of the Devil!" Where this came from, Heaven knows. But how it would have shocked Aunt Betsy! The fact is, he pores and ponders over Retsch's "Faust," and "Hamlet," and the like, as a child of larger growth. But he is as well and jolly and good-tempered as ever; and as he is so inclined to be busy with his little head, we don't urge him, but let him take his own course. So much for godma and godpa.

I cannot write more at present, as Mary is in the room, and she is a great listener. God bless you all!

Yours ever truly,

THOMAS HOOD.

P. S. — I shall thank Dilke for the two vols. of the "Athenæum" when I write to *him*, which will be after the tail of my review. The discovery at Trèves, &c., is stale — I mean the window story — six years old at least. Puff of the K. of P. to gull John Bull of some money.

P. P. S. — I forgot to mention that I had a little duel of messages with my "scandal-mongering" acquaintance * the other day. "Pray tell Mr. Hud," says she, "that I have no doubt but his complaint is a *scurrilous* liver!" (schirrous). So I sent her my compliments, and begged leave to say that was better than a "cantankerous gizzard!"

Chubb's Locks. O what a Goose!

END OF VOL. I.

www.ingramcontent.com/pod-product-compliance
Lightning Source LLC
Chambersburg PA
CBHW060516030726
47498CB00004B/970